THE DARE

THE BET BOOK 3

by

Rachel Van Dyken

The Dare
The Bet Book 3
by Rachel Van Dyken

This is a work of fiction. Names, places, characters, and events are fictitious in every regard. Any similarities to actual events and persons, living or dead, are purely coincidental. Any trademarks, service marks, product names, or named features are assumed to be the property of their respective owners, and are used only for reference. There is no implied endorsement if any of these terms are used. Except for review purposes, the reproduction of this book in whole or part, electronically or mechanically, constitutes a copyright violation.

To Grandma Nadine, for conveniently forgetting to censor herself ever since she turned eighty. ;)

Preface

I think it goes without saying... this series would not be possible without my real grandma, Grandma Nadine. She's amazing. I seriously want to be her when I grow up. I've never seen another 87 year old woman wear red lipstick or heels so ridiculously well. Swear, the woman has more energy than I do. Last time we were at a book signing together I was the one sitting on the bench while she grabbed my arm and tried to get me to sight-see. Naturally I gripped the bench with both hands and tried to stand my ground, but one does not fight against Grandma. She has secret powers that make it impossible to argue with her, so I ended up doing what she wanted and had blisters on my feet the next day.

To this day, I have a special place in my notes on my phone for Grandmaisms, and am happy to announce that every time she says something inappropriate she pauses and goes, "You aren't going to put that in a book are you?" *lol* I'm so happy you guys have fallen in love with her as much as I have.

This will be the last book in *The Bet* series...or will it? I'm tying things up nicely but I'm not so sure Grandma is willing to be done yet, I imagine she's going to drag me down another rabbit hole where I end up writing another three books.

Thank you so much for your support in this series! As always you can follow my adventures on Facebook (Rachel Van Dyken), Wattpad (Rachel Van Dyken), Twitter (@RachVD), or you can join my group *Rachel's New Rockin Readers* and get sneak peeks and bonus material, plus join in on the discussions!

As always, if you love the book, review it, if you hate it, review it. Reviews help me, even if they aren't stellar. :)

Love you all!

Hugs,

RVD

PROLOGUE

High School Prom 2000

I pressed my hands against the sleek white dress my mom had purchased for me. Char looked on, her eyes skeptical as she eyed the dress and then my face.

"Are you sure he asked you?"

"Char!" I rolled my eyes. "For the second time... yes, he asked me last week in biology class."

Like I would actually forget one of the coolest moments of my teenage life. My crush had actually spoken to me, and it wasn't even something stupid like asking me to do his homework or pass a note to the hotter girl. It was because he'd noticed me.

I knew the new clothes were paying off. It was the only explanation. I'd traded my old jeans for new designer ones and bought a few Abercrombie screen t-shirts.

"And you're sure?" Char's voice was high-pitched, meaning she was stressed out.

"Why do you keep asking me that?"

Char twirled a piece of dark wavy hair in her finger. "It's just that I could have sworn I heard that he was going with Jessica."

1

"Well," I spritzed some perfume on my neck and sighed, "you heard wrong. Now how do I look?"

Char smiled. "Beautiful. Like a fairy princess."

Giddy, I clapped my gloved hands together. Prom's theme was a black and white ball. My gown was a strapless white Cinderella-like dress with glitter across the bodice, and my gloves were black.

I couldn't contain my excitement. I was going to prom with Brett Xander. Basically the hottest guy at my school. He'd asked me! I mean, I wasn't a total nerd, but it wasn't as if I was high on the totem pole either. I was valedictorian and the president of the Future Business Leaders of America. But he'd noticed me, he'd asked me, and yesterday when he'd called me to finalize plans, I'd about died.

The doorbell rang.

I ran down the stairs, nearly tripping on the last one, before taking a deep breath and opening the door.

"Beth," Brett's smile dazzled, making me feel weak in the knees, "you look beautiful."

Licking my lips, I made a sound that sounded a lot like a girlish sigh and offered my arm. I'd specifically told my parents that if they as much as snapped one picture, I'd refuse to get married and give them grandchildren. So they'd reluctantly stayed in the study, allowing me this one moment, just for myself.

"So, you ready?" Brett took my arm and began walking me toward the waiting limo.

A freaking limo.

I was sighing again.

Unable to form a sentence, I nodded as he opened the door. The plush leather seat beckoned me. Maybe I was going to get my first kiss? Or a sip of wine? Or a—

"Hey, Beth!" a chorus of voices sang out.

Huh? I dipped into the limo and nearly choked on my tongue. Four girls were sitting demurely around, sipping soda. Each of them from my biology class. None of them were popular. If anything, they were less popular than me.

Confused, I looked to Brett for an answer, but the door slammed in my face.

"He's not riding with us?" I asked, full-fledged panic setting in.

"You're kidding, right?" One of the girls laughed. "Brett Xander? With us? Breathing the same air? Um, no, this is his good deed for the year. He was short a biology credit, and it seems Miss Sims has a soft spot for all us girls and the hard work we've had for our AP class. His extra credit was doing something nice for the biology department, and since it's Brett Xander, well, you can imagine what his something nice was."

"Us," I mumbled. "So what? He's taking all of us to prom?"

"Nope." The same girl slurped her Mountain Dew. "He picks us up in a limo, joins his girlfriend in the other limo, and walks into the gym with us. But at least we each get a dance with him. I mean, he is going to be Prom King. Everyone says so."

"Right." I licked my lips and debated whether or not I should jump out of the limo, but just as I was reaching for the door, the car started barreling down the road.

Suddenly, my dress felt too tight, and I felt like an idiot. After all, what guy would want a super-geek control-freak who had a preference for cats? Not Brett Xander. I was kidding myself to think he would even look twice at me.

"Hey, you want a soda?" One of the girls threw a Pepsi in my direction. I caught it but set it on the seat.

"No, thanks." I left out the long lecture about soda causing cancer and instead focused on my black gloves. The same black gloves my mom had spent over thirty dollars on because she was so excited I had a date.

I couldn't bail now. I couldn't go home and tell them the truth.

I'd just have to be brave and smile. One day.

One day, a guy hotter than Brett would notice me. I'd make sure of it. I wouldn't be the crazy cat lady, or the girl who went all through college without making out with at least a few guys.

I just needed to find the right one.

One that wouldn't break my heart into a million pieces.

One who wasn't too good-looking.

Scratch that. One who wasn't better looking than me.

And someone I could trust.

So basically, I couldn't date a lawyer, doctor, model, celebrity, or firefighter. And at all cost — I could never marry a politician.

I mean, who would ever be that desperate?

CHAPTER ONE

"You've been charged with the kidnapping of a United States senator. How do you plead?"

Grandma Nadine smirked. Amateurs. She winked at the FBI agent and answered saucily, "Why, guilty, of course."

Beth

My legs ached something fierce, my face was smashed against a soft pillow that smelled a heck of a lot like a rich politician, and I distinctly remembered eating at least three cookies, or maybe it was four?

With a groan, I tried to move, but everything in my body, not to mention my brain, told me it would be a painfully terrible idea. I moved anyway.

And screamed.

Again, not my fault.

"What the hell?" A deep voice rumbled from somewhere underneath me.

I closed my eyes.

"You can't close your eyes. I already know you're

5

awake."

"This is all a dream," I muttered, my voice sounding scratchy and unfamiliar. "I'm a figment of your imagination. Swear. In two seconds you're going to feel—"

"Shame," the voice said. "Isn't that what you were going to say? Absolute mind-shattering shame?"

I opened my eyes. "What?" I should have left them closed.

Really. It's the small things in life that get you. Close your mouth. Close your eyes. Pretend you don't see that. Crap. Some things just can't be forgotten.

And that face?

Those lips?

Bright blue eyes?

Blond hair that fell just below his ears?

Officially stored into my permanent memory until I died, alone with all my cats.

"I was kidding." Mr. Sexy chuckled. "I just thought I'd throw that in there to make you feel more comfortable."

Right, because lying across a complete stranger in nothing but a smile screamed, *Hey, let's joke around. I'm game*. I quickly grabbed at the sheet and pulled away, kneeing the poor bastard in the process.

After a few expletives, his muscled body moved away from my catastrophe to the other side of the bed. "You can't tell anyone you know."

Like I was really tempted to go to the media about my current state of undress.

"About?" I tried to make my voice all high-pitched and screechy like the stupid girls on TV. Basically, I was playing dumb.

"Really?" He turned; a dimple peeked out from the right side of his cheek as he eyed me with humor.

I giggled.

Hey, I didn't say I was good at playing dumb; I was a

chemist, for crying out loud! My version of playing dumb was allowing the opposite sex the opportunity of pushing the elevator button in hopes that he'd get laid by being so chivalrous. I believe it included twirling my hair and blinking more than once.

Yeah, that was my game.

"Well…" I shrugged. "I should, uh, be going." Why the heck couldn't I remember anything from the night before? I never did this. I was so NOT that girl. I quickly grabbed my bra from the floor, my bridesmaid dress from the chair — crap, and my heels from the bathroom, though they looked like someone puked on them. Great, was that my puke? Did I get drunk?

"Do you do that a lot?"

Sexy man-candy grabbed my arms, and that's when it happened. No, not what you're thinking. Gosh, I wish it was that easy: he grabs my arms, I swoon, fall into hopeless love, and get married in Vegas the next day to Chris Hemsworth's doppelganger.

Nope. Not my reality.

Again, let's revisit.

I don't do things like this.

I don't sleep with guys.

Correction. I've never slept with a guy. Ever. Never. Ever. Ever. Was that too many evers? Holy Batman and Robin, was I starting to sweat? How unattractive could I make myself to sex-god? And why the ever-loving heck was he entering into my personal space.

I closed my eyes to summon the memories of the previous night.

Bridesmaid's dress, good-looking groomsmen, Grandma giving me a drink. Cake, dancing, Grandma giving me another drink, and then Jace and me dancing, and laughing, and getting into a car and… aw, hell. Cookies.

Damn it, politician Jace!

He'd grown up since I'd last seen him. Correction, he'd grown into the type of man-candy that makes people weep. I'd never told anyone about that night — the night he'd basically saved my soul from getting crushed by the quarterback of our football team. Was this how I thanked him? I'd met him once in my life. Once! Of all the dirty politicians to fall into bed with, why did it have to be Jace?

The same Jace that Grandma Nadine had convinced needed soothing after my sister broke his heart all over the place.

Well, I'd soothed him all right. Pretty sure Grandma hadn't intended for me to seduce the groomsman then leave him ASAP.

Sleeping with a politician basically made me a whore.

Great, so I'd lost my virginity to a man who'd one day be president. Monica Lewinsky and I should be Facebook friends. Then again, I doubt she was a virgin if she and Bill got all—

"Did you hear me?"

"Yup." I nodded. "Loud and clear." I was so going to hell for lying to his face.

"Great, so let's just pack everything up."

Pack everything up? What? Like we had a sting operation going on in this hotel room? What happened to the Jace from high school? The one who'd rescued fair damsels and had ridden a white horse?

"I think it's what's best." Jace swore and grabbed his cell phone. "Just don't go outside. For the love of God, don't go outside. I'll have to call security. But I need to take a shower first. Eat a cookie. I know you like those."

"What?" I turned to face him. All of him. Another point in my life when I should have closed my eyes rather than ogled.

The only thing covering up his nakedness was a pair of black boxers. Everything else on his body? Fair game. I looked hard. Hey, don't judge me. Besides when would I ever get a chance to see perfection so up-close? I'd never seen a guy with so many muscles packed tightly around his midsection, or someone whose arms actually looked bigger than my head. Seemed Mr. Senator had a slight obsession with physical fitness, not that I minded.

I doubted anyone would mind the rippled six pack currently facing me in all its model-like glory.

"Beth?" Jace smirked. "You awake or are you sleepwalking?"

My head snapped up to his amused eyes. "Awake. Sorry, what was the question?"

"Cookies?" Jace smirked. "You cried into a box of them last night."

I officially want a do-over. I lose my virginity to a dirty politician, and I cried into a box of cookies? Where's the justice, God! The fairness! The—

"I think there's some left over in the corner." He pointed to the minibar.

Suddenly ravenous, I stalked over, still half-naked, mind you, and grabbed the small box. Great, so I officially consumed half my body weight of something that I know will most likely give me cancer in five to seven years. Stellar. I threw the box onto the ground. "I'm not so hungry."

"You should be after all that exercise."

"Excuse me?" I whipped around so fast that I had to steady myself with the mini-fridge.

Jace grabbed a shirt and threw it over his toned and tanned body. "Easy, Beth, not what I meant." His eyes twinkled with amusement.

Ha, this was me, amused. I kept my frown firmly in place and even put my hands on my hips to show my disapproval.

With a wink, Jace grabbed the half-empty box, pulled a cookie out, and dangled it in front of my face. "You were hungry. I told you to eat a cookie. You said no."

"So?" I shrugged.

"So, your reason for saying no was because you didn't get a workout in, so I offered to—"

"Pretty sure I know where that story ends." I held up my hand.

"Right."

Jace ate the dangling cookie and then another, making my mouth water. Dirty rotten Clinton-lover!

"But, you turned me down. Said squats are just as good as... you know." He cleared his throat. "So you proceeded to—" He waved the cookie in the air and smirked.

"Please," I bit my lip and closed my eyes. "Please tell me I didn't do a naked workout in order to eat cookies."

"Okay." He ate another cookie and headed toward the bathroom.

I breathed a sigh of relief when I heard the shower turn on.

I was about five seconds away from going into the fetal position when he called out, "You ate five cookies and, according to your extraordinary math, decided that thirty squats per cookie equaled to the caloric intake, though you did keep sputtering some sort of nonsense about how exercise doesn't kill cancer, and then you said a whole bunch of shit and finally passed out after yelling, *Die, mutated cells, die.*" Much laughter followed. "Oh, and you thrust your fist into the air. I think you were trying to be dramatic."

And utter silence.

And I wanted to die.

"That's what you get for waking up in Vegas." A voice sang from the shower.

Great and now he was mockingly singing Katy Perry.

Things could not get worse.

CHAPTER TWO

"Guilty?" The FBI agent sighed heavily and reached for his coffee. "You do realize you'll be going to prison."

Grandma shrugged. "Wouldn't be the first time I've gone to the slammer for the greater good."

"The greater good?" the man asked, his eyes narrowing.

"Why, yes. I served a few months in a Russian prison after The Cold War. I was a spy and guilty of poisoning a government official. Then again, they could never prove it. I'd slipped something into his mouth during a heated kiss." She reached into her leopard purse. "Breath mint?"

Jace

"Great, they're going to put *Cradle Robber* on my tombstone," Beth yelled, interrupting my rendition of Katy Perry as she made her way into the bathroom.

I was trying to lighten the moment until she started having a panic attack in the middle of the room. I was still trying to figure out how long it would take her to realize I was showering, naked, and she was standing there rocking back and forth like someone about to have a nervous breakdown.

"I can't believe I'm thirty and still can't make sound decisions!"

Something, I'm guessing was a shoe, slammed against the wall. More cursing. Damn, it was hot when she cursed.

"Why the hell don't I have that drunk text thing? Wait. Does that exist yet? Son of a—" More banging around. And then silence.

To be honest, the silence freaked me out more than the nervous breakdown. Yelling, I could deal with. I was a politician for shit's sake. I cut my teeth on people who yelled and bitched every day of their lives. But silence? Kryptonite. Superman was officially going to crash into the moon if Beth didn't pull herself together.

Her eyes were more green than I remembered them. Then again, my memory wasn't so great; it had been over ten years. Ten years, and I still couldn't get those damn eyes out of my head. Instinctively, I reached behind my ear and touched the scar; it may as well have been a blazing red sign that read *Danger*. Last time I had a run-in with Beth, I landed in the hospital.

So we'd shared a one-night stand. Big deal. People did it all the time.

I mean, I didn't. But *people* did. They had to, right? Where else would Hollywood get all that shit about one-night stands and waking up in Vegas, and the Ashton Kutchers falling in love with the Cameron Diazes?

I closed my eyes against the memories. Damn. It was her stupid dress that had done me in. It had reminded me of prom. It had reminded me of her sweet scent, and after a few drinks, I'd been done for.

"I'm going to die. And then I'll burn in hell," Beth wailed.

Well, at least she was talking again.

I cleared my throat and shook away the past regrets, burying them deep into the part of my brain where boxes sat with cobwebs. "Wait, why are you dying?"

The shower must have muffled my question because Crazy Pants just kept talking.

"No, scratch that. First they'll put *She Loved Her Cats Very Much, Cradle-robbing Hussy.*"

I turned off the shower, grabbed a towel, wrapped it around me, and stepped out.

"Still not following." I cringed when she almost slipped on a puddle on the floor of my own making. Whoops.

"Just..." Beth took a few deep breaths, pressing her fingers to her temples. "Help me turn on the shower, and you can leave."

"Not a fan of personal hygiene? Don't know how to turn on a shower? The hot water is this way." I pointed to the right. "Cold this way." I pointed to the left. "Easy as pie."

Beth's stomach grumbled. Her face flushed red.

"Ah, so the lady doesn't just like cookies, but pie as well?"

"The shower's too fancy," Beth grumbled, changing the subject. "Just help me so this nightmare can be over with, and I can go home and drink wine until I die."

"Death by alcoholism. Classy. You'd make a great politician."

Beth's eyes narrowed. "Just the shower, not career advice. I'm perfectly happy curing cancer, thank you."

"How's that working out for you?" I leaned against the doorframe, enjoying this exchange a little more than I should.

"Wh-what?" Her eyes darted between my bare chest and my mouth.

"Curing cancer."

"I, uh—"

"Wow, I can tell humanity is in good hands. Can't turn on a shower at a fancy hotel and answers *uh* to my questions."

"Never mind." She sighed irritatingly. "Move out of the way. I'll turn it on myself."

"There's a skill I'd like to see." I chuckled as I watched her step into the shower.

"What?"

"Turning yourself on," I teased.

"Were you this much of a jackass last night, or were my beer goggles just that broken?"

"Beer goggles," I stepped into the shower with her and placed my hand on hers, "give the impression that without alcohol you wouldn't have slept with me."

"So." She breathed, her hand shaking underneath mine.

"So," I slowly turned to the right, stepping out of the way, "alcohol had nothing to do with it."

The hot water poured out of the shower and directly onto Beth and her very white sheet. I had to bite my lip to keep from laughing at her horrified face as the sheet plastered against her naked body.

"Out!" she shouted hysterically.

"Leaving." I held up my hands, still laughing as I exited the shower.

I could have sworn I heard her talking to herself as I grabbed last night's clothes and started dressing. Maybe it was good to get it out of my system.

The whole getting drunk and sleeping with a bridesmaid at my good friend's wedding?

Yeah, I'd never done that before, but maybe I got extra points because I actually knew the bridesmaid before jumping into bed with her. Yes? No?

In my limited experience, one-night stands usually meant awkward mornings where reality set in, and you realize you aren't ready for a relationship. This usually involves the guy trying to get out of bed without waking the beast; the beast, upon hearing her mate moving, jolts to attention and latches on without a second thought to the male's inability to feel anything but the sharp talons of the female burying into his skin.

There are almost always tears, followed by yelling; and if the guy is lucky, the girl vacates the premises, screaming obscenities into the air. If he lacks any sort of good luck, he usually ended up with a bag of peas pressed firmly against his best friend.

His *other* best friend.

I let out a chuckle.

Yeah, so that one-night stand? Freaking perfect.

Though I could have sworn Beth was still talking to herself from the bathroom — at least she wasn't screaming or clawing my eyes out. Then again... I winced as I moved my shoulder back and forth, causing a crack to reverberate throughout my body. What the hell had happened last night? Everything was so fuzzy. The only thing I recalled was drinking and then Beth eating cookies. I only remember the cookies because she was so damn beautiful when she was eating them. I sound insane, but it was true. She hadn't mauled them; she'd taken her time with each one. And each time she'd bitten into the cookie, I could have sworn I'd felt that bite all the way down to my toes.

There had always been that special *something* about her, besides her obvious good looks, shiny dark hair, and damn cat eyes. I was drawn to her. I'd been drawn to her since I was seventeen. Shit, I felt like I was seventeen again. My body sure as hell responded like it.

Our brief encounter at prom shouldn't have been brief, which again gave me a clue as to why a one-night stand with her was a bad idea. Our last meeting? Had not ended well. Clearly, the feeling hadn't been mutual. I'd been like a moon-eyed starstruck teenager, and she'd been less than impressed that night. It was good I'd never made it. Seeing her again brought back the old feelings. Damn it! They were supposed to stay locked away. I was twenty-eight now. I was an adult. I was a senator, for shit's sake. I pinched the bridge of my nose. The problem? The details of our hot night together? More than fuzzy.

Which had to be a bad sign.

Then again, I had no hangover whatsoever. Not even a headache.

In fact, other than the sore muscles, I felt fantastic.

Whatever. Shrugging, I went in search of my suitcase. Then paused.

Why the hell didn't I have my suitcase? Details came rushing back. I'd been staying with the Titus family during the wedding, meaning my suitcase was still there, and I was... here? Whose hotel room was I actually in? Because it sure as hell wasn't mine!

I scratched my head then resorted to slapping myself in the face to jolt any sort of memory. But nothing. Still blank. Maybe Beth knew?

Right. That's what every woman wanted to hear: *"Hey, you're hot, but I totally don't remember what you look like naked. Even though we woke up that way together. Thanks for a good time? Oh, and P.S., whose room are we in?"*

May as well put the name *Jake Titus* across my forehead and do the walk of shame.

I wasn't some billionaire playboy like Jake. I was responsible. In control. Hell, I was the youngest damn senator Oregon had ever seen.

And that's when reality hit.

In a force so strong my eyes frantically searched for a paper bag.

Holy shit.

It was going to be in the newspapers.

If I couldn't remember being drunk or getting to the damn hotel, that meant I was sloppy about every single thing that happened.

I checked my watch. Six a.m. With a curse, I reached for my cell and winced. Fifteen missed calls.

I never put my phone on vibrate.

Then again, I'd never had a one-night stand, kissed a girl whose last name I can't even spell, or done a walk of shame Jake-style. So maybe I was turning over a new leaf. Or maybe Jake's whorishness had left him the minute he'd said his vows and floated into my consciousness.

Shit. Now I was freaked about being possessed? By what? The need to screw every female within a ten-mile radius?

A throat cleared. I looked up. Beth stood wrapped in a fluffy white towel, her dark wet hair clinging to her neck and shoulders.

Scratch that. Not every girl within a ten-mile radius. Her. Just her.

"What's your last name?" I asked, needing the distraction as she shifted from one toned leg to the next.

"You're kidding, right?" Beth's eyes narrowed.

"Yes?"

Yeah. It was definitely a day of firsts. For example, not only was I the first person in my family to make it into politics, but I was going to be the first male of the family to die before the age of thirty.

How would she do It, I wondered? Suffocation? Push me out the window?

"Why are you so pale?" Beth slowly walked toward me.

"I, uh…" Damn. I had nothing. My entire career was spent talking, and I had absolutely nothing. Words escaped me. My focus was on her lips as they moved. Fantastic. First I want to actually be the cookie she bites into, and now I'm obsessing over her lips.

But they had this naturally pink tint to them.

Which reminded me of bubblegum.

I had a thing for gum. It kept me from getting nervous during speeches.

I had a feeling Beth would do the same thing for me, if only I was given the chance for one, small taste.

One-night stand. One-night stand. Maybe if I kept repeating it to myself, my body would catch up. Getting lost in those gorgeous green eyes or looking at that amazing ass was going to get me nowhere in life. I needed a solid, committed relationship where both parties equally benefited from said partnership. Not a fiery green-eyed temptress who ate cookies at 3:00 a.m. and cried into a box of them when she discovered they were peanut butter instead of chocolate.

"Jace?" Beth reached out and cupped my chin with her hand, peering into my eyes.

"What are you doing?" I stepped back.

"I'm a doctor." Beth rolled her eyes.

Doctor my ass. I distinctly remembered hearing she played with diseases for a living; no way did I want her hands anywhere near my face. Then again, they'd probably been on other parts all night.

Mental note: *Scrub harder in shower.*

"You're a chemist. Big difference." I swatted her hand away.

"So you know I'm a chemist, but you don't know my last name?"

"You were doing the periodic table of elements in your sleep and were talking about curing cancer? Remember? Doesn't take much math to add that one together, sunshine."

Besides, part of my homework, given by the lovely Grandma Nadine, had been to do a background check on Char and her family. That woman was insane; she wanted no stone unturned. In the end, I'd broken at least four laws to get the information she'd needed. But I owed her. She'd pulled me out of my slump. I remembered Char from high school since we were closer in age. And Beth? I remembered her for entirely different reasons…

"Are you okay?" I asked, approaching the pretty girl in the white dress. Normally I wasn't so brave at another school's functions. After all, I played for their rival team, and I was quarterback. I kept a low profile. My cousin, however, had needed a

date for prom, and I couldn't say no.

"Yeah." She sniffed and then looked down at her hands. "Thanks."

That moment defined me, not because of anything special happening like fireworks lighting up the sky or romantic music floating through the air. It defined me because it was the first time in my life that a girl's tears had actually cut me to the core. I wanted to fix it, and I didn't even know her. It pissed me off that she was crying, and it pissed me off that I cared so much.

"Want to dance?" I held out my hand.

She looked at my hand like I'd just offered her pot.

"Just one dance," I urged. Why did I care?

"Sure." She stood. "Just one dance."

I hadn't known that my one good deed would come back to bite me in the ass. How could I know that, even then? Grandma's watchful eyes were on me like the damn *Lord of the Rings'* Eye of Sauron.

"Damn Grandma," I said aloud. I'd done my good deed for the year; I was ready to be finished with the entire Titus family and their insane shenanigans. The sooner I left, the easier it would be to walk away. Sound logic, I was aware.

"If you keep talking to me like I'm a child, you'll have a reason to call me sunshine because I'll be putting my foot where the sun don't shine. Got it?"

"Are you always this pleasant in the mornings?" I stepped away from the beast. Yes, we were back to name calling. "Or is that reserved especially for me?"

"Just you," she stomped over to her discarded bridesmaid dress and snatched it off the chair, "and politicians I don't vote for."

"You didn't vote for me?" It was out of my mouth before I could stop it. Deflated, I waited for her answer.

"Nope." Beth grinned, seemingly enjoying my shock. "Then again, I don't live in Oregon."

Idiot. Last words said. Gauntlet fallen. Game set. I

watched her disappear yet again into the bathroom.

CHAPTER THREE

"Ma'am, with all due respect. You've committed a federal crime. I don't believe a breath mint is going to solve that problem, and for the last time, no. Your dog may not serve as a character witness."

"It's because he's French, isn't it?" Grandma nodded knowingly.

Beth

I needed a paper bag and a do-over *Back-to-the-Future-*style. I leaned against the door and took a few deep breaths before opening my eyes.

Jace.

It had to be Jace. Out of every damn single man at the wedding, my ovaries had decided to jump into his pants? Really? Was I that desperate? It didn't make sense! I'd spent the better part of my shower trying to figure out the equation with logic.

Was it because he saved me before? Was I still holding onto the one that got away? To be fair, had he not run away like a scared child, I probably would have run myself. It had terrified me, made me feel things that an eighteen year old shouldn't. I'd spent the better part of my freshman year of college thinking about that kiss. Thinking about the way his lips felt against mine and wondering what would have happened had he stayed instead of run.

But he'd left, and I never saw him again.

It wasn't until a year later that I realized he hadn't even gone to my school.

I self-consciously tucked my hair behind my ear. Did he even recognize me?

Know who I was?

Why couldn't I have done something normal? Any other guy I could have forgotten — not him.

My eyes burned, my body hurt, I was starving my ass off, and I looked like I'd just gotten run over by a chicken truck. Taking a deep soothing breath, I focused on the previous night.

We'd both been at the wedding.

We'd both been drinking.

Did he remember anything? Or was I the only cookie-eating loser who had blacked out partway through our night of fun?

I would not freak out. I couldn't freak out. Ha, ha. I was officially losing my damn mind. Calling my sister was out of the question. Not only would she be massively disappointed in me, but she was supposed to be packing for her honeymoon.

Stepping away from the door, I placed the dress gently on the toilet and stared at it.

That dress had betrayed me.

Grandma Nadine had promised it would be magical. She'd said, and I quote, *"Beth, you just trust Grandma. She has everything figured out for you."*

Figured out. My. Ass.

I should have figured Grandma Nadine would have something up her sleeve. After all, the woman meddled in everyone's lives, thinking she knew what was best. She was like a freaking cupid, only she wore leopards instead of hearts, and even on her worst day she could still outsmart the CIA.

The dress glared at me.

I made a face.

The white sparkles reminded me of my senior prom dress. It had been white and looked like something a princess would wear. My stomach clenched at the memory…

"Will you dance with me?" Brett held out his hand.

Once I picked my jaw off the floor and my breathing returned to normal, I grasped his hand and leaned against his chest as KC and JoJo's "Crazy" came on the loudspeaker.

I couldn't believe I was actually dancing with Brett Xander. I tried to appear calm, but my heart was beating erratically against my chest. I pulled back and smiled. "Thanks for doing this for all us girls."

"No sweat," he responded, seeming to genuinely mean it. "I mean, it would have sucked to not graduate."

"Not graduate?"

"Right." He rolled his eyes. "My penance for being a jack-off for the last four years came in the form of my idiotic teacher saying I needed to learn how to be less self-absorbed. Unfortunately, my parents agreed. So not only did I have a shitload of homework to do to get my grade up, but I had to do community service."

"Which was what? Taking out all the AP girls in biology?"

"Hell no." He laughed.

I instantly relaxed.

"It was to pick girls who I knew wouldn't get dates and take them with me to prom. I mean, no offense, Beth. You're kinda hot in a nerdy, pent-up-sexually-frustrated-librarian-type way, but you're much too smart and intimidating for a guy to actually date."

"I'm too smart?" I repeated, stunned. I mean, I knew he was an ass for doing what he did and not realizing how much it affected the

rest of the girls, but still? To call me out? On a special night?

"Well, yeah." Brett nodded and pulled me close. "Maybe if you dumbed yourself down a bit, people would like you."

"People?"

"Yeah." He actually looked embarrassed. "I mean, it's not just dudes that walk the other way when you stroll down the hall. People think you're like one science experiment away from pulling a Carrie on the entire school."

"Right." My lower lip trembled. "Anything else?"

He squinted. "Wow, you're taking this really good."

"Yup." Lies. All lies.

"It wouldn't hurt to get a better rack. Then again, you probably haven't grown into your body yet. It happens."

The song ended. Brett leaned over and kissed my cheek. "Hey, you're pretty cool for a nerd. Thanks for the dance."

I stood motionless in the middle of the dance floor, unable to cry, unable to feel, really unable to do anything except look down at the white dress and wish for once I was the princess instead of the ugly duckling.

"Beth!" Jace knocked on the door. "If you're done freaking out, we need to go."

"Right." I wiped my wet cheeks and clenched the dress in my hands. It wasn't magic. If anything, it was just a reminder that I was exactly where I'd been when I'd graduated in 2000. A loser. A loser with a small rack who preferred math and science to Facebook.

"Beth, I'm serious. It's not looking good."

"Keep your pants on!" I yelled, irritated that he was making me hurry. With a curse, I pulled on the dress, put my wet hair in a quick pony tail, and opened the bathroom door. "What's the big hurry?"

Jace held up his phone. It said *Grandma Nadine*.

"Hello!" a loud voice yelled. "Jace! Beth! Hurry! Grandma has this all figured out."

"Famous last words." Jace nodded. "But we have no

choice."

"No choice?" I repeated. "What? Is the mafia after us or something?"

"Worse."

"I highly doubt that."

"Look." He pointed to the TV. Reporters were in front of a hotel, looking excited as hell.

"The news?" I asked. "Why is that worse than—"

"Special reports say the senator took a prostitute back to his room at midnight last night and has yet to check out! Which raises the question, has the senator truly put his murky past behind him? Sources close to the senator's ex-fiancée say the cheating scandal from two years ago nearly destroyed him. One more scandal won't bode well for the youngest senator in state history. Could a trust issue in his personal life have a reflection on his public one?"

"That's enough." I grabbed the remote from Jace's frozen hand and threw it onto the bed. Great. So not only had I lost my virginity to a politician, but now I was a prostitute. I reached for his cell phone and growled into it. "We'll have words later."

Grandma snorted.

"But get us out of here first."

"Say the magic words."

"Uh, please?" I nudged Jace out of his paralyzed state.

"Not *those* words."

I closed my eyes and allowed visions of my calm and sterile office to bring back the peace into my body. That didn't work. I needed to think about *Vampire Diaries*.

Damon Salvatore. Damon Salvatore. Damon Salvatore. And happy place found!

"I can't read minds. What words do you want me to say?"

Grandma chuckled. "Why, thank you, of course!"

"For?"

"How was he?" She giggled like a school girl. "Men with

power seem to have a special type of—"

"Thank you!" I all but shouted. "Now get us out of here."

"Roger."

The phone went dead.

I looked to Jace for help, but he seemed to be fighting a losing battle with his tie as he tried to pull it from his neck.

"Stop." I swatted his hands away. "You're going to hang yourself if you keep doing that."

He shrugged.

"What?" I loosened the tie. "No snappy retort?"

"Not feeling snappy," he said dryly.

I slapped him. I never said I was good with emotions.

"What the hell was that for?"

"Singing Katy Perry." I grinned. "Now snap to it, Mr. Senator. We've gotta make it out of this hotel without that skinny bitch reporting it on the evening news."

"Grandma?"

"The reporter."

"You understand my confusion," he added, just as someone knocked on the door. "Stay here."

"It feels like a bad movie," I whispered to myself as I chewed the nail polish off my thumb.

"Shit." Jace looked through the peephole and then said *shit* about five more times before slowly opening the door.

Why was he so upset? Why the hell would…

"Aw, shit." I repeated. Because there really wasn't any other word that existed in the English language that would fit as well.

So I repeated it again.

As did Jace.

Grandma shrugged and pulled off her sunglasses. "Let the fun begin!"

CHAPTER FOUR

"Yes. I'm secure in my masculinity, and for the last time, dogs cannot speak."

"That's what Jake said."

"Jake?"

Grandma nodded. "He doubted me once. But never again."

The FBI agent was silent for a moment then asked, "Did you kidnap him too?"

"No, but I did almost kill him. I had the shovel and everything."

Coffee spewed out of the agent's mouth. "Murder?"

"Luckily, when I petitioned God, He said He'd take care of it. Want to know what He said about you?"

Jace

Memories of my gold-digging fiancée, Kerry. Dead memories, ones I'd killed off with a bottle of Jack, threatened to surface. She'd only used me for my position, and when I'd found out about her inability to keep her clothes on, she'd gone to the news and turned the story on me.

My reputation almost hadn't survived. And my heart hadn't ever been the same. My tie felt too tight, the room too small. Luckily, Beth kept me from hanging myself, and for a moment I enjoyed it.

The feel of her hands on mine.

The promise that someone actually cared more about me than my pocketbook or ability to buy them things.

But mostly, the concern that etched around her face when she was helping me. People weren't usually concerned with my feelings. I was a politician; meaning, I didn't have feelings. Just opinions that only forty percent of the population in Oregon actually agreed with.

Maybe I was projecting past memories onto her present person. Who knows what type of person she was now? The girl from high school could be long gone, for all I knew. Hell, I wasn't the same person anymore, and I partially blamed her for it. Beth had made me believe in magic, until the accident changed it all.

Grandma put her hands on her hips. "Well, what are you two standing there for? We have to get out of here!" She threw two duffel bags at us and stomped into the room. "Now change."

"Change?" Beth and I said in unison.

Grandma reached for the box of half-eaten cookies and pulled one out, closing her eyes as she chewed. Several crumbs landed on her leopard scarf, acting like a tray underneath her mouth.

"Well?" Grandma opened her eyes and stared us both down. I wanted to duck behind Beth and or make a run for it, but something kept me in place — maybe curiosity, or possibly desperation. Whatever it was, it was annoying as hell.

"May I ask why you're wearing..." Beth swallowed, "that?"

"Oh, this little thing?" Grandma chuckled then put up a hand and meowed. "I'm a cat."

"We noticed." I coughed to hide my laugh. "Aren't we supposed to be incognito, though?"

"Cats have nine lives."

"Thank you, Wikipedia." Beth smiled tensely.

"People love cats, and people love me. It's really the perfect plan. I'm famous too, you know. They won't even notice you leaving through the back door once I walk into the lobby. I'm donating a horrendous amount of money to the Portland Zoo. They'll think it's a publicity stunt and well... now I don't have to do my own press conference."

I was silent. Thinking. Wondering if she was insane or had finally fallen off that rocker and gotten a blunt head wound. I was about five seconds away from calling Travis and begging him to put his grandma in a home. She wasn't only a danger to society but a danger to herself.

"Strip."

Well, if the catsuit hadn't done it, that one word had.

I shook my head. "Strip?"

Grandma rolled her eyes and grabbed another cookie. "You can't be incognito in a tux and a bridesmaid dress."

Okay, so Catwoman had a point. I looked to Beth, but she was already digging through the duffel bag Grandma had brought her. She pulled out a pair of jeans and a white t-shirt.

Following suit, I unzipped my own bag and found enough clothes to go to the tropics for at least two weeks on vacation. I pulled out a pair of board shorts. "And I'd need these because?"

"No questions," Grandma snapped.

"How did you get all of our clothes so fast?" Beth asked. "I mean, weren't they at the Titus house? Or in my case, the rental car?" Beth gasped. "The rental car!"

"Waiting outside." Grandma popped the cookie in her mouth and examined her nails. "Really," she chewed, "it's as if you two don't trust me. Grandma knows best, and that's all you need to know."

"You're wearing a catsuit," I pointed out.

Actually, it was more of a leopard jumpsuit with a long black tail, a leopard scarf that naturally matched, and a black beanie that looked a hell of a lot like something you'd see on a person just before they robbed you blind.

"Hurry up!" Grandma stomped her leopard heel and looked at her watch. It was also leopard. The woman probably had stock in the design.

Beth grumbled under her breath and stomped into the bathroom; within minutes she walked out and looked a bit like a guy's dream come true. Her white t-shirt was snug across her chest, her skinny jeans ripped in all the right places, and black-and-white Converse sneakers that made her somehow look younger. Not that I'd say that aloud lest she remove my balls with her fist. Apparently age was a sore subject. Not that I imagined she was much older. Then again, I wasn't a super good judge of anything lately, so I decided not speaking was probably a good call.

I went into the bathroom and threw on a black t-shirt and a pair of jeans I really don't remember being that tight. In fact, the jeans didn't look familiar at all. Whatever. I grabbed the cardigan and decided against the tie. By the time I emerged, we'd been in the hotel room for fifteen minutes with Grandma or crazy cat lady.

"Alright." Grandma clapped her hands together, only it wasn't loud because now she was wearing gloves. I had to look away. Looking directly at her was like reliving the time I'd done mushrooms in college. An experience I swore I'd never re-live.

"It's time."

****

The elevator dinged at the lobby level. Grandma pressed play on her iPhone and turned to give us a wink. "Side door, a car's waiting. I'll see you in a few minutes. Now let Grandma have the spotlight."

The doors opened.

And "Lion King" started playing. Grandma strutted down the hall and turned the corner.

My mouth may have dropped open as she started moving her hips in a way no woman at eighty-six should know how to move — in perfect cadence with the music she danced. The reflection of cameras going off was our cue.

"Come on." I grabbed Beth's hand and walked briskly toward the back door.

As Grandma had said, the rental car was running, and a gentleman in a Hawaiian shirt was at the wheel. "Get in!"

Not needing to be told twice, Beth and I tumbled into the back seat and barely had time to buckle our seatbelts before the old man hit the accelerator, causing the Chevy Malibu to squeal in protest.

"Um," Beth clenched my hand, squeezing it so tight I almost lost feeling. "Sir, where are you taking us?"

"Airport."

Beth released my hand, her body relaxing. "That's a relief."

"Don't I know it." The man went through a yellow light and hit the accelerator again, barely making it through the next.

"Mind slowing down?" I asked.

The man's answer was to turn up the music. Just our luck. Britney Spears' "Womanizer" started playing in the background and, of course, our insane driver knew every damn word.

Ten minutes later, we arrived at the airport. I wasn't really sure why I was there other than to help Beth get her crap out of the car. I was officially taking back every thought about one-night stands I'd ever had. No one-night stand should end with your friend's grandmother showing up in a catsuit. Not unless you're high on some sort of illegal substance, which I was ninety-nine percent sure I wasn't.

There was always that one percent, especially when Grandma Nadine was involved.

"Well," I handed Beth her bag, "it was fun."

As soon as the words were out of my mouth, I expected to be slapped.

Beth's eyebrows arched.

I tried again. "I mean, last night. The cookies, the, uh, exercise…" Oh, God, I was making it worse. "And—"

"Just stop." Beth held up her hand. "And thanks for the reminder that I consumed that many calories in your presence then promptly puked in my shoe."

Concern punched me in the gut. "You puked?"

"Not the point," Beth said through clenched teeth. "Just give me my bag, and I'll be on my way. Thanks for the best night of my life."

"Really?" I felt my face light up.

"You're such a guy. And I was being sarcastic, Mr. Senator."

I scowled." You can call me by my name."

"Gee, how noble of you, *Mr. Senator*. I appreciate it. Really. Now if you don't mind, I'm going to go back home and try to forget about the catsuit, reporters, cookies, and—"

"Me?" For some reason it was irritating. She was running away. What the hell? Did she remember me at all? Remember the kiss we'd shared? The dance? Anything? It was a damn good kiss, and why in the hell was I obsessing over it now of all times? What was with her? And what the hell was wrong with me? Holy shit, I was going to have a panic attack. I gaped at Beth, expecting her to say something like, *Oh hey, remember that one time you stuck your tongue down my throat? I still dream about it. Want to have my babies?* Okay, so maybe that was a bit farfetched, but for shit's sake! I'd obsessed over her for years! I was hospitalized even! The least she could do is acknowledge that there was a past between us. That's it. Maybe even a head nod or a blink. Wait! She was blinking, and her eyes seemed to narrow. She did remember!

"See ya on the other side!" the insane driver called, throwing my bag at my face before I could protest.

With that, he drove off.

Leaving Beth and me staring after him with confusion, and me wondering if Beth was going to talk about the giant-ass elephant in the room.

I was just about to open my mouth and speak, when I heard the daunting click-clack of heels hitting pavement. I'd come to recognize that sound as any normal animal on the food chain would when trying to protect itself from a predator.

I closed my eyes and waited for the footsteps to near.

When they got louder, I prayed. I finally understood what prayer was for. It was to ward off Grandmas in catsuits who thought they could rap. It was to save my soul from being possessed by her equally insane whorish grandson, and it was to keep myself from being caught up in the Titus family saga.

For some reason.

Even though I knew I wasn't Grandma Nadine's family.

Dread filled me to my core, suspicion turned into paranoia. I felt it in my body, in my very bones, in my soul if that was possible… I was her next target.

And it wasn't going to end well.

CHAPTER FIVE

"Where is he?" The FBI agent sighed heavily. "Just tell us where he is."

Grandma grinned. "I imagine he could be in a great many places."

"Location, ma'am."

"Your ass."

He spit out his coffee again.

Ah, this was turning into a delightful afternoon!

"I'm running out of patience."

"And I'm running out of lipstick. So what else is new? Tell you what," Grandma leaned forward, "I'll make a bet with you."

"I don't gamble, ma'am."

"Well maybe," Grandma tapped her fingernails against the table, "it's time you did."

Beth

Grandma approached, only this time she wasn't wearing the catsuit. Somehow she'd changed into Victoria's Secret sweats and had magically appeared out of thin air.

"Let's go." Grandma grabbed Beth's hand.

"No." Jace stood his ground. "Listen, I appreciate the, uh, help, Grandma, but I'm going to go at it alone, alright? This is my home. I'm not going inside the airport only to be tricked into boarding a plane for Vegas and getting married. I'm not going to be part of your schemes, and I'm sure as hell not going to allow myself to be manipulated. I saw what you did to Jake. Hell, I participated. Not this time, Grandma."

"You're certain?" she asked, a warm smile spreading across her wrinkled but pretty face.

"Yes."

"Fine." Grandma pulled out her cell and texted something then slipped it back into her purse. "Let's get a Starbucks. Beth, how would you like something warm to drink? Grandma will even slip in a bit of the vodka."

Going with Grandma meant getting away from Jace; it also meant drinking at 7:00 a.m. But who was I to judge? I looped my arm in hers and followed her into the airport.

Out of curiosity, and I swear it was nothing more than that, I turned and stole one last glance at my one-night stand also known as Thor or Mr. Senator. He was looking directly at me, a small smile at the corner of his mouth. I wanted to run back. But more than anything, I wanted to remember what it felt like to have his lips on mine, because the memory from high school wasn't enough. He'd been young, and years had a way of doing that to people. Ripping away the memories of a person until all you remember is the slightest of touches and how that one touch changed you forever.

That one touch had destroyed my idea of what a kiss should feel like. It had taken the movie-star and romance-novel kiss and turned it into something suddenly achievable. In ten minutes, Jace had taken my expectations and put them on a level that no man would ever meet.

He'd made me want to wait for the prince or the white knight. And every year that he'd been a no show, I'd collapsed a little more into myself. Because unlike other women, I knew it was possible. I'd experienced both the save and the kiss that followed, and even though I'd been only eighteen, it had stayed with me.

Hanging by a thread.

I hoped that this would banish the curse he'd put on me since my senior year. See? Look Beth? He's not perfect. If I looked really close I could see a slight limp, and I could have sworn there was a tiny scar by his eyebrow. And let's not forget that he probably has gas problems and halitosis.

I squeezed my eyes shut. I was going to give him a damn incurable disease if it was the last thing I did! He needed to be gone, so I could either move on with my own Prince Charming or adopt Charlie, the calico cat.

If I didn't hurry up and get over him and over the fantasy I'd created, I was going to turn into one of those creepy girls who stalks celebrities and tries on all their clothes and jewelry, convincing themselves that they're in a serious relationship.

I wasn't going to be one of those girls.

I refused to be Warren Bates.

So I kept walking.

And I didn't turn around again.

Not even when my entire body felt like it was shaking from the desire to do so.

My stomach clenched. Was it so wrong to want the fairytale? What was so bad about striving for more? Was I being punished for wanting the knight in shining armor to actually have a soul? Most men I'd met were either so shy they cried when I said hi or so boring that I did formulas in my head. The really good-looking ones? Well, they acted a lot like Char's new husband, Jake. Granted, he'd cured his own whorish nature by falling in love, but still. If the good-looking ones weren't gay, they were total players with no souls and the inability to attach to another human being.

I wanted a good one. I wanted to experience what it was

like, just once in my adult life.

Just once before I finally gave up.

Thirty, but I figured if no man had been interested in the real me by now, I may as well throw my entire existence into my career, rather than waiting around for someone to rescue me from my castle.

"Dick!" Grandma yelled at the top of her lungs.

Horrified, I looked up.

The barista's name was Dick.

Heat flooded my face.

"Dick! Dick! Dick!" Grandma kept repeating as I slowly stepped away from her embrace. Only her wiry arm came out and pulled me against her body like glue. "It has been an age! An entire age! How are the kids?"

"Good." Dick smiled and shrugged. He looked around forty. "I can't complain. Now what can I get you lovely ladies?"

"Two GNs, extra shot of you know what."

"Got it." Dick grabbed two grande cups and began making the drinks. Then when the other barista wasn't looking, pulled a flask out of a cupboard and put a shot in each of the drinks.

My mouth dropped open. I'd thought she'd been kidding. Joking. As in, *Hey, let's get wasted.* Ha ha. Not seriously wanting to drink vodka!

He topped the drinks with whip and scooted them toward us.

"What's the damage?" Grandma leaned over the register and smiled.

"You know the special's always free, Nadine. Always." He winked and grabbed her hand, kissing it gently before nodding in my direction and asking for the next person's order.

Grandma handed me my drink and took a long swig of hers.

"How is it possible that you just ordered something that doesn't even exist on the menu?"

"Oh, but it does." Grandma placed her hand on my arm. "It's just complicated. It's like a hidden menu only for me. Howie knows what I like."

"Are you talking about Howard Shultz?" She was kidding, right? Was I getting punked? Light bulb. I must be on the show *Off Their Rockers!* It was the only explanation.

"Oh look, there they are! And just in time."

Grandma took another sip as Travis, Kacey, Jake, and Char briskly walked through the airport, all of them totally oblivious that shit was about to not only hit the fan but fill the airport to the brim, until everyone within the vicinity suffered a slow smelly agonizing death via Grandma.

"And there he is..." Grandma's voice dropped as Jace walked briskly behind them, paparazzi taking pictures of him until Travis and Jake basically rescued him. Airport security removed the remaining paparazzi.

"What did you do?" I asked.

Grandma took another sip of hot coffee. "He still don't want me."

"Who?"

"The man upstairs." She sighed. "It seems my work isn't yet done. You'd think He'd be pleased. I mean, I basically saved the world."

"How do you figure?" This I had to hear. After all, I was curing cancer, how could what she'd done be any better than that?

"I saved the world from STDs. The way that grandson of mine was going, he was going to be solely responsible for coming up with a new strain. Mark my words. The little slut." She sighed. "But I love him. I may have ruined him, but Grandma fixed all the broken, whorish little pieces, and now look at him." She pointed. "Happy as a clam."

"Right." I backed away slowly.

Grandma's hand shot out and grabbed my arm. "Now drink your coffee and follow me."

"Do I have a choice?" I asked, looking around for a quick escape that wouldn't end up with me being hit by oncoming traffic.

Grandma paused and looked directly into my eyes. "My dear, we always have a choice. The question is never if you have a choice. It's whether your options are better on your own or with my help. Choices come and go. But chances? Only once in a lifetime." She winked. "So why don't you jump?"

"I don't like heights."

"I don't like loud breathers. Doesn't mean I smother people with pillows when I'm irritated," she joked. "Sometimes, my dear, we need a little push."

"Is that what you are? A little push?"

"Hell no." Grandma snorted. "The little push is your conscience. I'm a damn atom bomb. Now are you coming or not?"

I could go home. I could choose safe. I could choose white walls and a sterile environment. What I should choose was the exact opposite of what she was offering. But she was right about one thing: I'd probably regret not taking that old wrinkled hand in mine. So even though I was pretty sure I was making the biggest mistake of my life, even counting the time I tried to dye my hair bleach-blond, I grasped her like a lifeline and prayed to the Man upstairs that I wasn't going to be sent home in a body bag.

****

"I need to disappear for a while." Shaking, Jace let out a loud curse and looked like he needed Grandma's special coffee more than I did.

Grandma released my hand and pushed through her grandsons. "Did I hear someone say something about escape?"

A resounding groan was followed by four horrified faces as Grandma walked up to the ticket counter.

Grandma started firing off questions about her grandsons' honeymoons. I say honeymoons because Travis and Kacey had just gotten married, and in a very strategically set of planned events, so had Char — to Jake, the one she constantly referred to as the whorish grandson. Money had exchanged hands; a preacher, who will have to face consequences once he gets to heaven, married the couple without their knowledge. And the weird part? Jake and my sister Char were so happy it made me a little nauseated.

Char had gotten fired from her job, not that it mattered since the Titus family had more money than God, and now she was taking a honeymoon with Jake Titus, reformed playboy and GQ's Man of the Year.

Clearly, she'd gotten the looks in the family.

Whereas, I'd gotten the brains and less-than-stellar vision. Yay me.

"Beth! Beth dear! Come over here. I need your ID."

All eyes turned to me. Whoever said doing the walk of shame was, well, shameful lied. This? Walking by both Titus brothers the morning after the wedding, looking like I hadn't slept and being with Jace? Let's just say it wasn't something I ever wanted to repeat. I felt naked. And not a good naked, where you feel free and happy and at peace with the world. No, it was a bad naked. The type of naked where people point and laugh, and you have nothing to cover yourself up with but your hands, and even then you only have two of them, so where's the justice in that?

I took a few steps toward Grandma and Jace. He looked too worried to be irritated that Grandma was manipulating. Maybe that's how she worked. She wore you down so much by the time she offered the little crumb that I'd like to refer to as the *gateway drug into crazy land*, you were so desperate to escape you didn't just take it and examine it. You freaking ate it and asked for more.

Damn.

I was eating her crumbs.

So was Jace.

"ID?" Grandma snapped.

I pulled my driver's license out of my purse and handed it over.

Jace rubbed his face with his hands.

"It seems the only seats we have next to one another that are available are in the back of the plane."

The ticket lady's pinched expression gave me the impression that they were bad seats.

"We'll take them," Grandma announced. "And I'll take first class with the honeymooners."

I wasn't really sure what was so bad about the back of the plane. I looked to Jace for help, but he was busy scrolling through text messages like someone who'd just taken a shot of espresso and didn't know how to handle the jolt of adrenaline that followed.

"Thank you, Ilene. As always, you're so helpful." Grandma patted the lady's hand and smiled.

"Do you know everyone?" I whispered so only Grandma could hear.

"Oh, honey," Grandma handed me my ticket, "what's the use in doing the Lord's work if you don't have the connections needed to pull it off?"

Sound logic. Damn her.

"Yoohoo!" Grandma called and then whistled.

I winced. Travis cursed. Jake shook his head and seemed to be speaking in a different language, and Kacey just laughed.

"It's time to go through security." She turned her attention to Jake. "Son, hide your drugs."

"What?" His eyes widened.

"Kidding." Grandma pinched Jake's cheek and let out a giggle.

Nobody joined in. That shit could get you arrested.

"Sense of humor!" Grandma slapped her leg and laughed again. "Oh, sometimes I just kill myself."

"I've tried," Travis grumbled. "No cockblocking."

Did he really just say that? Out loud? To his grandmother.

Embarrassed, I looked away. Who spoke to an elderly woman like that? Did she even know what that meant?

"Sweetie," Grandma dug through her purse and pulled out a tube of red lipstick, "I'm already finished with you. You can have all the sex you want. You too, Jake."

The last time my face had felt this red was when I was in the sixth grade and accidently tucked my skirt into my tights.

"Uh, thanks?" Jake answered.

"Besides, I'm finished with you two. My work is done. Now your wives can continue in my footsteps. Actually, that's not true. If I don't see great-grandchildren in a year, I may have to re-evaluate my five-year plan. At any rate. My eyes or the Eye of Sauron—"

"Ah, *Lord Of The Rings'* quotes... of course," Travis interjected and pointed a finger at Jake. "That's what you get for making her watch all the movies after the wedding. You get an eighty-six-year-old woman thinking she has some sort of wizardly magic."

"As I was saying, the Eye is on these two."

Grandma pointed in my direction, and I could have sworn I felt the laser beam from her polished nail.

I stepped behind a very pale Jace, hoping that the whole finger-pointing magic would drain directly into him and leave me the hell alone.

I peeked around him, only to find both Titus brothers giving Jace knowing grins.

"Word of advice." Travis walked up to Jace and slapped him on the shoulder. "Don't drink it if it tastes funny."

"Also," Jake chimed in, "the law doesn't apply to her. So

if you call the cops, know it will probably be you behind bars before it will be her."

"She likes Benadryl," Kacey added.

"And she will win." Char nodded.

"This game isn't about skill." Jake put his arm around Char. "It's about knowing when to admit you've failed."

"And failure?" Travis laughed. "To that one?" He pointed to a silent-yet-smiling grandma. "Isn't an option."

"Best bet." Jake sighed heavily. "Put all your chips on the table."

"And then what?" I asked, curiosity killing me from the inside out.

"Oh that." Travis grinned. "You still lose. But at least by putting it all out there ahead of time, you know what you're losing."

"And what's that?" Jace spoke for the first time since getting his ticket. "A shitload of money?"

"Nah," Jake answered for Travis. "Something a lot more valuable."

"The question," Grandma piped up as she strolled toward security, "is never what you lose. But if you care that you're losing it in the first place."

"I think you've all lost your damn minds," Jace said, his voice hoarse. His panic-stricken eyes found mine as he rubbed the back of his head and cursed.

CHAPTER SIX

"I'd rather not make a bet with a convicted felon."

"Convicted?" Grandma gasped. "Bite your tongue! I'm just visiting until this little misunderstanding is over."

"I wouldn't call a white van with no license plates, a ransom note, and enough ruffies to put out a grizzly bear..." he put up his fingers in air quotes, "misunderstanding."

"Call it whatever you want. But I'm innocent."

"And I'm Charlie Sheen."

"I knew you looked familiar!" Grandma giggled. "Tell me, how's that sexy father of yours?"

Jace

The first thing I thought of when I got on the plane was alcohol. The second? All the sex I *wasn't* having that the media was convinced I *was*. Funny, because at this point, if I was engaging in said extra-curriculars with prostitutes, I sure as hell wouldn't be so dumb about it.

The only evidence they had was a scorned ex-girlfriend and Beth showing up at the airport with me. My publicist had

44

sent me a text and said not to worry — as far as everyone was concerned, I've been meaning to take a vacation. All they'd needed to do was explain I was at a wedding and catching up with an old friend. An old friend that I hadn't seen in over ten years and had seduced right out of her bridesmaid dress. Funny, because I doubted anyone but Beth and I really knew that we'd met before. And even then, why was I vain enough to believe that, out of all the guys Beth most likely had had fawning over her in high school, that I'd be the one kiss she'd remembered.

I groaned. The truth was… I had been holding on by a thread already. I'd worked my ass off to get where I was, and it terrified me to think that it could all be taken away. I'd graduated from college early. Completed my masters in less than a year. Studied through endless nights. Spent millions of my trust fund on campaigning, and for what? For people to wait for me to fail? And then throw me out of office onto my face? All because they believed a woman who had… my heart clenched. I could still smell the house.

I'd come home from a meeting in DC.

A fire had been lit in the downstairs, and I could smell a roast and potatoes cooking in the oven.

I'd taken the stairs two at a time. Eager to see Kerry, to hold her in my arms and forget about life for just a few minutes. Really, that's all I'd ever asked of her. I'd used her to relax and, in return, she'd looked good on my arm.

My time was precious. After dating awhile, we'd joked around that two minutes was like me handing her hundreds of dollars.

To me, time was the most valuable thing we had as humans. I wanted to make the most of every moment.

Maybe I shouldn't have.

Because if I hadn't taken two steps at a time.

If I hadn't come home early.

My life would be different. Granted, I'd be living in

ignorance, but still. I wouldn't be carrying around scars, and I wouldn't want to run the other way every time a woman smiled at me.

I cleared my throat and snuck a look at Beth. She was reading *People Magazine.*

What did I really know about her? Good kisser. Nice ass. And a hell of a laugh. Unless she'd somehow turned into a chain smoker, causing her laugh to sound more like a hack. But that was it. For all I knew, she really had been a prostitute at some point in her life. Maybe she had dirty little secrets just waiting to pop out. Who didn't? Furthermore, how else did she put herself through med school? I didn't say my logic was sound, but I was also under an extreme amount of stress, which is probably why, as the plane took off, I blurted out, "Are you a prostitute?"

Unfortunately, when they seat you at the back of the plane, what they really mean is they're seating you next to all the crying and screaming kids that nobody else wants near first class, where Grandma and everyone else was drinking and laughing.

If I breathed hard enough, I could imagine that the shit I was smelling wasn't from the little kid in front of me, but some sort of — oh, who was I kidding? I was in hell. And I had five whole hours to wallow.

A few parents turned angry eyes in my direction. I was too tired to care. So what? I'd said prostitute.

"Prostitute?" Beth repeated, louder than I'd initially said it. "And just how did you come to that conclusion, Mr. Senator?"

"Okay, if you keep calling me that, I'm going to start calling you Cookie Monster, and we both know how you feel about that."

"Bastard."

"I'll take it. Anything's better than Mr. Senator."

Beth rolled her eyes and looked back at her magazine.

"Are you going to answer my question, or do you want me to see if the flight attendant has any cookies?"

"Do I look like a prostitute?" Beth snapped.

"Well..." If I said she did, that basically meant I was calling her slutty, and if I said she didn't, I had an inkling she'd take that as me saying she wasn't attractive enough to be one. Maybe I was overthinking things a bit. I tugged at the collar of my shirt. "No."

"Exactly." Beth's face fell, just enough for me to notice. She turned away and looked down at her magazine but didn't turn the page. Because she wasn't reading or looking, she was hurt. Somehow me insulting her had turned into me hurting her, and I hated hurting people, especially ones who didn't deserve it.

"Look," I closed her magazine and whispered in her hear, "I'm not saying you couldn't be one if you wanted to be. You're sexy, alright? I'm not asking because I'm trying to insult you, and I'm not trying to be a complete asshole. I just need to know about your past. If you have any dirty secrets, if you as much as sneezed on your high school teacher and accidently fell over and exposed your pink underwear to a punk in your class and got a detention for sexual harassment. I need to know these things. Because they won't just attack me, they'll attack you too."

Beth's lower lip trembled.

I was fascinated. I hadn't ever been a lip guy. I was more of a full-package type of man. But her lips looked like soft pillows, and I hated myself that I couldn't remember the sensation of my tongue parting them last night.

"Well, no worries on that end, Jace." Beth's voice shook a bit. "In high school my nickname was Boring Beth. I had exactly three friends, including the lab rat that I had to train for AP Psychology, and was a pity date for my senior prom. So, sexual harassment? Prostitution? Selling my body or my wares or whatever you call it? Nothing. Not even a freaking parking ticket. Or a speeding ticket for that matter."

What? How was that even possible? She was freaking gorgeous, and even in high school I'd been intimidated.

I shifted uncomfortably and tried to open my mouth to speak, but she kept talking. Was she talking about the same girl I'd danced with all those years ago?

"In college I made out with two guys. One was a McDonalds' employee. He smelled like fries. I hate fries."

Mental note: She hates fries.

Who the hell hates fries?

"The other had a preference for garlic. He said it kept the vampires away. As you can see, I only dated nerds because, news flash, I am a nerd. I'm a chemist. I like safe. I like white walls. I drink wine and watch Netflix on the weekends, and I already have my eye on two cats at the shelter. I may as well settle into spinsterhood early. Now can we please stop having this discussion? It was embarrassing enough waking up without no memory of my first time with a guy, let alone..."

I tried not to react. My loud inhale mixed with a gasp probably didn't do well to shield my shock.

"Just forget it." Beth opened the magazine.

"Beth, look." I licked my lips. "I didn't know. I mean, I didn't..." Well, shit. How in the hell was I going to get out of this one? Or make it better. I did the only thing I could think of doing or maybe it was for lack of thinking that I pulled the magazine out of her hands and pressed my mouth against hers.

Again, let's revisit the situation. Being under severe amounts of stress can cause a person to make bad choices. Clearly. Because kissing her was probably the worst idea I'd had in the last hour. But she'd looked sad, and she'd basically just told me that she'd given me her virginity, and then her green eyes had gotten all glossy with tears, and I'd panicked. Yes, I, Jace Brevik, US Senator, panicked in the face of a woman almost crying.

Her lips were just as soft as I remembered. I coaxed them open and moaned as her tongue shyly touched mine.

"Are you married?" a squeaky voice asked.

I pulled back and glanced up. A girl who looked to be about eight was hanging over the seat in front of us, staring. Her pigtails bobbed on the side of her head as the plane hit a bump of turbulence.

"No," I said, eyes narrowing, body still pounding with lust. I was kissing a complete stranger. Kind of. Well, not really. Damn it.

"My mommy says that boys and girls should only kiss when they're married."

"You're mommy's living under a rock," I grumbled.

"No, she's right here." The girl pulled back and then shrugged. "She's sleeping. Sometimes she puts special juice in my cup so she can sleep on the planes."

"I want special juice," Beth said under her breath.

The girl giggled but still didn't turn back around. And I was left to wonder how a soccer mom had been able to sneak alcohol by security. Why hadn't I thought of that?

The girl kept staring.

To be honest, it was freaking me out. Don't get me wrong. I liked kids. I patted their heads and kissed their cheeks during photo-ops, but in my mind there was nothing freakier than a horror movie with a little girl in it. It gave me the creeps.

And this little girl looked exactly like one who could star in her own horror movie.

Clearing my throat, I tried to look away, because the longer she stared the more I was convince she was going to take the plane down with her. In a moment of clarity, I reached into my pocket and pulled out a piece of wrapped candy and held it out to her. "Want some candy?"

"Stranger danger, nine-one-one, stranger danger, nine-one-one!" the girl started wailing.

"Just a guess," Beth said, an amused smile plastered across her pretty face. "But I'm gonna bet her mommy also told her anyone who offered candy was living in an unmarked van down by the river."

Within seconds, mama bear turned around and glared at both me and Beth. I held up the candy like a white flag, hoping the woman wouldn't slap me, or worse, assume I was really going to take her daughter. Masking tape her mouth? Possibly. Kidnap? Hell no.

"You give my daughter candy?" she asked in a gruff voice.

"I was trying to be nice." I gave her my best politician smile.

"Be nice to someone else. We're all full here, and if you offer her candy again, I'm voting Republican next term."

"Nice." Beth chuckled once the woman turned around.

"What?"

"She knew you! Yay! Another vote in your favor." She held up her hand for a high five.

I glared.

And that was it.

Note to self: *Life isn't like the movies, and Beth isn't like any other girl I've ever met.*

I'd just had my tongue in her mouth, and we weren't sitting there having a conversation about what it meant for our new relationship. She wasn't doodling my name on her magazine. There were no birds chirping above her head, and no, Celine Dion had not started playing randomly throughout the plane. Instead, she was acting like she had amnesia.

She was acting like she didn't care that I'd just kissed her.

What did it mean? Why the hell had I kissed her? Did that mean we were sharing a room? Was I dating? I didn't date! I tugged at the collar of my shirt again and gasped for more air.

Holy shit.

Not only was I following in Jake's footsteps.

But I'd turned into a woman.

I half-expected birds to start chirping around my head as cheerleaders danced down the aisle with tampons.

Because for the next hour all I could think about was not putting my arm on the armrest for fear that it would brush against hers, and she'd think I was doing it on purpose.

And then I was too nervous to drink soda, because then I'd have to piss, and I'd walk by her, and she'd see that I was sweating.

I was losing my cool.

And my entire career was based on the very principle that I could be cool in any situation.

Except this one.

The one that got away was officially sitting next to me on a five-hour flight — and was immune to me. Like a damn antibiotic. Shit. I was a disease.

I groaned and put my head in my hands, leaning on the small tray.

My second hour in hell ended with the little girl in front of us turning around again and asking if I had gas. And that when she has gas, she moans too.

Side note: *I was never reproducing.*

CHAPTER SEVEN

"I'm not saying I didn't get a little help." Grandma shrugged. *"What woman doesn't want to look twenty years younger? These old things still have some perk left."* She pointed to herself and winked.

"I'm sorry, but what does this have to do with our national security?" The FBI agent took off his glasses and groaned.

"Oh, it doesn't. I was just bored with all the silly questions about kidnapping and death. So depressing! You wouldn't happen to have any wine, now would you?"

Beth

I'd read the same stupid article at least fifteen times before I finally realized I wasn't going to absorb any information at all. The only helpful piece of information I'd pulled from the two sentences I'd managed to repeat over and over again was that there had been another plane crash in Europe. Thanks, *US Weekly*. I really appreciate the terror you've just invoked into my life. Not only was I sitting next to Jace, but the plane could go down at any minute. Because, let's be honest, I wasn't the luckiest girl around.

After all.

I'd just admitted to Jace he was my first.

I was also thirty years old. Though he didn't know that, not exactly. It wasn't as if I was wearing a sign across my chest that said *Thirty-Year- Old Virgin.*

If they made a movie about my life, it would consist of a pantry, full of cookies, chips, and soda, followed by a Netflix addiction and a poster of *Vampire Diaries* in my living room.

There would be no leading man. The secondary characters would consist of cats and an aloe vera plant named Waldo.

I closed my eyes and willed my mind to stop thinking and just... relax. But his kiss had again reminded me of what I'd been missing. Of what I'd clearly missed the night before when I'd been eating cookies and throwing myself at him. It was terrifying to think that I'd never been intimate with someone, and that the one time I had, I couldn't remember it. At least I wasn't boring anymore! I already knew people accused me of being boring on account of what I did. It didn't help that it had been my nickname while growing up.

Boring Beth. I hated that humiliating nickname. Brett had called me Boring Beth when I refused to give him a thank-you kiss after prom. When he'd tried again, I'd threatened to poison him. Scowling, I put the magazine in the seatback pocket and tried to close my eyes.

"So... your first?" Jace whispered.

I opened my eyes. Yes, I was officially that girl. The girl who opened her eyes when she should have kept them nailed shut, the girl that said yes rather than no, and the girl that, given the chance to kiss the same sexy man all over again, would do it without hesitation.

He really did look like Thor.

He had to know that.

I was almost tempted to tell him that, but I doubted that he needed to be reminded of his own good looks. He'd grown into them too well. In high school he'd been smaller. Cuter. Now he was beautiful. Muscle and sharp planes formed his body into perfection.

Licking my lips, I stole a peek at him out of the corner of my eye. He was leaning against the window, his hand placed on his chin like he was in deep thought. Full sensual lips pressed in a firm line as he continued to stare at the seat in front of him.

I quickly looked away, and that's when the full force of my choices smacked me in the head. I was on a plane for Hawaii, with an almost-stranger, and I had no idea what the heck I was going to do.

"What are we doing?" I asked.

Jace tilted his head toward me. "Pardon?"

"Why are we going to Hawaii? This is insane, you know that, right?"

"It's not." He grimaced. "It looks like we're taking a trip with family. It gives my publicist time to smooth things over, and well, by the looks of it, Grandma isn't going to go down without a fight. Things are better when she's not faking strokes and tricking the clergy into fraud."

"Sound logic." I nodded. "But what are we going to do once we get there? I only had a week of vacation when Grandma called me to come to the wedding." Okay, so I was lying. I'd taken two weeks off, but he didn't know that.

"So, your first?" he asked again.

Is that what he'd been in such deep thought about? I instantly felt my face heat crimson.

"It's not up for discussion," I snapped.

"Fine." Jace turned in his seat, his eyes appearing strained as he silently seemed to work through the situation. "Call your boss when we land, explain the situation, but don't tell the whole truth. Say you had a family emergency. Your name wasn't leaked to the media, and I doubt anyone will be able to tell who you are by the fuzzy pictures they were tossing everywhere on TV."

"Okay, so that solves one problem, but what about Grandma?"

"You called?"

A disembodied voice sounded from behind me. I hoped I was imagining things, but by Jace's irritated expression, I knew that prayer wasn't getting answered. With a slow turn, I faced Grandma. She had wine in her hand and looked cheerful as all get out.

"Did you need something?" Jace asked smoothly.

"You're good." Grandma's eyes narrowed. "I'll have to be more careful with you than I was with the other two. You almost had me fooled, Jace Antonio Brevik."

Somehow I felt like I was in the middle of some sort of silent battle where either Jace won and Grandma walked away, or Grandma won and burned a hole through the plane, and we fell to our deaths.

"Anyway," Grandma's attention snapped back to me, "I know this is such an inconvenience, but I have to admit I planned it."

"You don't say," Jace said in a dry voice.

"I admit when I'm wrong." Grandma glared. "And I was wrong to drug you."

"Drug?" I repeated in a weak voice. "When did you drug us?"

"Honey, you should be more careful about who you let give you drinks."

"Right." I bit my lip. "I should be weary of eighty-six-year-old women with date-rape drugs? Is that what you're saying?"

Grandma stretched to her full height. "I can neither deny nor confirm your suspicions. But I will apologize. I think my matchmaking ways have rattled this old brain. That being said," her face fell, "all I ask is that you let me make it up to you."

"We're not getting married." Jace groaned.

"Oh you!" Grandma tittered, taking a long sip of wine. "I'd like to take you out to dinner once we land, just the three of us. And then you may both enjoy the rest of your week, all expenses paid. Beth, I know how you enjoy hiking."

"You hike?" Jace asked in a shocked voice.

My nostrils flared in irritation. "Don't sound so shocked that I like exercise and nature, Mr. Senator. Sometimes I get bored with all the white walls in my office. I like getting dirty."

His eyes dilated.

On instinct I leaned in, my hand gripping the armrest between us like it was the last barrier before I jumped onto his lap and ripped his tie off. I'd always wanted to do that. Attack a man and have wild crazy—

"And, Jace," Grandma said, ignoring our exchange, where I was daydreaming about taking advantage of him and he was most likely assuming I was suffering an aneurysm, "eating has always been at the top of your list. Don't deny it. You're basically obsessed with fine wine and dining."

"Do you wine taste?" It was out of my mouth before I could stop myself.

Jace's face lit up, the dimple at the corner of his mouth distracting me from breathing. "My family owns a few wineries near the Oregon Coast. I love it."

I'm so marrying him for his wine. Don't judge me. Girls have needs.

"Interesting." I scooted closer, inhaling his scent, allowing his wine-loving presence to wash over me, and then in an instant, Jace jerked away from me and glared at Grandma.

"I see what you're doing."

"What?" Grandma examined her nails.

"She likes wine. I like wine. She likes hiking. I like hiking." He rolled his eyes. "Oh look!" He laughed dryly. "It just so happens I have a priest waiting to marry you. And a special license! Well, I'll be damned." His eyes narrowed. "You belong in a home."

Grandma's icy glare could have single-handedly ended global warming. "The only home I'm going to is the White House, and it's only to be sure to secure your failure should ever try to run for office."

"Try me."

"Already have."

"Guys." I placed my hand on Jace's chest and let it shamefully stay there an extra few seconds while I gently pulled Grandma's talons out of my arm.

Jace's face broke out into one of those creepy politician smiles, you know the ones I'm talking about, where you see too many teeth and the eyes get all small. "You're right. Where are my manners? Let's try this again." He cleared his throat. "I don't do relationships. I refuse to be played by a woman who eats blood-pressure pills like candy and cheats at Bridge."

"Why I never—"

"I won't play your games, and now Beth knows that as well."

"We all know that," the lady from the seat in front of us chirped in an irritated voice.

"Drink your damn happy juice," Jace fired back under his breath then crossed his arms. "Grandma, stop meddling. Yes, we'll do dinner, and then this," he pointed at me and her, "is done."

For some reason, I felt like crying. I wasn't really sure why. I mean, I agreed with every single thing he'd said, but that didn't lessen the sting or make me feel the rejection any less.

But the thing about women and how we think? Regardless of what a guy said about not wanting commitment or the stability of a relationship, deep down, every girl imagined that if he just found the right one, he'd change his ways. So hearing that he'd met me, kissed me, slept with me and still wasn't willing to change his ways? Yeah, it stung.

Maybe Jace wasn't trying to reject me, but that was what it felt like. It felt like the final nail in my relationship coffin. If I couldn't perk a politician's interest, really what did I have going for me? I swallowed thickly and gazed up at Grandma.

"Beth? Do you agree?"

Her eyes held magical powers. I could have sworn I felt her reach into my brain and touch the truth with one of her bright red nails. So I looked away for a brief moment before nodding, giving her my best fake smile. "You know me, Grandma. I'm all about my career. Settling down really isn't in my future."

"Well," Grandma slumped, "if you're both sure."

Jace reached for my hand. "We are. And we appreciate the effort."

Okay, suddenly I wanted to punch him in the face.

"Jace," I said in a sickly sweet voice.

"Yeah?"

"If you don't stop speaking on my behalf, I'm going to use your body as my own personal Frankenstein experiment when you're sleeping, got it?"

He pulled back and smirked. "Got it."

"Well," Grandma sighed loud enough to wake up every single child under eight in the back of the plane, "I guess what's done is done. And again, I'm so very sorry for the inconvenience. We'll be landing around dinnertime. I've already apologized to the kids for crashing their honeymoon. They've agreed to take your bags back with them to the hotel while we go have our peaceful dinner, then we can meet them there for a nightcap."

"Fine." I smiled tensely.

"Ta-ta." Grandma waved and walked back down the aisle.

With a sigh, I slumped back against my chair, trying to

look at the positive side of things. Just because Jace didn't want me didn't mean I was a loser. It just meant I was... single. Still single. Did it mean I was bad in bed? Possibly. It also meant that I was probably a terrible kisser. Who could blame me when my practice had been with Vampire Lover and McDonalds' Employee of the Month?

"She's up to something."

"Jace," I swore, "stop being so..."

"So what?"

"So... suspicious. She apologized. We get a free vacation. Leave it at that."

"But—"

"I'm going to sleep."

"Okay." He sounded disappointed.

I wanted to see the look on his face. I wanted to dissect every single look, every touch, every sigh, but I knew in the end the equation would still equal out to be zero. No matter how many tallies I put in his favor, he still wouldn't want what I had to offer.

Because in the end, I wasn't even sure what I had to offer, except for my heart. And for thirty years — even that hadn't been enough.

CHAPTER EIGHT

"You mean to tell me he wanted to be kidnapped?"

Grandma nodded. "Yes, that's correct."

"And he wanted to be ruffied?"

"Of course."

"And he asked you to give him some time before you revealed his location?"

"That's what I'm saying."

"Did you murder Senator Brevik?"

"Oh honey, if I'd had murdered him. I wouldn't have gotten caught — that's why I'm here."

"You're here because you got caught."

"I let you catch me. To give him time."

"Fine. I'll bite. Time for what?"

"Love."

Jace

Once the plane dropped down in Honolulu, I was beyond ready to lose my cool. The little girl in front of us had, for the past hour, chattered about school, life, her mom, her

60

gas — really anything that she'd thought might interest us. But the real kicker had been when Beth had started coloring with her.

And I'd been left to watch.

I'd watched her hands glide over the paper.

I'd watched her delicate fingers as they held the color blue.

I'd watched when her face lit up from the praise the little girl had given her.

And then I'd ruined it by scowling when the child gave her a high five, and I'd been left out.

Irritation pierced me in the chest. And I was ready to lose my damn mind over it. Every time I tried to imagine a reason for me to be upset that Beth wasn't giving me attention, the more upset with myself I became.

I probably should have apologized for my bluntness, but things were better that way. She needed to know it had been a one-time thing. Yeah, she was beautiful, but that didn't mean I was ready to hand my balls to her on a silver platter.

Been there done that. Never again.

So what if that made me insensitive? I had my job. I loved my job, and I intended to do anything to keep it.

I turned on my phone and looked down at the screen.

Rick: *Call as soon as you land.*

I texted him back instead, knowing I didn't want to be that annoying guy who started talking loudly when everyone was trying to grab his bag and make it down the narrow aisle.

Me: *Landed. Can't talk. Everything okay?*

Rick: *Define okay.*

Me: *Did the problem go away?*

Rick: *If the problem you're referring to is an attractive thirty year old that works for the company whose bill you just rejected because you said it wasn't soundly written, then yeah. Sure. Peachy.*

Me: *What?!*

Rick: *Like I said, call me when you have time. We need to make this go away. Approval ratings can drop overnight. Good news? People think you're getting married, and the news is loving it. So stay put.*

Cursing, I put the phone back in my pocket and rubbed my temples.

"Bad news?" Beth blinked her green eyes innocently.

"Thanks to you, yes." I was trapped. I couldn't leave, and if I stayed, I stayed next to Beth, and the longer I was in her presence, the more I wanted to attack her — in a totally sexually pent-up, frustrated way. One where there was biting and fighting and—"

"Me?" Her eyebrows shot up.

I tried to look pissed instead of aroused.

"Any chance I can pay you an obscene amount of money to kick me in the balls on national television and say you're mentally insane?"

Beth's eyes narrowed into tiny slits. "Tell you what, I'll kick you in the balls for free. As for the rest of it, go screw yourself."

"Ha," I said dryly. "Chemist's got some personality after all." I was being an ass. I knew I was being an ass, but I was pissed. I'd specifically asked her if she had a past. I'd specifically asked about any sort of drama in her past, and she hadn't even thought to tell me she worked for GreenCom? Technically, it had been my fault. I hadn't looked at her work history, just her title. And honestly, it didn't matter that much. I was more upset over the fact that I could smell her damn perfume, and it was choking the bachelor out of me.

"You're an ass," she hissed, pushing past me and walking down the aisle. By then, people had basically vacated the plan.

With a curse, I got up and walked slowly down the aisle.

I'd been drugged by an eighty-six-year-old woman.

Couldn't remember my one-night stand.

Had been accused of sleeping with a prostitute.

On a last-minute vacation where I felt slightly manipulated and possibly kidnapped.

And my approval ratings were going to hell.

Things couldn't get worse.

I finally reached the gate where Travis, Kacey, Char, Jake, and Beth were waiting.

Clearly something was wrong because they were frantically dialing their phones, and Kacey looked like she was ready to cry.

"What?" I asked stupidly. "Did someone die?"

All eyes turned to me.

"We can't find Grandma." Beth's voice was strained. "She said she had to use the powder room and just disappeared."

"I'm sure she's fine," I soothed. "After all, this is Grandma Nadine we're talking about. I'd feel sorry for her attacker. Hell, I'd probably watch the entire episode and order popcorn."

The group seemed to relax a bit.

That is, until we heard honking.

And then a splash of leopard flew by me at top speed.

"I think I found her." I pointed.

Grandma parked the airport cart, giving herself whiplash in the process, and stepped out. "Sorry, dears, it took me the longest time to find one of these things."

I winced. "Grandma, I think it's illegal for you to drive that without assistance from the airport staff."

My body gave an involuntary shudder as Grandma's pointed stare met mine. "I am the law."

Ho-o-oly shit. What had I gotten myself into?

"Get in." Grandma put the cart in reverse, nearly killing two elderly people in the process, then pulled out her lipstick and began applying in the rearview mirror.

Great, so she used mirrors for lipstick application and not driving. We were in such good hands.

The last thing I wanted to do was go to dinner. Sleep. That's what I wanted. Sleep. And to hear from Rick that everything was fine.

I picked up my bag and made my way to the cart, eying Beth as she leaned on Char. Was she crying? Had I done that? Feeling like a jackass, I moved toward her, only to be stopped by Jake and Travis, both of them looking like they'd rather shoot me in the face than let me even near their family.

"Listen, punk," Jake started.

I laughed. I couldn't help it. Punk? Really? That's what he was going to go with? And then he punched me in the stomach. I doubled over, not a proud moment. Travis pulled me by the shirt and leaned me against the wall so it looked like I hadn't just gotten the wind forced out of me.

"Listening." I glared.

"We will end you." Travis smiled as if he was excited about the idea of killing a state senator and going to federal prison. "Leave her alone."

"Her?" I repeated. "You mean Grandma?"

"Grandma?" Jake snorted. "That woman could run circles around you in her sleep. Hell, I don't even feel sorry for you. We're talking about Beth."

"Hey," I held up my hands, "I didn't do anything wrong."

"You slept with her."

"I'm not sure," I answered honestly. "I can't exactly... remember the details."

Travis nudged Jake. "Performance anxiety?"

"Hell no," I growled. "I think I was too drunk or—"

Wrong thing to say.

I got punched in the stomach again.

My stomach had dropped to my balls — well, at least I wasn't hungry anymore!

Travis swore. "Don't play games with her. Leave her alone. Let her have a relaxing time in Hawaii and be nice."

"I'm nice." I defended myself.

"You're a… *politician*." Jake made mock quotes. "That basically means it's your job to be nice and make everyone feel confident in your abilities, but I see through the bullshit. I saw through it when you were after Char, and I see through it now. Leave. Her. Alone."

"Or what?" I sneered. Okay, so I wasn't actually going to do anything, but I was pissed they were threatening me.

"Oh, that's easy." Travis stepped away, smirking at Jake as if they had this giant-ass secret I wasn't a part of. "You don't leave her alone, and we let you fend for yourself with that one." He pointed back to the cart where Grandma was currently thrusting her phone into the air and yelling.

"I have no service! Damn third-world country!"

I'd last five minutes alone with that woman before committing a federal crime. "Fine, but for your information, I was going to leave her alone anyway."

"Sure you were." Jake rolled his eyes. "That's why you've been staring at her ass for the past ten minutes."

Naturally, my eyes went directly where they weren't supposed to, and I was gifted with another hard slap to the stomach.

"Glad we understand each other." Travis smacked my cheek.

"Shit, you're like Grandma's mafia."

"She'd be one hell of a mob boss." Jake whistled, thrusting his hands into his pockets. "Oh, and by the way, have fun at *dinner*."

"Damn." Deflated, I watched as the group got on the cart and wandered down to baggage claim, leaving Beth, Grandma, and me.

"Well!" Grandma clasped her hands. "Isn't this nice! Now, how about that dinner?"

CHAPTER NINE

"How long do you plan to keep this up?" the agent asked pointedly.

Grandma grinned and leaned forward over the metal table. "How long do you have, sugar?"

Beth

I was a blubbering idiot. The only explanation I had was PMS or something like it. Char and Kacey enveloped me in a few side hugs and told me men were asses. It helped. Kind of.

I could only assume they'd seen my fallen face and were trying to offer their support in any way possible, which to girls basically meant bashing on the guy in question until the crying girl stopped crying and started joining in.

But I didn't want to join in. Because, regardless of how harsh Jace had been with my feelings — at least he'd been honest.

Honest, I could do. It was the men who lied about who they were that really bothered me. I'd dealt with honest most of my adult life. I could work with it; logically I could explain it.

Maybe it was my hair.

I'd always been told the brown was too dull.

Or possibly my eyes? But, in my opinion, they were really the only thing I had going for me. Dark lashes fanned the emerald green of my eyes, giving them an almost exotic look.

But that was it. No, seriously. It was all I had. My body was normal, not too big, not too small. And I officially sounded like Goldilocks from *The Three Bears*.

"Was he mean to you?" Char squeezed my hand. She'd always been the type to fight first, ask questions later.

I loved her for it.

"Nah," I lied. "He was a perfect gentleman. Not too bad for a senator."

"Senator my ass," Char hissed. "He's slimy, that one."

"I thought you liked him," I argued.

"Liked." Char sniffled. "Past tense. I liked him before he stole you away from the wedding reception. I liked him before I found out you were plastered against his naked chest for hours on end. And I liked him before he started staring at your ass as if it held secrets to national security."

"He was staring at my ass?" I asked in a much-too-hopeful voice. Bad Beth. Very bad.

"Not the time, Beth." Char's eyes narrowed. "Remember what happened with Brett? And Steve? And John?"

"Stop naming men from my past before I kill myself," I muttered.

Kacey didn't say anything. She watched our exchange with interest, her mouth turned upward in a smile as she looked between Jace and me.

"He *is* cute," she finally said.

Um, actually he was a god. No really, ask Marvel Comics.

"Kace..." Char warned. "Cute is for puppies. Not politicians."

"Let's go!" Grandma shouted above the boys fighting and the girls laughing next to me.

"Go get 'em, tiger." Char pinched my butt. "Make him work for it."

"Work for it?" I asked innocently. I had a sneaking suspicion she didn't mean actual work, as in giving him math formulas and solving for Z. But something way harder, like actually trying to be sexy.

Char's answer was to nudge Kacey and laugh. Was I missing something? Shrugging, I summed it up to being overly exhausted and tugged my purse over my arm. Dinner. One dinner. And then I was going to find some Hawaiian man in a loincloth to rub coconut oil all over me and say big words like electromagnetic and ionic… bummer. I was my own ionic bond. No matter how many times I'd wished I could stick to something, it hadn't happened.

Crap. I had no charge. I so *wanted* to charge. I *needed* a charge.

"You okay?" Jace asked, once we fell into step behind Grandma.

"Do I have a charge?"

"Huh?"

"A charge," I repeated.

"Like a card?"

"Like a bond."

"I think I'm confused."

I sighed heavily. "Ionic bonds. They're formed when charged particles stick together. I think I'm chargeless."

Jace's face lit up with humor. "Chargeless, huh? Is that your professional opinion?"

"I'm going to the ladies' room! Damn wine!" Grandma yelled and stomped off, leaving Jace and me in the very romantic spot people like to call the wall between the ladies' and men's restrooms. Toilet flushing was our romantic music, and the smell of Mexican food floated through the air.

Again. Clearly I was chargeless.

"So…" Jace leaned against the wall.

"So?"

"Your professional opinion. Is that it? That you have no charge?"

"Yup." Another toilet flushed. Awesome. I almost wanted to cheer for that person. I mean if you can't cheer for someone having a successful bowel movement, really, what can you cheer for?

"Great." He grabbed my arms, pulling me into his embrace. Toilets continued to flush, but I focused my attention on his lips as they moved. "Now, here's mine."

His kiss was tender, elusive. I leaned into him, and I was rewarded for my efforts as his hot mouth pushed harder against mine. Without warning, he pulled back.

"Beth." His hoarse voice washed over my body, giving me chills. "You're looking at it wrong. The problem isn't your damn charge. It's that you don't even realize you had it in the first place. If you don't know what you have, how can you use it? So you want to form an ionic bond? I call bullshit. Why would you want to bond with another person's energy when you have your own? Why bond when you're a continuous spectrum?"

"You used big science words." Right, that's all I had after his speech.

Jace's eyes flashed with amusement. "Sometimes. It happens. I did go to school, you know."

"It was like dirty talk, only hotter." I leaned in closer as his smile grew.

He leaned forward, touching his forehead to mine. "There's more where that came from."

"You called me a continuous spectrum." I grinned, feeling all warm and fuzzy all the way down to my toes.

"It was a compliment."

His lips were so close I could almost taste his peppermint

gum.

"I know."

"Beth," he gently pushed me away, "stop worrying about attracting things you don't want to attract." He cleared his throat and ran his hand through his overly long blond hair.

Was he referring to himself? Was I attracting him?

"Trust me, the right guy will come along, and when he does, it will be amazing. Until then, just keep shining. You're beautiful, you're smart, and you have a lot going for you. Don't let yourself become your worst enemy."

Stunned, I could only stare at him and wish... that's what I was doing. I was willing or wishing him to say *screw it* and kiss me again. I wanted him to want me, and I hated that I was so weak that I felt like I needed a person of the opposite sex to affirm that I was attractive.

"Well!" Grandma strolled out of the bathroom and swore. "Some people just can't handle dairy products, and that's that!" Her eyes narrowed. "What's going on here?"

"Science lesson." Jace put his arm around me. "A little ionic-bond lesson."

"Damn bonds." Grandma hauled her giant leopard purse over her shoulder and winced. "I'll tell you about bonds. The government makes you buy them, and then you wait years — years, I tell you!"

"And an economics lesson," I added. "What a day."

"I'm a starved lion. And I about croaked in that Godforsaken hellhole they call a bathroom. Let's go." Grandma pointed to the doors and scurried away.

Jace chuckled and followed after her, leaving me trailing behind the two of them. Why did he keep kissing me if he wanted to keep me away? And why did I care? Thor was kissing me. This was cause for celebration not contemplation. But, of course, in true spinster fashion, all I could do was focus on the fact that he'd told me I was a spectrum, and sadly that was one of the nicest thing any man had ever said to me.

CHAPTER TEN

"Ma'am, what does Justin Timberlake have to do with anything?"

"Justin Timberlake is the answer to everything," Grandma said solemnly.

"How do you figure?"

After a long pause she answered, "Because he brought sexy back."

"I'm sorry I didn't take a sick day today."

Jace

So I'd kissed her twice. Big deal. I licked my lips for probably the twentieth time, hoping, no praying, that I'd still be able to taste her on the tip of my tongue. Damn, she tasted good. I couldn't get her smell or her taste out of my consciousness, and I really needed to be focusing on important things like trying to get my career on track, rather than flushing it down a shithole.

With a haggard groan, I licked my lips. One last time. Just to remember.

How many times had I kissed a woman and experienced nothing?

Shameful to admit when a man is so ridiculously turned off by the female species that he stops responding all together. That's what Kerry had done to me. She'd broken me. And I hated feeling like a broken misused toy that no longer functioned properly. It pissed me off and made me feel like less of a man.

But Beth? She made me feel alive. Too bad the things that make you feel alive eventually kill you. Drugs, alcohol, bungee jumping. Okay, fine. I was being dramatic, but still. Women were predators. They couldn't help but want to trap men and eventually destroy the relationship in the process. Maybe it was fear, but I imagined it was so much deeper than that.

Arranged marriage. That was my future. At least in an arranged marriage I could pull the strings; I could use it for my benefit. I'd have the perfect little senator-wife, and I'd have my dream.

The only problem? The longer I spent with Beth and that damn grandmother, the more reality was pushed away from the forefront of my mind. I needed to get back to the mainland, and I needed to call Rick. Beth made me lose focus.

I never imagined myself a romantic. That dream had been killed over ten years ago. I was so young and stupid, naïve to think that Beth would remember the magic of our kiss. The magic of the moment we'd shared. I'd fallen head-over–heels. In exactly three minutes, I'd had our wedding planned, while she hadn't been able to wait to get away.

When I'd told Grandma Nadine I'd help get Jake and Char together, never in my wildest dreams had I thought that I'd get pulled into the Titus-family drama. And not once, had I thought I'd end up in bed with Char's sister. Especially after all those years wishing for that very thing.

I stole a glance at her.

She was beautiful. But I'd been surrounded by beautiful

women, and none of them, not a single one, made me want to fight.

She did.

And it made me pissed as hell that I had somehow given her that type of emotional power over me. I'd done it once with Kerry, let my guard down and found her in bed with my best friend. But even with Kerry, I hadn't felt the sizzle I'd felt with Beth.

Which was terrifying. If it was this easy for me to want to be with her, then that meant she had that much more power to destroy me. And the sad part was, I'd probably let her, because even though I wanted to be that guy that was tough as shit and didn't give a damn. I wasn't him.

I'd always known that once I fell for someone — once I fell in love, it would destroy me from the inside out. My mom had always joked that I wore my heart on my sleeve. In my profession it helped. People genuinely trusted me. They liked me. And in return, I tried to do my best for them.

Them. I needed to keep remembering what I'd been born to do. Lead others and sacrifice. At least, at the end of the day, I'd still have my job. Logistics, voting, politics, they were topics that, given the chance, would take over a person's life, leaving no space for anything else. I needed my life to be that way in order to be able to control things.

Groaning, I decided to put my mind to rest.

For tonight.

I was going to focus on getting through dinner. It would be hard enough fielding Grandma's ministrations. I'd need all my energy for that woman. I swear, God had done a number when He'd made her.

"We're here!" Grandma shouted as if we were at the World Cup.

"Yay." Beth pumped her fist into the air and gave me a tired smile.

Poor girl. She was probably just as tired as I was. It

wasn't as if that flight had been something made out of dreams. It had been hell, hell on earth. And it truly had made me question my desire to procreate.

"I'm so hungry I almost ate the three-week-old candy I found at the bottom of my purse," Beth murmured so only I could hear her.

"What? No sharing?"

"It had fur on it." Beth sighed. "Fifty-fifty chance I would have died from some sort of fungus poisoning."

"More science." I sighed. "Hot."

"Fungus. Always hot."

"Where's the damn boat?" Grandma put her hands on her hips and stomped down the dock, while I closed my eyes and pinched the bridge of my nose.

Grandma yelled obscenities into the night sky, but I wasn't paying attention, because Beth had somehow managed to lean against my shoulder, and my shoulder had decided in those brief seconds that it liked being leaned on. So I stayed, paralyzed by her touch, debating whether or not I should put my arm around her or just stand there like a limp idiot.

"You kids stay here. This is just..." Grandma didn't finish; instead she continued yelling and walked off down the beach, cell phone in hand.

Beth didn't move. Instead, she leaned further against me while I closed my eyes and let the smell of the islands permeate my senses. The air was thick with the humidity of flowers. For the first time in two years, I felt semi-relaxed.

That is, until a horn sounded in the distance.

I blinked a few times at a boat. Scratch that, it was more like a freaking yacht. Of course, when dealing with Grandma Nadine, what else could I expect? The woman didn't do small, in any capacity, so if the Titanic suddenly arose from its watery grave and made its way across the ocean to our destination, yeah, I wouldn't even blink. As the yacht got closer, it was harder and harder not to look away. I'd always had a thing for them, and this one was beautiful. Stark white with its lights reflecting off the water. I could retire on it and live comfortably for the rest of my life. The side said *Titus Enterprises*. Maybe we were having dinner on it? . A man in a blue Hawaiian shirt pulled up to the dock and waved us over.

"I think that's our ride," I whispered in Beth's hair, shamelessly allowing myself a few deep breaths.

"Hmm..." she answered and started walking down the dock.

I blindly followed, hypnotized by the sway of her hips as she made her way down toward the water.

The captain helped her into the boat. She was tired, but I was at least still functioning.

"Where are you going?" I asked.

"Are you Jace Brevik?"

"Yes?"

"And Beth Lynn?" He pointed to Beth, who looked absolutely dead on her feet.

"Yeah..."

"Great!" He clapped his hands together. "I'm your captain. Your grandmother is going to follow in the next boat. She said something about needing to use the restroom again, so I was given the go-ahead to drop you kids off so you can eat."

"Food." I grunted. "Fine, How far away is it?"

The captain gave me a funny look then answered, "Things are only as far away as you allow them to be. Now sit back and relax. There's rum punch in the back. Help yourself."

"Alcohol." I nodded. "Score."

"Right, because that hasn't caused us any problems in the last twenty-four hours," Beth joked sleepily.

Ignoring her, I grabbed two paper cups and went to the little mini-bar at the back of the boat. Filling both cups to the rim with the pink juice, I grabbed a bag of salty chips to share with Beth and returned to where she was sitting.

"Eat." I handed her the chips.

"Food!" She snatched the chips from my hands and opened them.

"You respond like this to all types of food, or is it just junk food, like chips and cookies?" I laughed.

Beth closed her eyes and slowly placed a chip on her tongue then closed her mouth and started chewing. Who the hell ate chips like that?

"All food," she said, still chewing. "I love salt."

Well, that explained the weird chip placement. She reached for another chip and did it again. I swore and looked away. What the hell was my problem?

I lifted the rum punch to my lips and took a sip. The liquid was cold and sweet, but not too sweet. It had a hint of ginger and basically tasted like heaven after that flight.

"It's pretty." Beth sighed, drinking her punch.

"What is?"

"The sky. The hotels. The water." Beth pointed to the shoreline as all the hotels of Waikiki Beach lit up the dusk night sky. "I've only been here once. I promised myself I'd come back after graduation, but then I got a job, and you know how that goes. Ten years later, you wonder why you haven't ever taken a vacation."

I snorted. "Know what that's like."

"Anyway," Beth cleared her throat, "I've been thinking."

"That can get you into trouble."

"I know." She played with the half-empty cup in her hands, twirling it around a few times before leaning back against her seat. "I know this situation isn't ideal. I know you have a lot going on. But, I think this is what I needed. A vacation. To get away for a bit. I'm just sorry that you got drug into it."

I threw my head back and laughed. "Honey, it was my own damn fault. I actually said yes to Grandma." Shrugging, I continued. "I was, uh, supposed to hit on your sister and get her to like me. There was a certain wager going on between Grandma, Kacey, and Travis. They wanted someone good for Char, and Grandma wanted to win the wager. Clearly, Grandma succeeded. Jake and Char seem happy."

"So you are still a white knight, sweeping in just in time to save the day." Beth sighed.

I, in turn, panicked. "What do you mean? White knight?"

"I remember." She broke a chip in her hand and popped it in her mouth. "Senior year. You were at prom with your cousin."

My palms got sweaty all over again as I rubbed them on my pants and waited for what was next.

"You swept in and danced with me when I was pouting all by myself."

I laughed. "Believe me when I say, there was nothing white-knightish about your rescue."

Her face fell. "What do you mean?"

"Truth?"

She nodded. "I thought you were really hot."

The sound of Beth's laughter filling the crisp night air may as well have been a damn explosion inside my chest — I would have been happy to listen to her laugh all night.

"Thanks." She smiled. "That made my night."

"That's a shame." The word were out of my mouth before I could stop them. "Because as far as compliments go, it was pretty shitty. I hope that you've been told that you're more than hot. I hope guys use the big words with you. You're a big-words type of girl."

Beth's smile tightened; she shrugged and looked away. "Char says Jake gives good compliments. It's sweet."

With a frown, I set down the cup. "You don't seem convinced that it's sweet at all. If anything, your entire body just slumped further into your chair, and your shoulders fell forward. Don't you like Jake?" Personally I thought he was a spoiled ass, but he was working on it, and I respected him for that.

"It's not that."

Beth shook her head and stared down at the damn cup in her hands. Irritated, I grabbed the cup, forcing her to look up.

"It sounds ridiculous when I say it out loud."

"What does?"

Beth rolled her eyes. "I don't even know you. I'm not going to get all emotional on you."

"Lies." I smirked. "I've danced with you for at least three minutes and shared a few hours in bed with you. And if Grandma has her say about anything, we're most likely engaging in some sort of Hawaiian wedding tradition where sharing rum punch means we're married."

"Valid point."

"Tell you what. This is a free pass. Besides, we're on the ocean. Nobody can hear us, no cell phones are going off, and there's no media. It's just you and me. You want to howl at the damn moon, just say the word. I've officially made the ocean Switzerland."

Her mouth curved into a smile. "Neutral? Hmm, can senators do that?"

I paused then snapped my fingers. "Just did."

Beth laughed.

I held my breath. It was that beautiful. I didn't want to ruin it by making any noise at all.

"Fine." She chewed her lower lip, tilting her head to the side. "I think it's jealousy."

"Jealousy?" I leaned forward so our knees were touching. "How so?"

"Travis had been in love with Kacey since he was little. Char was in love with Jake. Each of them had their past, their own story, and a Cinderella-ending with a fairy godmother in the form of a lipstick-wielding grandmother."

I chuckled. "And?"

"And," Beth leaned forward and sighed, "I have science."

"Rock on." I nodded encouragingly.

She smacked me in the arm. "I'm serious!"

"I thought you liked your job."

"I do! I just…" She started twirling a piece of her hair. "I just… sometimes, I just wish for the Cinderella story. I want the happy ending, I just want… more."

"More isn't always better, Beth. Remember that. It's easy to watch from the outside. Especially when you're lonely. Hell, it's easy to assume people have the perfect life. You make up a fantasy about how lucky they are and how perfect they are. But truth? Life sucks. It's freaking difficult. Most couples bleed and fight and burn to stay together. That's what it takes. It isn't a fairytale. And I don't think that's what girls want in the first place. They may say they do. You may say you want easy, but believe me when I say you want hard. You want a guy to fight. You want him to be willing to go to battle for you. Don't for one second envy a situation you know nothing about. Instead, be at peace with where you're at in life and know that when the right time comes, it will happen. And when it happens, it's going to be hard, and you're going to have to ask yourself if it's worth it."

"Do you think it is?" she asked in a small voice. "Worth it?"

Sometimes I hated my own honesty. "Most of the time." I swallowed and looked away, feeling guilty about what I was hiding from her. "No. I don't think it's worth it. And even if it were, I can say with absolute certainty that I wouldn't stick around to find out."

"Whoa," Beth said. "Brutal. But honest."

"Who says politicians can't be honest?" I joked aloud, even though my heart thumped in betrayal. "I hope I didn't let you down. I just don't think I'm made that way." Lies. All lies. I had been made that way, at one point, but people change. Things happen.

"What way?"

"Like Prince Charming." I elbowed her. "Walking straight into love just seems like a bad gamble to me. It doesn't make sense. Why willingly walk into a situation where the odds aren't in your favor? Why take the chance that things won't end up happily ever after? Why not just do what you're good at and be successful? To me, success makes me happy, I don't need another person in my life to know that I'm a good person. And I don't need approval from the opposite sex to feel like more of a man."

"So..." Beth smirked, "you're okay with dying alone?"

"If I don't get assassinated first," I teased.

The boat approached a dock. That was quick. Someone walked toward the boat and helped the crew tie it up. A line of Tiki huts lit up the front of the shore. Things didn't look abandoned, but it wasn't as if there were tons of tourists.

"She sure took us a long way just for dinner," Beth said.

"That's because you aren't here for just dinner," the captain answered. "Your bags will follow in the next boat with your grandmother. Everything has been taken care of. Enjoy your stay."

"Stay?" we repeated in unison.

"For six days." The captain scratched his head and checked his clipboard. "Yup, says here you have Romeo and Juliet Honeymoon Suite. And wedding be, oh yes, Saturday. Now is there anything else you needed?"

"Wedding!" Jace yelled.

"Chill. Hang loose, man." The captain laughed. "I love pulling that trick on tourists. Gets 'em every time. No wedding. But you do have the suite. It was the only hut available."

"Hut?" Beth enunciated the T with vengeance.

"Sure." The captain smiled. "Though here on the island we just call them fertility huts."

"Holy shit. Grandma's trying to get you knocked up." I chuckled. "Not gonna happen."

Beth's gaze snapped to mine; her eyes narrowed.

"Not because I wouldn't want to sleep with you. I mean, I think we can both say it was... fantastic." If only I could remember just how fantastic. Kill me now.

"Up you go!" The captain grabbed Beth and hoisted her onto the dock. "Just keep walking straight until you reach the main lobby."

The minute I followed suit and stepped onto the deck, the captain grabbed me and whispered, *"Keiki, keiki, keiki."*

Was he saying kinky or keiki?

"What the hell are you doing?" I pushed him away.

"Cursed." The captain slapped my back a few times then tugged my ear.

Swear, I almost kneed him in the nuts.

"Keiki, you have *keiki*, and you'll be happy for all eternity. Six days." He smiled. "For six days you will be cursed with her scent, her laugh, her walk, her smile. If, at the end of the six days you decide to walk away, the curse be broken, and you not feel pain from her parting. If you choose her as your mate, you be blessed."

My mouth dropped open. "Are you high?"

"Keiki." The captain nodded and slapped my back again. "Good luck, my friend. Aloha." He put a large necklace over my neck and kissed my cheek.

I reared back, ready to push him into the ocean, when Beth yelled my name. The breeze picked up as I turned to face her.

And my heart froze in my chest.

Her green eyes were glowing in the moonlight. My body reacted like she was my universe; it was as if everything around me faded, and all I saw was green.

Green eyes.

Beautiful eyes.

The wind picked up again as the smell of coconut floated through the air. I could taste it on my tongue. Hell, I could taste her. Damn, I wanted her. I wanted her so bad that my body was having trouble functioning.

Shit! The man, the beads, the curse. I turned to yell at him for putting his voodoo crap on me, but the boat was already gone.

When I turned back around, Beth was smiling.

And I knew.

She would pull.

I would fall.

And in the end I *would* walk away.

Because she deserved better, and I didn't believe in second chances, even when it came to the one who got away.

CHAPTER ELEVEN

"We don't have alcohol on the premises." The agent rubbed his forehead again and groaned. "And even if we did, I'd use it before I'd give it to you."

"Well, that's rude." Grandma sniffed.

"Can you help me at all? Can you give me anything? Any information?"

"Yes." Grandma sighed. "I suppose I can, but it will cost you."

"Bribery? Of a government agent?"

"I kidnapped a US senator. You said so yourself. Do you think the law applies to me? Furthermore, do you think I care?"

"Ma'am, I can say with absolute certainty, that you are under the illusion that no law or rule applies to you."

"Why, thank you! How sweet." Grandma leaned back in her chair. "Where shall I start?"

"The beginning."

"It began with a curse."

"Shit."

"Don't worry, it was a good curse. And it wasn't real, but he didn't know that. You see, sometimes we just need to be given permission to do things. We need to be told something is okay."

Beth

Jace looked like he'd just seen a ghost. I waved in front of his face; he sucked in some air and began choking wildly and tugging at the beaded necklace around his neck.

"When did you go shopping?" I fingered the necklace.

"Don't touch it. I'm cursed!" he shouted.

I'd never witnessed a nervous breakdown. But I was almost one-hundred-percent sure that's what was taking place. Jace pulled at his neck, nearly choking himself in the process and kept holding his breath.

"Get it off!" he yelled again.

"Jace. Breathe," I demanded.

His wild eyes looked everywhere but my face. Finally I grabbed him and pulled him into a hug. "It will be okay. It's just six days."

"You can't touch me. I'm serious, Beth. This is serious!"

"Right. You and your necklace are cursed." I patted his back in a motherly fashion. "You're under a lot of pressure right now. It's okay to freak out every once in a while. Just take some deep breaths, and we'll get some food in you."

"I'm not..." He started hyperventilating. "What the hell kind of perfume do you have on anyway?" He pulled back, eyes wild.

"I'm not wearing perfume."

"Aw, shit!" Jace finally pulled free from the necklace and threw it into the ocean, nearly popping his arm out of the socket in the process.

"Better?" I crossed my arms.

"Immensely." His chest was still heaving from exertion. "Sorry about that."

"Oh, it's fine. I've always wondered what it would be like to watch someone completely lose their mind." I smiled.

And was rewarded with a middle finger.

"Whoa there, Senator, manners."

His eyes narrowed. "The damn captain cursed me. He cursed me with you!"

Mad as hell, I smacked him on the arm. "Then why don't you just go back to your perfect life with your ridiculous amount of money and leave me the heck alone! I need this vacation, and I don't need you here being all—" I pushed him again, "angry!"

"Fine!" Jace shouted, and then he pinched the bridge of his nose. "I mean, you're right. I'll leave. I just. He just—"

"Aloha!" A lady approached us on the dock. "I don't mean to interrupt what I'm sure was a very healthy and emotional conversation where you're both searching for your feelings deep down inside and—"

"Who are you?" Jace interrupted.

The lady was wearing all black and had a name tag that said *Dr. Z.*

"I'm the manager of this fine establishment, and I've been expecting you." She couldn't have been more than five foot two, was of Asian descent, and had black-rimmed spectacles that covered half her face. "Now if you'll just follow me to the center."

"Center?" I repeated. "I thought it was a hotel?"

"Oh, it's so much more! Here at Ocean Breezes Couples' Retreat, we pride ourselves on being up-to-date on the latest couples' therapy, relaxation treatments and—"

"Back up." Jace held up his hand. "Couples' therapy?"

"Of course." Dr. Z nodded. "That is why you're here, is it not?"

"Not," I answered for both of us. "Not, not, not, not."

"Strange." She folded her arms. "I've had your reservation for over a month."

"A month!" I yelled. This time Jace braced me as I lunged for the innocent doctor.

"Come along." She ignored my violent outburst. "Dinner starts in about ten minutes, and we need to get you in your clothes first."

"You have our suitcases?" That was the best news I'd heard all day.

"Oh no." Dr. Z snapped her fingers. Two men came running; one handed her a packet, and the other handed her a key. "Here at Ocean Breezes Couples' Retreat, oh my, that is a mouthful. Here at OBCR, we value equality over style. Both men and women wear the same white outfits every day to show their commitment for a clean slate."

"Clean slate?" Jace gave me a nervous look.

"Ah, here we are." Dr. Z led us down a pathway to a large hut. "You'll find a change of clothes inside. Please hurry. As you were dropped off later than expected, we do not want your dinner to get cold."

With that she closed the door, leaving Jace and me alone in the hut.

After a few moments of silence I said, "I think we were played."

"You think?" Jace snapped.

"Don't try to pin this on me!" I stomped over to him. "Besides, it's not like we could have made an escape, what with you grabbing at your chest like you had fleas or something. *My necklace, a curse, a curse, a curse!*"

"Not funny. I was cursed!" he argued.

"Yeah, with a nervous breakdown, and now we're at some mental institute for unhappy couples! Screw you and your advice on the boat. I want the fairytale, you hear me!" I pointed up at the ceiling. "I want the fairytale, damn it!"

"Who are you talking to?"

"God."

"Why?"

"So he can tell Grandma I want a do-over."

"Nice." Jace smirked. "And I'm the one with the nervous breakdown."

"Don't push me." I pointed at his chest and held up my

fingers. "I'm this close, this close to snapping."

"Well, we don't want to see what that would look like, you snapping. Hurry up and hide the cookies."

"Aghhh!" I pushed him against the bed, causing it to slam towards the wall and him to fall backwards on top of the mattress. And then I realized I was on top of him. Straddling him. And he was warm. And great gods of Asgard, my body savored it.

"Nice thighs." He smirked. "They're strong. Mind unleashing me before I have to get both legs amputated from blood loss?"

"Please, like it's your legs you're worried about."

A knock came on the door. "Five minutes!"

"She's just going to keep coming back." Jace grunted from underneath me. "I say we hurry up and change, get some damn food in our bodies, and then call Grandma. We can take the next flight out of here and still have time to have a nice quiet vacation."

"How brave! You're running away with your tail between your legs."

"Are you saying you want to stay here?" Jace lifted his arms into the air helplessly.

"No, that's not what I'm saying." I put my hands on my hips. "What I'm saying is I can handle staying here. I have balls of steel. What do you have?"

"Balls. Normal ones. Ones I'd like to keep intact, and if I stay here much longer, they're going to pull back up into my body and render me a eunuch. You want that to happen? You want that on your conscience?"

"Three minutes!" Dr. Z shouted.

Beth threw a set of white clothes at me. "You're ball-less, just like I'm chargeless!"

"Excuse me?" he shouted, reaching for his pants.

Was he going to show me? Was this a pissing contest? Seriously?

"You heard me!" I peeled off my shirt and threw it onto the floor. "You don't want to stay because you know you couldn't take it!"

"Is that a challenge?" He took two steps toward me. "Hmm, Beth?"

"It's only a challenge if the other person stands a chance."

"What do I get if I stay?" His eyes roamed greedily over my chest.

I crossed my arms and glared.

"Not that."

"Like I'd have to ask."

"You're an ass!" I hissed, pulling the white linen shirt over my body and following with the white linen pants.

"I'm a politician, sweetheart. I've been called worse."

"Time's up!" Dr. Z said, knocking on the door again.

"So what do you say?" I held out my hand. "We have a bet?"

"Wager."

"Dare."

"Deal," we said in unison.

"You stay for six days, and I help you with the whole *I'm a prostitute* situation. I'll say whatever I need to say to those nice little cameras. I'll even kiss you on national television."

"And I'll…" Jace frowned.

"You'll give me six days." I licked my lips out of nervousness. I hadn't meant to ask for that, but the more I thought about it, the better the idea became. After all, it was his kiss I hadn't been able to get out of my head for twelve years; his touch I'd been thinking about every single time another man put his arm around me. If anyone in that Godforsaken hut was cursed, it was me. Cursed with memories of a man that made me wish for the fairytale. I'd been feeling sorry for myself for too long. And Jace was probably right. Maybe the fairytale wasn't real, but I wanted to experience it just for a little while. And he was going to be the one to deliver it.

"Pardon?"

"A real six days. No strings attached. Six-day vacation with food, drinks, fun, and…" I felt heat rising to my cheeks, "just six days. Six days of being a normal girl in a normal relationship with a normal guy." If the normal guy happened to look like you could break boulders off his abs.

"Stop saying six." Jace swore. "It sounds like sex, and I just watched you take off your shirt."

I felt my cheeks heat.

"And it makes me want to slam you against the wall and rip it from your body, so when you ask for six days, know that you're asking for a real six days. I'm not going to keep my hands to myself."

"Fine." My lower lip trembled. "I just want to be romanced."

"You want the fairytale," he said in a low voice.

"Yeah. I do."

"I can do six days," Jace whispered. "Just don't hate me on day seven, because I will walk away."

I snorted. "Easy, Jace. You aren't that irresistible. It's a risk worth taking. I want to put Boring Beth away for awhile." Besides, he'd walked away before. What's one more time?

"Beth." Jace sighed. "You're not boring. Look, maybe this isn't—"

A whistle sounded, and then Dr. Z opened the door. "Ready?"

Jace held out his hand to shake mine. I touched it, feeling the sizzle all the way down to my toes.

"Ready."

CHAPTER TWELVE

"This ship captain, did you pay him to curse the senator?"

"Of course not!" Grandma shook her head. "No money exchanged hands."

The agent took a long sip of coffee.

"However," Grandma paused, "there are other ways for payment."

The agent choked. "Ma'am, prostitution is illegal."

"I would never sell my body." Grandma shook her head vehemently "Besides, the captain's already tasted the goods. Past lover, you understand. He was only too happy to... aid me in my quest."

"Your quest for love?" The agent's eyebrows narrowed.

"Yes. Let's call it that. It has a certain ring to it!"

Jace

I'd just made a deal with the devil. I'd signed the contract in blood, and now all I had to do was live through the next six days. The good news? I could save my career. And Beth was right. She was the answer. I'd send a text to Rick as soon as I could.

As for giving her six days of a fairytale? I imagined it would be like babysitting, more or less. Lavish her with gifts, feed her, give her enormous amounts of wine, and wait for her to fall asleep at night. Okay, so maybe if I wanted to get arrested, it would be like babysitting. I just needed to keep her happy, repeat for six days, and home free. How hard could it be? To woo a woman? I wooed people on a twenty-four-seven basis. Then again, most people I wooed weren't ones I'd been pining for since I'd gone to my first dance.

The other issue would be that damn curse. I wasn't an idiot. I didn't believe in curses, but the man had been right. Thirty-two minutes ago we'd gotten to the island. And for thirty-two minutes, I'd done nothing but stare at Beth's mouth, watched her hands as she gripped her silverware, and closed my eyes when the breeze carried her scent into my personal space.

Shit.

Six days.

Less than a week.

I could do anything for a week.

"Jace." Beth's soft voice carried across the table. At least she didn't sound pissed anymore. "Did you hear anything I just said?"

"Sure." I sipped my wine.

"So you agree?"

"Absolutely."

"On the neck, don't you think?"

"Uh..." Well hell, that's where daydreaming got a person. "The neck is perfect."

"How long should it be?"

"Long enough." I was the king of vague. I could field questions all day long without actually giving an answer. Point, Jace.

"And color?"

"I think bright colors are the best." I nodded. "They seem to… attract attention." I gave her my best politician smile.

"Hmm, maybe you're right." She looked down at the paper in her hands and started scribbling. "Tomorrow good?"

"Sure." I leaned over to see what she was writing down. But she jerked the sheet back. "I need you to sign."

"What am I signing?" I asked, giving her another polite smile.

"You said you were paying attention." She handed me the pen.

"I was. I am."

"Good. Sign here."

I was ashamed to admit I signed only because I didn't want to look like an ass.

Dr. Z approached the table. "I take it you filled out the information?"

"We did." Beth grinned.

"Fantastic." Dr. Z took the folder and pulled out the sheet I'd signed. Her eyes widened slightly. "How very brave of you two!"

"We thought so." Beth reached for my hand.

I had a bad feeling.

"A twin dragon tattoo! And on your necks! How lovely! The dragon is the symbol of being connected. It's rare for couples to be so committed upon arrival!"

"That's us," I said in a dry voice. How the hell was I going to talk myself out of that one? I'd signed the damn document. "Committed." I kicked Beth under the table.

She winced as Dr. Z examined the rest of the papers. "Alright, I'll just schedule the rest of your week and slip the paper under you door this evening. Your first session is with one of our newer therapists. She's absolutely lovely."

The sound of Dr. Z's heels clicking against the tile floor felt like a noose getting tighter around my neck.

"Tattoo?" I tilted my head. "You think you're funny,

don't you?"

"You weren't paying attention."

"I was." Sort of. If watching her mouth move was paying attention, and memorizing her scent was my pop quiz, yeah, I was paying attention.

"No, you weren't. We shook on it. Six days. I don't want you ignoring me. I don't want you texting. I want the fantasy. God knows, it's only six days." Her face fell a bit before she smiled to cover up her disappointment.

Shit.

"You're right." I reached for her hand. "I'll do better. It's just been a long day." And if she kept saying six, I was going to six the hell out of her in a public forum.

"I know." Beth stared down at our hands.

I should have pulled back. I should have run. Instead, I placed my other hand on top of hers and whispered, "Why don't we go back to the room. I'll draw you a bath and romance the hell out of you."

Which also meant I was going to be rewarded with sainthood for not trying to seduce her the minute we were alone.

"I thought you were gifted with words?"

"Exhaustion. It's set in. Plus, I'm cursed. Don't expect perfection."

"Who said I wanted perfection?" She winked. "I just want the fairytale."

"Didn't we already have this talk? They're the same thing."

"No," Beth stood, "they aren't. And that's why you're so bitter. Some things aren't always black and white, Mr. Senator. Now romance me."

"Day one." I smirked.

"Day one," she agreed.

I held her hand the entire way to the hut.

****

"Sure, I'll dance with you." She put her hand in mine. I walked her to the dance floor, unable to take my eyes off her glistening dress or pretty brown hair. My cousin was going to kill me if I bailed on her, but the pull was too strong.

"You're really pretty." I pulled her into my arms and tried act smooth, even though I was pretty sure my hands were shaking. "What's your name?"

"Beth." Her head tilted back, enough for me to see her crazy green eyes. "What's yours?"

"Jace." My voice cracked at the end. Great, I'd just give away my age. No doubt she was a senior and thought I was about as cute as seventh grader with a cold.

"Thanks."

She leaned her head on my shoulder. At least I had my height going for me.

"For what?"

"The rescue." She laughed. And a part of me that had been dormant for a lifetime flared to life. God, she was beautiful.

"I'll rescue you anytime. Day or night."

"Is that a promise?"

Her smile was deadly. It made me want to kiss her, and the last thing I needed to be seen doing was kissing a girl from another school while I got my ass handed to me by the defensive line of the football team. It was their territory, not mine.

But I couldn't stop the words from coming. "Of course."

My head descended; she met me halfway. Our lips touched, and I kissed her hard. Harder than I'd ever kissed a girl before in my entire life. It was a hello and a goodbye kiss, because I knew it wasn't something I'd be repeating. She was way out of my league. As it was, I was playing with fire even kissing what I'm sure was the quarterback's girlfriend. But I couldn't help myself.

"Brevik," a male voice sneered from behind.

I pulled away from Beth and slowly turned to face, who I was *sure, would be the largest kid in school.*

Instead, it was the coach from the football team. Aw, hell. He only knew me because I'd unintentionally put one of his players out of commission for the rest of the season.

"Who are you here with?"

"My cousin." I swallowed nervously.

He peered around me at Beth and chuckled. "She doesn't look like your cousin."

"Not her." I ground my teeth together. "She's just... a friend."

Behind him, my cousin waved frantically.

"Look, I gotta run. My date needs me." Geez, it wasn't like I was getting secret plays from Beth or anything. I turned and gave her hand a quick squeeze. "It was fun."

She gave me a sad nod, and I walked away.

When I looked back, she was gone.

The sound of the alarm jolted me out of the dream. Why the hell was I dreaming about that now? I smacked the alarm clock with my hand and peeked over at Beth. She was sleeping like the dead, too beautiful for her own good, and I was horny as hell from that damn dream. I shouldn't have walked away. I should have gotten her number. Not that it would have changed a damn thing. People didn't date in high school and then get married right away anymore. At the time, I'd still believed in love at first sight. Hell, I'd thought it had been love; the rest of the memory was painful as hell. My therapist had said my mind somehow pushed the rest of the night out of my consciousness; he'd said accidents had a way of doing that. I was protecting myself. But from what? I wasn't sure.

When I'd woken up in the hospital, I was changed — everything had changed. My parents had said I wasn't the same, but I had no idea why. It had made me even more paranoid about pleasing them, about getting things right. Getting my career right.

Speaking of careers, I grabbed my phone from the nightstand and was rewarded with a low-battery signal. I got up to grab my bag then remembered that I didn't have a bag. The same checked bag that had yet to appear.

My guess was that Grandma was holding it hostage. Or maybe Jake and Travis. Those bastards must have known. And how the hell did the woman have this planned a month ahead of time? A month ago I was saying yes to her scheme with Char and Jake.

A light bulb flickered on in the darkness of my brain.

I'd said yes.

That's where I'd gone wrong. I should have stayed far, far away.

Russia. I should have moved to Russia.

"Beth." I nudged her a bit.

She was lying on her stomach, wearing the outfit from the night before. She stretched, her shirt inching up on her body, exposing her flat stomach and a slight scar where her appendix had obviously been.

She moaned again and lifted her arms high above her head.

The shirt followed.

So did my eyes.

I blinked a few times, fascinated with how smooth her skin looked. I wanted to touch it — to hell with that, I wanted to lick it. Had I licked it the other night?

"Jace.

Her voice was low, sexy as hell, raspy. Shit, I was in trouble.

"What?"

"Do we have to go to couples' therapy?"

"Aw, sweetheart, backing out already? Where's your balls?"

"I don't want balls." She yawned. "I just want a damn charge. I have girl parts. I talk a big game. I use big words. Right now, I want a big-ass coffee and a big sleep."

"Stop saying big."

My body was responding to that word in a very *big* way, and I was already struggling after watching her yawn and stretch and mew all over the place.

"Fine. Large. I want a large coffee, a large—"

I covered her mouth with my hand. "Let's establish mornings as quiet time. A time of reflection, and thinking, and—"

She bit my damn hand.

"Coffee."

"Bite marks." I showed her my hand.

"Woo me."

She fell back onto the bed in a heap, and I had to admit I liked the bossy attitude. I got up and started fumbling with the Keurig.

The shower turned on.

"I'm so proud!" I yelled without turning around. "You turned it on all by yourself."

And I turned myself on by saying *turn on*. Damn curse! I gave myself a little shake and placed the cup under the spout.

"Aghhh... mother of—"

Thump. Thump. Thump. Thump.

Absolute silence then an ear splintering, "Jace!"

I ran toward the bathroom.

"So big!" Beth yelled.

The shower was one of those walk-in ones, where there was no curtain or door or anything to hide any scratch on your body.

Beth was standing in the corner with a shampoo bottle in her hands, pointing at the opposite corner.

The first thing I noticed was her nakedness, but it was quickly trumped by another shout and a shampoo bottle flying by my head, causing another thump.

"Get him!"

A spider that looked a hell of a lot like a shrunken MMA fighter barreled toward me. Now, I wasn't a fan of spiders. I didn't hate them, but that didn't mean I particularly enjoyed the idea of something hairy sinking its fangs into me. So I did what any logical man would do.

I looked for a gun.

And when I realized I wasn't James Bond, nor did I live in a spy novel, I grabbed the next best thing.

The hair dryer.

It wasn't plugged in, but it was big enough for combat. I smashed the hell out of the spider until all that was left were pieces of legs and tufts of hair.

"Did you get him?" Beth came up behind me, shivering.

"Yeah" I wiped my brow with my arm, "it was a battle. Lots of lives lost. Bloodshed. But… I got him."

"My hero," she whispered, wrapping her arms around me from behind.

I froze.

Not because she was calling me her hero. Please, I wasn't that narcissistic. It was because she was naked. And she had forgotten about her nakedness at a very fortunate time.

Men everywhere: Applaud. I didn't even react. Not one gasp or shudder. I simply basked.

Basking: *Another word for utter stillness when a lady is pressing against you in such an erotic way all you can do is close your eyes and smile.* **See also: Euphoria.**

"I'm naked." Beth released her hold. My body immediately tightened in all the wrong places, and I'm ashamed to admit, I let out a pathetic whine, or maybe it was a growl. *The next thing I knew, I was turning around and pushing her into the shower, up against the wall, and taking her like a—*

Great, so not only had I frozen in a euphoric state, but I had resorted to daydreaming.

"Thanks." I saw movement out of the corner of my eye as Beth leaned back under the shower and closed her eyes.

It was like watching my own personal Pantene Pro-V commercial, only the girl was hotter and available.

But not to me.

Not in reality.

"Are you going to watch me, or are you going to get ready?" Beth said, water dripping from her face.

"Do I get a choice?" I half-pleaded.

"No, but you'll get a knee to your balls if you don't leave in five seconds. The spider's gone, you've saved the world, now take your hammer and go."

"Uh, hammer?"

"Hammer, hair dryer — same thing. Go, Thor. Go get your cape on. We have therapy."

Men. We're easy. No really, we are. She'd basically called me an Avenger, which, in my book, meant I was like two steps ahead of Iron Man, and a hell-of-a-lot better looking.

I sported a smug grin the entire time I got ready.

****

Thanks to the water-stealing princess, I wasn't able to shower in time. And Doctor Z had specifically said that we needed to be on time. Not wanting to start off therapy on a bad foot, I took one for the team.

"It's only an hour, and then we have what the schedule states as *Couple Fun Time* by the pool." Beth checked her watch and handed me the map of the place.

I locked the door to our hut and turned the map sideways.

"North," I said, examining the red circle that said *Serenity Circle.*

"I don't like that name." Beth snorted. "It sounds like a place to get high."

"If they have drugs, just say no." I stuffed the paper into front pocket of my lame-ass linen shirt and grabbed her hand.

"What are you doing?" She tried to pull away.

I held tighter. "What does it look like I'm doing?"

"Holding my hand." She squeezed back, and then a girlish smile appeared, all sense of hostility evaporating instantly.

"That I am." I pulled her closer and inhaled. Damn, her shampoo smelled good. "You said you wanted six days of a fairytale. I thought holding hands was a good place to start."

"Oh."

Her face turned crimson, and I instantly felt it in my gut as if someone had taken a baseball bat and beat me crapless.

She'd never had her hand held.

I'd bet money on it.

Girls didn't blush over things like that. Most girls didn't give a rat's ass. What type of man wouldn't hold her hand? What type of man wouldn't first at least try to woo the shit out of her?

Wrong wording. One should not woo shit out of anyone, but I digress.

Sighing, we walked hand-in-hand toward the building, and I made myself a promise. One I knew I would most likely regret this time next week.

I was going to actually try. I was going to leave my baggage at the door, check into the happy romance hotel, and make her feel wanted.

And when it was time to leave, I'd do so without looking back. But I'd also do so without any regrets, and that was reason enough to take the leap.

CHAPTER THIRTEEN

"How did the senator take to being cursed?"

"He wasn't tickled pink, that much I know. He threw my very expensive fertility necklace into the ocean!"

"Tragic loss," the man said dryly.

"Oh it was!" Grandma pounded her tiny fist onto the metal table. "One can't simply purchase fertility necklaces anywhere!"

"I wouldn't know."

"Well, I would." Grandma sniffed. "After all, I've spent years collecting them, storing them in my grandsons' cars, houses, offices, boats—"

"Ma'am, are you saying you've been this way for... years?"

"What way?"

"Insane."

Grandma smiled. "Some people's definition of insanity is genius. What's your take, Gus?"

"My name's not Gus."

"You look like a Gus. I'm going to go with Gus."

The agent looked longingly back at the glass window. "I think it's time for a break."

Beth

Holding hands with Jace was like riding a school bus for the first time. You were all sixes and sevens with your own body. Not sure who to sit by, not exactly positive you were at the right stop, so you kept looking out the window to make sure you didn't miss your own house. And then when you did per chance miss your stop, you couldn't care less because you'd already made friends with everyone and were really enjoying the ride.

"This is it." He let go of my hand.

The stupid bus stopped.

And now I had the infamous children's song, "The Wheels on the Bus," playing in my head like a broken record.

"I think we just go in." I clenched my hands together and moved to knock when the door was pulled wide open.

"No. Way." Jace swore and then kicked the doorframe.

Grandma pointed at the ground. "I think you killed an ant."

His nostrils flared. But he said nothing.

Grandma clapped. "Oh good. It's still alive, look." She pointed down.

Jace looked and stomped at least five times before regaining control of his body again.

"Oh dear. Well," Grandma touched her hand to her cheek, "I guess he's dead as a doornail now."

Jace stomped again.

Pretty sure Grandma was driving him over the edge. I grabbed his hand and squeezed. At least he stopped stomping.

"Come in, come in!"

Grandma opened the door wide and led us into a small office with a trickling waterfall and two black leather couches. The wall facing the door was a floor-to-ceiling window that looked out onto the ocean. All in all, if this had been my office, my life would be complete.

"Sit," Grandma said sweetly.

Jace released my hand and sat on the leather couch. I waited for him to start rocking back and forth.

He didn't.

I exhaled.

"So," Grandma took a seat opposite us, "tell me about yourselves. Why have you chosen Ocean Breezes Couples' Retreat?"

My mouth dropped open. She was kidding, right?

"You. Put. Us. Here," Jace said in slow, curt language.

"Poppycock." Grandma lifted a cup of tea to her lips and chuckled. "I do love that word." With a sigh she took another sip. "Tea?"

I took the tea just so I'd have something to do.

Jace took a long sip and closed his eyes. He was probably trying to find his center, or whatever people called it.

"Is it bedroom trouble?"

Jace spit out his tea all over the table.

"Oh," Grandma's face fell, "how difficult that must be for you, Beth, to have a man who can't..." she cleared her throat then mouthed, *perform.*

"That's it."

Jace lunged for Grandma, but I mom-armed him and handed him his tea again, much like a mom would hand a kid a ball to keep him distracted.

"Listen, Grandma..." I used my calm voice, which sounded a lot like my pissed-off voice, only not as loud. "You drugged us, brought us here under false pretenses, forced us into a couples' retreat where we have to go to therapy as if we're a real couple, and now this? You, as our therapist? Excuse us if we aren't exactly in a great mood."

Grandma set her tea down and sighed. "Grandma Nadine isn't here at the moment. Hold one second." She reached for her purse and pulled out a leopard scarf then proceeded to wrap it around her neck, put on another application of lipstick, and then popped a cinnamon Tic Tac in her mouth. "Alright, now you may refer to me as Grandma Nadine. I have to separate the two titles for HIPAA privacy issues, you understand."

"Fine. Grandma," I clenched my teeth together, "you said you put your meddling behind you, and you're worse than ever!"

"I see that you're confused." Grandma shook her head. "I apologized for drugging you, brought you here to protect you from the media and give you a vacation, Beth, and used my own money to give you a free stay at one of the US's top ten honeymooning locations. Now, did I leave anything out?"

My mouth snapped shut.

Jace's eyes narrowed.

"Nobody said you had to participate in therapy." Grandma shrugged. "I just thought it would be beneficial. Take it or leave it."

"We'll leave it," Jace answered, standing up.

"Alright, I'll let Dr. Z know that you've refused treatment." Grandma smiled into her tea.

"Wait." I held up my hand. "What happens if we refuse treatment?"

"Oh nothing, dear, don't be such a worrywart." She licked her lips and hid her smile behind her teacup.

"Jace," I tugged his shirt, "sit."

"No, I'm not—"

"Sit, or so help me God, I'm going to revive that goliath spider and put it on your pillow."

Swearing, Jace sat back down.

"What does therapy entail?"

"Communication," Grandma said smoothly. "Knowing your partner."

"But we aren't partners."

"Six days," Grandma whispered.

"What?" Jace asked. "What did you say?"

"Nothing." Grandma clapped twice, the lights dimmed, and classical music began playing in the background. "Now close your eyes."

Jace swore again.

"Stop swearing, son, it makes you sound simple-minded."

"Did she just call me stupid?" Jace whispered next to me, his lips grazing my cheek.

"Pfft." Grandma chuckled. "If I wanted to call you stupid, I would just say it to your face."

"Right."

"Jace?"

"Yes, Grandma?"

"You're being stupid."

Jace cursed again.

"See?" Grandma grinned triumphantly. "Now, both of you, close your eyes. I'm going to give you a sample of what therapy will do for you. Take it or leave it, but don't make your decision until tonight. Agreed?"

"Fine," I said, teeth still clenched.

Jace nodded.

"Good." Grandma clapped once more, causing the shades to pull down the large window, blanketing us in utter darkness.

Great, just what we needed, to be vulnerable in the dark with Grandma.

"I want you to feel," Grandma instructed. "Beth, put your hands on Jace's legs."

Slowly, I stretched out my hands and placed them on Jace's thighs.

"Jace, turn toward Beth so it feels more comfortable."

His body shifted so we were facing one another on the couch. My hands were placed awkwardly against his thighs, and I could feel the heat of his body through the linen pants. I could almost feel his heartbeat as blood hummed through his system.

"Now, Jace," Grandma said softly. "I want you to touch Beth's face with your hands. I want you to be gentle, and I want you to memorize the way she feels."

I felt the heat of Jace's hands just before his fingertips grazed my chin then my cheekbones. His hands roamed across my face; his touch was so gentle it almost hurt. I leaned toward him as he moved his hands down my neck and to my shoulders.

"Feel how her body responds to you," Grandma coached. "Feel her skin, every sensation, every touch. I want you to memorize her face so well that if asked to draw a picture of her likeness you could do so blindfolded."

My fingers dug into his thighs as he continued rubbing my face, dipping his hands into my hair. With a gasp, I bit down on my lip as he brought his head closer and closer to me.

"Now," Grandma whispered. "Beth, I want you to do what Jace was doing but start on his legs, move up his torso until your hands are placed firmly on his chest."

And so my torture in hell began. I say torture, because every movement my hands made across his thighs caused my hormones to spike to deadly levels. Muscles I didn't even know existed were now a permanent fixture in my memory. My body cheered with delight when my hands made their way to his abs. They were tight. And I was ready to maul him for no other reason than touching him felt so good.

By the time my hands reached his chest, it felt like I'd just gone into a sauna with a wool coat on and was confused on how to get it off. My breathing was erratic. I was leaning so close to Jace that I could smell his cologne.

Grandma clapped, and the lights came on. I was practically in Jace's lap. His face was one inch from mine, and my body was tight, so tight it was ready to explode. I wanted him — everywhere — and I didn't even feel guilty that I was sweating like a whore in church.

"All done." Grandma clapped again, and the lights went full-blast, making me pull back.

"I'd say the first lesson went very well." Grandma rose from her chair.

"What was the lesson?" I croaked.

Grandma turned away from us and laughed. "I'm sure you can figure it out."

Jace grabbed my hand. "She finds joy in torturing others."

"No," Grandma turned to face us, "I find joy in inspiring others and, by the looks of you," Grandma looked Jace up and down, "I'd say you're about as inspired as they come."

"Pool," Jace blurted. "We should, uh, go swim."

"Okay."

Jace pulled me out of the office and stalked down the hall, tugging me behind him with such force my arm almost came loose — not that he'd notice. The man was on a mission.

We jogged to the pool area.

Jace pulled off his shirt and jumped in, leaving me gaping after him.

"What's wrong with you?"

"Inspiration." Jace cursed. "Too much damn inspiration."

CHAPTER FOURTEEN

"You drugged them... again?" The agent scratched his head.

"Well, what was I supposed to do, Gus?"

"Um, how about not drugging them?"

"Oh, you're no fun, Gus. Tell me, when have drugs ever done more harm than good."

"You're kidding, right?" The agent looked around, "You have to be joking."

"I don't joke." Grandma sniffed. "And I stand by my decision. Every man needs help every once in a while."

"Shall I add drugging to your kidnapping charges?"

"Well if you must. I don't want to have to give you too much paperwork, Gus. I really don't want to be a bother."

Jace

"Um, Beth." I swam to the edge of the pool and tried to think of a way to tell her that wouldn't sound crazy.

"What?"

I'd been swimming around for a good five minutes while Beth went in search of towels, but now that she was back, I

108

had to tell her. Damn it. Damn Grandma!

I shook my fist at the sky.

"You okay, Jace?"

"No." Embarrassed, I closed my eyes. "I think there was something in my tea."

"What do you mean?"

"I think I was drugged."

Beth's eyes widened. She took a step toward the edge of the pool and leaned down so she was on her hands and knees, talking to me. And let's be honest. I the state I was in, it was doing more harm than she even realized.

"What type of drug? Do you feel funny?"

"I wouldn't say I felt funny..." I looked down. "Just... inappropriate."

"Huh?"

"Viagra. She put Viagra in my tea."

Beth burst out laughing. "Jace, I highly doubt she would do that. You're a young, healthy, virile—" Her eyes widened. "Oh, Lord."

"What. Do. I. Do?" I grasped the edge of the pool like it was my lifeline.

Beth's grin grew. "Clearly you have a little problem."

"Can we call it a big problem?" I hissed. "You know, for my self-esteem and all? Can we not refer to it as little or small or miniscule or—"

"I got it." Beth held up her hand. "We have a tiny problem."

"Damn, should have seen that one coming."

"Just..." Beth waved, "make it go away."

"Just make it go away?" I repeated. "Make IT go away? How do you imagine I go about that, Beth? In a public place? In a public pool? Under the watchful eyes of God? Hmm?"

"Whoa. Easy, sinner. I don't mean for you to fornicate with the pool toys or anything. I'm just... thinking."

"Can we come up with a better idea? One that leaves

pool toys out of this whole conversation?"

"Don't be so touchy," Beth snapped. "We'll just wait it out."

"Right." I nodded. "Great. So I'll just stay in the pool for four hours in hopes that the situation alleviates, and if it doesn't, what then? Call 911?"

"Well they do say that if an erect—"

I covered her mouth. "There's an easy way to fix this." Without thinking about the ramifications of my actions, I pulled her into the pool, clothes and all.

When Beth came up for air, she screamed. "I'm not really a prostitute, Jace!"

Luckily the only other couple at the pool were by the swim-up bar, partying it up.

"Stop yelling!" I pulled her to the furthest corner of the pool. "And I didn't call you a prostitute. I accused you of having a shady past. There's a difference." But if she were thinking about a career change, now would be the time to fully commit.

"This is SO not the fairytale." Beth smacked me in the shoulder once we reached the other side of the pool by the waterfall.

Thunder rumbled across the sky.

And then sheets of rain started tumbling out of the sky — it wasn't a normal rain. It was a Noah rain. The type of rain that makes it almost impossible to see the person in front of you without blinking the drops out of your eyes.

Beth tilted her head back and laughed.

I couldn't laugh. The laugh was stolen from my chest the minute I saw her close her eyes as the water dripped down her body. I would never need Viagra in that woman's presence. Ever.

Just put Beth in front of all the test subjects for ED. Problem solved. I should get a medal.

"Come here." I growled, pulling her close to me. She

didn't fight. She wrapped her arms around my neck and her legs around my waist.

I groaned as she pressed against me. I was ready to beg, I'd been brought that low. Weeping? Yeah, it was going to happen. A grown man was going to weep; jury was still out whether the weeping would be from ecstasy or pain.

"I'm still not helping you." Beth smiled. "But there is this one thing I've always wanted."

"There's several things I want at the moment," I said in a hoarse voice as I moved against her. "But what's your one thing… tell me."

"I want to be kissed in the rain."

I touched my forehead against hers and nipped her lower lip then whispered against it. "I think I can do that."

Our mouths touched.

And it was like lightning had struck the pool. My entire body hummed as Beth's mouth worked against mine. I pushed her against the wall of the pool and then jerked her hard against me when she moaned into my mouth.

My body didn't just ache for her — it burned from the inside out, the outside in. Every time her teeth grazed my lips or her tongue collided with mine, I was burning hotter and hotter. Ready to explode. Happy and satisfied to be kissing her, even though my body had physically wanted more, I was finding ecstasy in her touch.

Rain poured down our faces as I walked her through the water, back underneath the waterfall.

I tripped with her in my arms; we both laughed as I managed to get us into the little cave.

My lips were about to find hers again when I heard a low voice say, "Beth?"

Beth moved her hands toward my pants, so I ignored the voice.

"Beth, is that you?"

Growling, I pulled back to yell but stopped when Beth's

face visibly paled. "B-Brett?"

"Hey!" He waded through the pool and pulled her in for a hug. "How are you? It's been so long!" He released her.

I tugged Beth closer to me and shielded her; I would have peed on her to mark my territory if my body would have allowed it. Seriously, the guy needed to back the hell off before my fist ran into his face.

"I'm good." Beth gripped my arm tight. "And you?"

"Awesome! Just on vacation for a few days." He held up his hand. "Hold on, you have to meet my fiancée."

He left. Beth's grip tightened. She looked like she'd just seen a ghost — and not a friendly one like Casper — one that feeds on the souls of small children.

"Make a run for it?" I whispered, tugging her away from the man with too much chest hair. Did he get implants? Did guys do that? To look more masculine?

"They'll see us," she said through a fake smile.

Brett reappeared with a plastic Barbie doll look-alike in nothing but a string bikini and smile.

Wonders never cease.

"This is Paris."

"Of course it is," I said under my breath. Beth elbowed me and held out her hand.

"Pleasure to meet you, Paris. I'm Beth."

Paris shook her hand, but passed Beth over as if she were a tiny little bug. Instead her eyes were glued to me and my naked chest. Of course they were. I'd be looking at me too if I had to date someone who used the same comb for his hair that he did his chest.

"Senator Jace Brevik?" A predatory smile made its presence known on her Botox-infused face.

I gave her points that she could still manage to move her mouth, let alone bust out a smile with all that swollen puffy skin.

"Yes. Yes, I am."

Brett laughed. "I knew you looked familiar! What are you doing here? Beth, holy shit, that's so cool you work for a senator?"

"Work?" Beth repeated. "What do you mean?"

"Well, you know." Brett waved her off. "You always were so smart. I just figured you were here to offer support to the senator and his wife or lover or whatever. Say, where's your significant other?" Brett looked around. "I would really love to meet her. Honestly, it would be an honor."

"My Brett's in politics too." Paris kissed Brett's neck and sighed. "He's the mayor of our town."

How nice. Brett thinks being a mayor means he's in politics. I should punch him in the balls and get it over with.

"Oh yeah?" Beth's lower lip trembled.

Why the hell did she look like she was going to cry?

"Yeah, mayor of Bellingham, but I have aspirations for more." He puffed out his chest.

Bellingham, Washington? Right. Good for him. If he kept at it, he could run against me for president, said no person ever.

"Anyway, we won't take any more of your time, but if your better half or whatever shows up while we're all at the pool, it would be cool to do a photo op."

"Why not now?" I found myself saying.

"But your girlfriend—"

I should have stopped talking. Instead, words were coming out of my mouth without my permission, and my arm wrapped protectively around Beth's shoulders. "She's right here."

Paris's mouth dropped open, and Brett turned bright red. Take that, sucker.

To add insult to injury, Beth chose that exact moment to grab my face and kiss me so hard that my mouth almost went numb from pleasure. When she pulled back, I tried to kiss her again, but she laughed and hugged me instead. The Viagra was still in full effect, and my body didn't understand that this wasn't the most appropriate of times to attack her.

I shot a look to Brett that basically said, *That's right, bastard. She's mine. Be an asshole elsewhere. We're full up here.*

"Wow." Brett smirked. "I, uh, I wouldn't have guessed."

"Why not?" I said smoothly. "Beth's one of the leading chemists in the field of research and development for GreenCom, she graduated with honors from Yale, and has more schooling than both of you combined. I'd say it makes sense." I pinched her ass.

She stomped my foot.

"Besides, she's sexy as hell."

"Well." Brett cleared his throat. "I guess we should take that picture then?"

Beth elbowed me again.

I glared.

She pointed down.

I cursed.

"Something wrong?" Paris purred, her talons resting on Brett's hairy chest.

Wasn't she afraid her fingers were going to get trapped? She scratched a bit; some of the hair covered her pink nails. I puked a bit in my mouth. And problem? Gone. Wow, and to think all I needed was a Botoxed woman touching another man's chest hair.

"Actually," Beth gripped my arm, "we were just on our way back to the hut for a nap, but we'll be here all week. I'm sure we'll see you later."

"Dinner," Brett said.

Would he never give up?

"Uh..." Beth looked to me for help.

"Sure," I answered without looking at Brett. "But just so you don't think we're flaky, we haven't been eating much. This trip is all about proper hydration so we can spend all day and night in bed. This is the first daylight I've seen in hours.

And I intend on keeping this one…" I swept Beth up into my arms and kissed her hard on the mouth, "very, very busy."

"Geez, get a room," Brett said under his breath.

"Oh, we have one." I smirked. "With a California king and a plunge pool. See you later, Rhett."

"It's Brett!" he called.

"Okay, Rhett!" I ignored him and walked with Beth in my arms all the way back to the edge of the pool. "Now we make a run for it."

"Now?" Beth winked.

"Don't make me chase you."

"If you catch me, you get a prize," she teased, lifting herself out of the pool and crooking her finger at me.

"I like prizes." I lunged after her, well okay so I lunged as well as my body would let me, but she was too fast. Me being a very aroused man, thanks to the tea, didn't help matters. Sadly, my run was more of a hop, cover up, hop, and sprint. So basically I looked like a drunk Hunchback of Notre Dame running towards the church bells. Then again, running towards church seemed wrong all things considering. Right, that was the last thing on my mind.

"Hurry!" Beth laughed.

And so I ran after her, hoping I didn't run into any poor soul on the way and get arrested for indecent touching.

CHAPTER FIFTEEN

"Let's go over this again. Besides the drugs, did you do anything else to harm the senator?"

Grandma rubbed her hands together as her eyes darted around the room.

"Ma'am?"

"Oh, alright!" Grandma let out a heavy sigh. "I may have helped them along in their relationship."

"Helped?"

"Lavender in the hut, fertility beads under the mattress, a dreamcatcher by the plunge pool, oyster appetizers every afternoon, and a Michael Bolton love mix."

"Michael Bolton?" the agent repeated.

"Don't knock it until you try it." Grandma smirked.

Beth

I ran to our hut, thrust my body against the door, and let myself in with the dangling key.

Jace was hot on my heels.

And I was out of breath.

But I wasn't sure if it was from excitement or embarrassment.

My past was coming back to haunt me. But it's not that it was a hard past where I'd done drugs or suffered from anorexia or anything like that. It had everything to do with insecurities, ones I'd never faced. And that was the crappy thing about insecurities: they never actually went away until you dealt with them. And I'd never dealt with mine. Ever.

And Brett? He'd just resurfaced every last one of them...

"Boring Beth, Boring Breath, Boring Breasts!" some of Brett's friends chanted and then high fived one another.

They all walked off. Every last one except JP.

"So, Beth." He smirked, and a piece of dark hair fell across part of his face. "Now that you know Brett wants nothing to do with you, considering you freaking plastered yourself all over the star of a rival football team like a total and complete slut," he took a deep breath, "I figured you'd go out with me."

"Go out with you?" I said in a small voice. "Like on a date?"

JP smirked and then burst out laughing. "I'm sorry I can't do this. The guys paid me ten bucks to ask you out, but the look on your face is priceless. I have a girlfriend, she puts out, why would I go for a virgin nerd with glasses, who makes guys run away screaming?"

My body crumpled against the floor. The cold tile helped alleviate the massive heat stroke that had attacked my body. I tried breathing in through my nose and out through my mouth, when I felt strong arms wrap around me and pick me up.

I snuggled into Jace's embrace and closed my eyes, angry at myself for allowing a bad high school memory to render me completely helpless.

Within seconds we were outside, and Jace held me as he walked into the plunge pool and sat. I was in his lap, arms wrapped around his neck.

"Thanks," I said in a small voice.

Jace's face was still, angry, tight. His jaw clenched as he

looked away from me and swore, slapping the water with one of his free hands. "What the hell did that guy do to you?"

"Nothing." I tried to squirm out of his lap, but his arms tightened, trapping me all the more against him.

"Beth."

"It's so stupid." My voice caught. "I don't think I've ever been so embarrassed. I'm sorry I freaked out. I just—"

"Beth," Jace's hand traced my face, "you have no reason to be embarrassed, but if you don't tell me what happened within the next ten minutes, I'm going to get charged with murder, and US senators don't do well in federal prison."

I gave him a weak smile. "It's a boring story."

"I happen to like boring," he whispered.

If any other guy would have said that, I would have taken it as a slam to my personality. But the way Jace had said it? Well, he'd made it feel real, as if he'd been saying that he liked me, had seen beyond what others had.

"Me and a few other nerds were his pity-dates at prom. I danced with him. He was really nice and then basically told me I was cool for a nerd. I refused to kiss him goodnight, and for some reason, it pissed him off that I wouldn't put out." I didn't want to tell him the truth, but there really wasn't any other way. "A few of his friends saw you and me kiss, and he was angry that I'd kissed you, a lowly sophomore from another school, and not him. He started a rumor that I'd hit on him, he'd rejected me but felt sorry for me, and that I'd asked him to take my virginity."

"Asshole," Jace hissed, rocking me back and forth in his arms. "I never thought…" He sighed against my neck. "I never thought my kiss would cause so many problems."

If he only truly knew how it had wrecked me.

"The rest of the year was absolute hell." I shrugged, ignoring the tiny voice inside that said I should tell him exactly how much that kiss had affected me, how much it had altered my view of dating and waiting for the right one.

"Notes in my locker from random people calling me a slut, whore, bitch, goody two-shoes. It was like I couldn't win. I suddenly didn't fit in anywhere. My smart friends were afraid it was true because Brett was so popular. And the popular people just thought it was pathetic. My freedom came when I graduated and went to college."

"Beth," Jace's thumb grazed my lower lip, "tell me what you want."

"Huh?"

"One," Jace continued tracing my lips, "I could go kill him and go to jail, but I think we've established that as only a last resort."

I laughed.

"Two, I can run for president someday then have the CIA handcuff him to a bed with stuffed animals and a few pornographic magazines, ending his political career for good."

"And three?" I leaned into his warmth.

"Three's my favorite one," Jace whispered. "Care to know why?"

I nodded, drunk off his scent.

"Because it involves you and me, lots of kissing, possible drugging, and a hell of a good time. What do you say?"

I kissed his cheek. "I say it may be a good thing we have Grandma here, since she seems to be her own pharmacy."

"Excellent," Jace whispered, his gaze roaming my face then resting on my lips. "I'm going to kiss you now."

"You don't have to." I leaned in anyway. The draw he had on my body should have been illegal. Either that, or they should somehow bottle it up and sell it to single women.

"That's the problem, Beth." His lips grazed mine. "I don't have to, but I really, really want to."

"Oh." That was all that escaped my mouth before our tongues tangled together. I gripped his long hair in my hands and jerked his body closer to mine as he growled low in his throat, his hands fumbling with the wet linen shirt that was still plastered to my body after being pulled into the pool.

I wrapped my legs around his body and hovered over him as he pulled my wet shirt off and threw it onto the ground, attacking my lips with renewed fervor.

"You're beautiful, Beth."

"Jace, just kiss me. You don't have to compliment me and—"

He reared back, his eyes nearly black with desire. "Don't tell me what to say or what to do. If I pay you a compliment, you say thank you. I don't do that often to women. I do it enough in day-to-day life. Hell, it's my job to make people feel good. But you? It's not my job to make you like me. It's my job to make you like yourself, and damn if I'm not going to try to get you to see how gorgeous of a person you are inside and out before these six days are up."

He threw off his own shirt and grabbed me by the waist, lifting me up onto the side of the pool. His lips met my neck and then my shoulder as he pulled down my bra strap and kissed the skin near my collarbone. His kisses were a mixture of sweet softness and urgency. I couldn't get enough of the way his lips felt against my skin and decided that even if I only had twenty-four hours with this man, I'd take it. Id' take it all, and I wouldn't regret it.

How could you regret something you've been dreaming about your whole life?

His hands moved to my thighs as he pulled me closer to his body, grabbing my legs and wrapping them around his waist as he rocked against me.

"Yoo-hoo!" A voice yelled.

Jace swore and reared back.

"Knock, knock!" the voice repeated.

"Dr. Z." Jace's eyes narrowed. "If we ignore her, she'll leave."

"Right," I said breathless as Jace kissed me again.

The knocking stopped and then suddenly a form

appeared on the other side of the privacy fence by the plunge pool.

"There you are!" Dr. Z's head bobbed up and down in relief. "I have your luggage!"

"From Grandma?"

"Grandma?" she repeated, sounding confused as her eyebrows pinched together. "No, this luggage is from a Travis Titus?"

"Ass!" Jace splashed the water with his hand again.

I laughed. "Thanks, Dr. Z. Just leave it at the door, and we'll grab it."

"Alright, and perhaps you should make use of the bathing suits rather than your undergarments." She winked and disappeared.

I looked down. My purple bra shone like a beacon in the pool.

"Whoops." I said out loud.

"Please." Jace's teeth grazed my shoulder as he kissed me again. "Like this was a whoops."

"Stop." I laughed, pushing against him.

"That's not a word I hear often." He winked then lifted himself out of the pool, but not before dropping his linen pants into a heap on the floor, leaving him oh-so-gloriously naked. "Whoops," he called as he padded all the way to the bathroom and shut the door.

I chose that moment to reflect by dunking my entire person into the cold water.

CHAPTER SIXTEEN

"Romance aside, what happens if your little love plan doesn't work?"

Grandma's smile fell as she placed her hands on the table and rose to her full height. "I don't fail."

"But surely you've thought of the possibility that—"

"Listen, Gus." Grandma's penciled brows furrowed together. "I've been doing this for a long time. I've got moles older than you, so don't get your panties in a twist, son. My ways may be..." she waved flippantly into the air, "unique. But I always make my match. Always."

Jace

Cold shower? Not working.

Cold shower. Grandma? Hairy-chested men named Brett?

Working.

Definitely working.

I leaned against the tiled wall and focused on evening out my breathing. I'd set out to make Beth feel better and where had that left me? Sexually frustrated enough to want to scream.

Or maybe I just wanted her to scream? My body seemed to be confused, because at that point I had to keep telling myself that in five more days I was walking away. Until then, all bets were off because I hadn't realized until that moment how much Beth needed the chance to see how spectacular she could be. Hell, I'd only known her for days, and even I could see it. How was it possible that when a person looked in the mirror all they saw was what they'd been told by other people their entire lives?

Beth was drop-dead gorgeous. With billowy lips, gorgeous thick brown hair, exotic eyes and a figure that started wars — it was no wonder that Brett had been an ass to her in high school. He'd been intimated, and that made me want to cause murder.

I was intimated and nothing intimidated me.

Was it so wrong to feel smug that, out of all the men in the world Beth could have asked to help her, she'd asked me? Granted, we were kind of stuck together, but still.

It was me.

And I didn't fail. Grandma and I had that in common.

I turned off the shower and wrapped a towel around my waist. When I opened the door to the bathroom, Beth had already brought our luggage in and was pulling out her own charger for her phone.

A moment of genius chose an opportune moment to make itself known. I swiped her phone and put it back in her suitcase. "No phones."

"How is that fair?" Beth tried to dig for her phone charger, but I held her hands hostage.

"It's fair because I won't use mine either."

She didn't look convinced. Her eyebrows shot up in shock. "Right, you're just going to refuse to answer your phone after the media portrayed you as a dirty rotten politician?"

"Rick will take care of it," I said evenly. "No phones. Just you and me. You want the fairytale. Pretty sure Prince Charming didn't have a Twitter account. We unplug. All week. Deal?"

Her eyes narrowed.

I held out my hand.

She took it. "Deal, but no cheating."

"Please, I don't cheat."

"Says the senator," she sang.

"Low blow."

"You make it too easy."

With a grin she patted my chest, and, if it were at all possible to be more aroused, it happened. All because she'd placated me; she'd patted me like a small child, and here I was ready to throw caution to the wind and take her on the bed.

"Jace?"

"Huh?" My head snapped up.

"Lunch?"

I pulled my watch off the nightstand and exhaled, giving my body enough time to calm the hell down. "You're right. It's still early. Let's do it."

Beth pulled out a sheet of paper and frowned.

"What?"

"It says we have three restaurants to choose from, and that we have some sort of mixer tonight for dinner? What do you want to do?" She twirled a piece of hair between her fingers as her mouth fell into a pout.

Hell and damn. I wanted to pull her hair.

That's what Viagra does to you. It makes you think about doing things you shouldn't be doing during the daylight. Like asking if you can pull a woman's hair, just to see what her face would look like when you're doing it.

Her eyebrows pinched together as she mouthed the restaurants and then bit down on her lip.

Never mind. I wanted to pull her hair and bite her lip. Or maybe I'd bite her lip first then pull her hair.

"Jace? Thoughts?"

"Sex," I blurted like a pubescent twelve year old.

"What?" The paper floated out of her trembling hands onto the bed.

Bed, bed, bed, my body taunted. Damn it!

I winced. "I'm glad we're going out instead of having, uh, sex?"

Yeah, she didn't believe me. Her mouth cracked into a silly grin as she crossed her arms and gave me a very judgmental look. So I said, "I'm a guy. I can't help it." Right, like that was a solid excuse. I may as well have pulled down my pants and pointed, "Look! Me boy, you girl," and grunted.

"The Viagra making a comeback?" she teased.

"Yeah, let's blame it on the tiny blue pill crushed into my tea." I had a moment of panic when I wondered if Grandma had slipped anything else into there, like a stupidity pill, because I sure as hell wasn't earning points toward Mensa membership.

"Tell you what." Beth picked up the paper again. "You pick where we eat. After all, this is my fairytale. I don't want to know all the surprises."

She had a hopeful look on her face, the same look girls get on Valentine's when they expect you to be the one guy to do something other than flowers or chocolate.

Smiling through my nervousness and intense need to impress her after the Viagra incident, I took the paper from her hands and examined it. All the restaurants sounded good. But good wasn't good enough. It was food. I wanted more than food, and I figured she did too. After all, how romantic can a person get over a hamburger and fries? Especially considering she hated fries? I should probably get to pull her hair for remembering that.

Beth stretched her arms above her head.

Down boy. We needed to get out of the hut before it turned into the hut of shame, and I made a complete ass out of myself by getting on my hands and knees and begging. I crumpled the paper onto the ground and stalked over to the phone and dialed the concierge.

"This is the concierge desk. How may I help you?"

"I want to romance my girlfriend," I said evenly into the phone, using my best politician voice. "Does this hotel have any excursions we can participate in?"

"Of course." The man chuckled. "When would you like your outing to take place?"

Beth bent over to pick up something off the floor. Holy shit.

"Now!"

"Alright, you don't have to yell."

"Sorry." I croaked. "I thought I saw a... turtle."

A turtle? Beth mouthed.

"Sir, testudines aren't predators."

"I know, I just..." I licked my lips in irritation. "The excursions? Please?"

The man was silent for a minute. "At this moment, all we have available is the noon excursion to a few of the sugarcane fields with a lovely picnic and a horseback ride through the waterfalls."

"Sounds perfect."

"Great, but I should warn you that—"

"Money isn't a problem," I interrupted. "We'll be in the front lobby in ten minutes."

I hung up the phone with a smug grin. Yeah, I was basically kicking Iron Man's butt. A horseback ride? Hiking through sugarcane fields? And a picnic? Slap my ass and call me charming. Fairytale, here we come!

****

"Jace?" Beth gripped my arm and stepped on my foot for the second time in five minutes. I winced in pain. "Sorry."

"What?"

"I think we're lost."

"We're not lost," I snapped. "We're exploring."

Exploring: A word men use when they're lost. **See also: Stubborn as a mule.**

"Oh." Beth sighed.

I took a sip of water from my water bottle and soldiered through. The picnic had gone pretty well. But now we were supposed to be touring the sugarcane fields, and in a moment of pure genius, I'd taken a step in and asked Beth to follow me. After all, how big could a sugarcane field possibly be?

It was like being in a giant cornfield, only the spiders were bigger than Mars and had fangs that made them look like tiny vampires ready to feed on our souls.

Note to self: Sugarcane fields are where people go to die. **See also: Hell.**

I pushed through some more sugarcane stalks and swore when I realized we'd have to go back the way we came. There was no way we could walk out of this place and actually make it back to the van in time for dinner. I wasn't Bear Grylls, and I could have sworn I saw a spider waving at me a few minutes ago. No way was I giving him a chance to get up close and personal.

"Jace..." Beth whispered.

"Not now. I'm trying to decide what direction we're facing," I snapped and looked up at the sky. North was ahead of us. The hotel was south—"

"Jace!" Beth swatted my back.

"Beth, seriously, don't interrupt a man when he's exploring. It's like our natural habitat, okay? Throws us off and freaks us out when women try to help."

She swatted me again, this time hitting me in the back.

"Beth, *seriously*." I turned around.

Her eyes were big as saucers, and then everything happened in slow motion. A tree-trunk-shaped hairy leg appeared in my line of vision. Beth screamed and started running in the other direction, and then something I can only describe as a species not yet discovered on this planet began crawling down my face.

Not a proud moment when a man screams like a small child and begins pulling off all of his clothes.

"R-uuun!" I shouted.

Beth had already taken off.

The creature bobbed against my line of vision as I ran. I swatted against it to get it to fall off of my face, but somehow it managed to cling to my arm. I imagined its tiny fangs sinking into my skin just as the sugarcane parted into a clearing.

Beth was hunched over, breathing hard, and I was still shaking my arm, trying to get the creature or spider or whatever the hell it was off.

"Shh..." A Hawaiian man approached, hands high in the air. "You're scaring Frank."

"Frank?" I stopped moving my arm and looked at the offensive creature.

"Very old," the man nodded, "very wise guardian of the cane."

"Oh, dear Lord."

"You mustn't remove Frank," our guide said in low tones. "He removes himself when he's ready."

"Would that be before or after he kills me?" I asked. "Just curious."

"He does not *kill*." The Hawaiian man actually looked upset that I'd even suggested such a thing. "He brings life into the cane and guards it from evil."

"So I'm evil?"

"No." The man took another step forward. "He must have been attracted to your scent. Tell me, are you aroused?"

I blinked a few times. Was this real? Or was I

hallucinating?

"Hell. No." Was he accusing me of being sexually attracted to spiders? Is that what was happening?

"During mating season, the spider senses can often be affected by the scent of arousal. Have you and your lady friend been…" He coughed.

"No," Beth chimed in. "Lady friend says no."

"Interesting." The man finally stopped in front of me. "But you want to with your lady friend?"

"Uh…" Oh, what the hell. "Yes."

"It could be the Viagra," Beth chimed in.

I sent her a seething glare while Frank clenched harder onto my arm.

"A young man such as yourself? Needing Viagra?" The guide chuckled. "No wonder Frank's attaching himself to you. He smells your desire."

"I AM NOT ATTRACTED TO MALE SPIDERS!" Yeah. I'd snapped. I'd take that assassination attempt any second now.

"Nobody said you had to mate with him." Beth giggled.

"You." I pointed and made a cutting signal with my free hand — you know, the one that wasn't getting humped by the spider. Words I thought I'd never utter.

"Perhaps Frank senses your desperation. Maybe you should stop prolonging the inevitable and mate with your lady friend." He pulled out a carrot and began gnawing on one end of it. "Besides, you only have five days to decide your fate. That curse must be working. It's magic."

"Curse?" I repeated.

"Yeah, your *keiki* is off."

"My *keiki* is fine."

"Frank's upset," Beth piped up. "He's getting on his haunches."

"Shit!" I waved my arm again. "First off, Frank," I pointed to the offending spider, "is still attached to me.

Second, how do you even know how long we're staying, and third, are you, or have you been in the past hour, high as a kite? And were you the one that cursed me?"

"I give drugs, not hugs. Hang loose, man." He grinned and reached for the spider. "Most guests only stay six to seven days, but you two were easy to peg. I read it in your reservation you made this morning. And my cousin's the boat captain." He grinned and took another bite off his carrot then held out his hands to Frank.

The spider slowly crawled off my arm and into the guide's waiting hands. The minute his hairy ass was gone, I ran toward Beth and shook my entire body.

When I approached her for comfort, she took a step back.

"Oh no, you don't. You could have more Franks in your pants. No way I'm taking a chance of one of them touching me. Who knows what voodoo that Viagra cast on you."

"So many things wrong with that sentence, Beth. So many things."

"Be free, Frank!" The guide let the spider loose and turned to face us.

"Bye, Frank!" Beth waved.

"Stop waving." I grabbed her hand.

She jerked free of my grip. "Chill. It's not like he bit you."

"And you noticed that when? Before or after you took off screaming, leaving me to die in the middle of the sugarcane field?"

Beth's eyes narrowed. "You're just pissed because you're the worst explorer ever, don't know where North is, and would totally get voted off *Survivor Island*."

"I would rather bomb the island with me on it, than have to run through a sugarcane field again. But if you wanna try out for *Survivor*, be my guest."

"Ahem." Our guide cleared his throat. "If it is okay with you two, we'll continue our expedition with the horseback ride."

"Saddle up, cowboy." Beth winked and slapped my ass. "Or are you scared of horses too?"

"I will ride that horse so damn hard…" I stopped talking. My body had failed me earlier today, and now it seemed my mind was last to go.

Beth's eyes shone with humor.

Our guide brought over the horses. I assumed the short ugly one who looked like a hundred years old was Beth's, but she was already getting on a different one, leaving me with Donkey from *Shrek* and a sinking feeling that one of us wasn't going to make it through the jungle alive.

CHAPTER SEVENTEEN

"Do you feel guilty?" the agent asked.

"For?"

"For potentially harming innocent people with your schemes and ministrations?"

"I'm sorry." Grandma shook her head. "I don't understand the question."

Jace

"How's the ass?" Beth called behind her as I let out another streak of swear words into the trees.

"Angry."

"Maybe he's hungry."

"No, I'm going to go ahead and go with angry. I'd be pissed if a two-hundred-pound man was riding me too."

"Maybe you should stop talking for awhile." She laughed. "You're not doing so well with the whole stringing-words-together thing."

"Damn mating spiders threw me off."

"And again, point proven. Maybe this should be quiet

time where you stare longingly at me and say I'm beautiful and irresistible and—"

"Can we switch animals?" I complained as Donkey let out a fart that smelled like dead chicken and enchilada. How was this supposed to be a romantic excursion?

She turned around and smirked as Donkey made another grunt and tried to catch up. "No."

"Please?"

"Be the prince, Jace!"

"My noble steed's older than Grandma! I need a steed!"

Donkey farted again, this time gifting me with the smell of roses — if roses smelled like burning flesh.

"Such a stud." She chuckled. Her posture was perfect on the horse as it galloped ahead. It made her look like some sort of avenging princess storming the castle.

Shit. Did that make me the damsel?

"Beth…" I growled. "I take it this isn't impressing you or making you feel like you're living in some damn romance novel."

She stopped the horse and turned around. "Take off your shirt, and we'll talk."

"No." I shook my head firmly. "I have to draw the line somewhere. I'm not going to take off my shirt while riding an ancient donkey through the jungles of Hawaii."

"Fairytale." Beth coughed, her damn eyes lighting up with humor, while mine narrowed with self-loathing and defeat.

"Why yes, Channel Six News, I am a prostitute. Want to see my client list? Oh, Senator Brevik? He's so extravagant!"

"Well played." With jerky movements, I finally managed to get Donkey to stop walking and peeled off my shirt. "Happy?"

"Immensely." She sighed happily. "Now mush."

"Not at the Iditarod," I called after her.

"So what are we supposed to say?" she grumbled. "Our

guide is too far ahead of us, and I'm not getting lost again."

"I don't know. Say please?" I really had no experience with animals or nature. My hikes had been by the Columbia River, not in spider territory.

Hybrid Metrosexual: *Man who likes showers more than dirt but still knows how to smoke cigars and chop wood.* **See also: Tom Hardy.**

"Go!" Beth pulled on the reigns and then kicked her heels into horse's sides.

Of course, it reared up.

And, of course, it took off in a gallop.

She wanted a fairytale ending?

"Donkey! Go!" I kicked the donkey's sides. It turned its head and looked at me like I was some sort of irritating fly, buzzing around his overly large ears. "Donkey, go!"

"Well, *shit*."

The donkey hee-hawed and took off into a gallop after Beth. I held on for dear life as the ride jolted my teeth near out of my head. Really? *Shit* was his word?

"Beth!"

The donkey slowed.

"Shit, donkey. Shit!"

Hello, second wind.

"Jace!" she called from behind her. "What do I do?"

The guide had stopped his own horse and was looking on. He took an apple out of his bag and bit into it as juice ran down his chin.

"A little help!" I yelled as Donkey decided to slow down to a walk.

"The horse will stop when it wants to stop," the guide yelled back.

Tour guide, my ass. Had we even signed release forms?

"Beth, pull on the reigns!"

Donkey was gaining on her. Okay that was a lie. Mold grew faster than the animal was moving.

"Tug them back and say halt!"

"Halt!" Beth yelled, pulling on the reigns.

The horse reared up again, this time causing Beth to fall out of the saddle and down the horse's backside, directly into a puddle of water.

But hey, the horse stopped. So I counted it a win.

"Whoa there, boy, whoa."

The donkey screeched to a halt or, if you were watching, slowly took one last step and began chewing on the grass next to Beth's foot.

I jumped off and ran toward her, much like a prince rescuing the fair damsel. You know, if the prince rode an ass and used a hair dryer to fight off spiders, then sure, I was the prince. "Are you hurt?"

"I don't think so." Beth touched her fingers to her temples and shook her head a few times. "But I'm going to have a bruise on my entire backside for at least a month."

I couldn't hold my laugh in any longer. "Some excursion, huh?"

"Yeah," her eyes narrowed, "some excursion." She pulled me into the rather large puddle and splashed me with water.

Laughing, I pulled her into my arms and kissed her. It just seemed like the right moment — you know, with Donkey looking on and farting and the mud caked to my chest and face.

"I'd get up if I were you." The guide suddenly appeared with his horse and damn half-eaten apple.

"Oh yeah?"

"Yeah." He took another loud bite of his apple. "Puddles are a mating ground for mosquitos, and those bites swell as big as watermelon around here."

Beth and I both jumped up as fast as we could. The ten year old in me wanted to push her back into the puddle, point, and laugh. *Fairytale, fairytale.* I clenched my teeth. I really needed to start trying harder. The sooner things went well, the sooner I could put the six days of spiders, donkeys, and mating mosquitoes behind me.

"Well," the guide scratched his head, "guess you'll need to wash off. The waterfall is just over that ledge right there. I'll hold the animals while you guys explore. Return in a half-hour so we can make it back in time for dinner."

"Great." I held out my hand. "Let's go Beth. I don't think Donkey wants to carry both of us, and I don't trust the horse."

She slipped her hand in mine. We were silent as I led her around the ledge and down toward the water.

"Wow." Beth breathed. "That's gorgeous!"

The waterfall was at least thirty feet high with jagged rocks near the bottom. A pool was behind the waterfall and there were steps that led into it.

"Huh, that's kinda cool." I pointed. "People must come down here for — oh, dear Lord."

"What?" Beth's eyes followed where I was pointing.

A very large hairy man had just appeared from the lagoon; he must have been taking a dip because when I had originally looked, the water hadn't really been moving.

It sure as hell was moving now.

"Um..." Beth chewed her fingernail. "I'm trying to decide if being clean is worth it."

I looked down at my muddy jeans and dirt-caked arms. "It's worth it."

"Okay," Beth peeled off her shirt, "but let it be known: if it makes the six o'clock news that you were bathing under a waterfall with a large naked man, I'm not coming to your defense."

"Thanks," I muttered. As I unbuttoned my jeans, a moment of panic hit me swiftly in the gut. Was I really going to jump naked into the water? And why the hell was I suddenly nervous about being naked?

"Last one in's a rotten egg," Beth yelled.

I looked up. And nearly had a stroke as I watched her

perfect body catapult into the water in a perfect dive.

"Well, shit," I mumbled. A distant hee-haw from Donkey followed.

Great. My sidekick was an ass. At least he had good hearing.

I threw off my boxers and joined Beth in the water.

The man had disappeared again under the waterfall, leaving us alone in the main part of the pool.

Beth popped up out of the water, but in my fantasy-like state, everything was happening in slow motion. She shook her head. As water droplets fell across her body, she bit down hard on her lower lip and then blinked the water away from her eyes before giving me a come-hither glance.

Hell yes.

I felt like I was experiencing my own version of Peter Pan when he gets rescued by mermaids. I don't care what guy you ask — the mermaids in that story were hot as hell.

Side note to parents:, *The reasons kids like that story is because there are no rules in Neverland, and the mermaids are hot.*

Screw Tinkerbell. Just give me mermaids.

Or Beth.

Beth as a mermaid.

Beth in a mermaid costume under a waterfall holding a bottle of—

"Jace?" Beth snapped her fingers in front of my face. "Are you sick or something? You're all flushed."

"Viagra." I nodded. "It's, uh, probably still in my system."

"You do know you can only use that excuse possibly one more time, right?"

"I'm aware," I croaked, reaching out to touch her smooth clean skin. "I'm also frighteningly aware of you."

"Frighteningly?" Beth repeated. "Is that a compliment? Or does that mean I look scary."

"You look beautiful," I said honestly. "Scary beautiful.

The type of beautiful that guys are afraid to touch. The type of beautiful that makes men want to risk everything for one taste, one touch, one night. Mix that with your brains, and you're the epitome of why men fight wars."

Beth's smile lit up my world. "Are you saying men fight over intelligence as much as they fight over beauty?"

"Yes," I whispered, pulling her body against mine as I took us closer to the waterfall. "Because you wear your intelligence, it's part of your beauty. You can't separate the two. I admire both. I'm attracted to both."

Her breath hitched as a blush stained her cheeks. "Nice words."

"True words." I cupped her face. "You may be asking for the fairytale, but I wouldn't lie to you just to make you feel better."

She tried to jerk away from me. But I held her face captive.

"If you could see what I see," I traced her jaw with my fingertips, "you would fully understand why you are the most frightening woman I've ever met."

"I do see what you see." Beth sighed. "That's the problem."

"I disagree."

"Big shock."

"Listen to me." I pulled her flush against my body. "You see boring. I see brilliant. You see brown hair. I see brown hair with honey highlights. You see normal pale-pink lips. I see bubble gum."

"Bubble gum?" She smirked.

"That's what you taste like." I nipped her lower lip with my teeth. "Damn bubblegum that never loses its flavor. I could taste you all day and still crave your sweetness." I was struggling between my own honesty and feelings. I wanted her to see herself how I did, but at the same time, telling her these things? It didn't change what I would do. I would walk away. I would. I would. I had to keep telling myself that.

"Why don't you?"

"What?" I snapped out of it.

"Conduct an experiment."

She trailed her fingers down my chest. I felt it in all the places I was trying to ignore, so I kept her virtue intact. Knowing a hairy middle-aged man was most likely watching us was literally the only thread holding my arousal together.

"What kind of experiment?"

"A taste test." Her arms wrapped around me, which meant we were chest to chest, her softness against every plane on my body.

"I like tasting." My mouth collided with hers before I could form another thought. I wasn't sure if I leaned in or she leaned in, or if I was seriously hallucinating from having been drugged by Grandma.

In that moment, I didn't want to be honorable. I really wanted to be a manwhore like Jake. I wanted to be the guy who didn't apologize all the freaking time. I didn't want to be the stuffy US senator, who half of the state hated. I didn't want to have to worry about someone watching me, or ruining my reputation.

I just wanted to *have her*.

And I was selfish enough to want to take her any way I could — even if that meant that I'd be giving her nothing in return. It made me the worst type of man to willingly walk into something, knowing that I wasn't going to stay. I may not be lying to her about my actions. But I knew that actions helped people form opinions, and my actions would lead her to believe I wanted more than the next few days — and that was the last thing I could afford. A relationship past the few days we had.

"Sorry to break this little love scene up," our guide said from the shore. "But if we're going to make it back in time for your dinner reservation, you gotta wrap this here up. How much longer you need? Five? Maybe ten minutes?"

I jerked away from Beth and grumbled, "Five minutes? Really, man?"

"At least thirty." Beth winked, bless her heart. "But we'd have to charge for the show, so we may as well get out now."

"Damn, I would have liked a little show," another voice chimed in from behind us.

I slowly turned to see the giant hairy man who, no doubt had a giant hairy spider like Frank as a pet. He was grinning from ear to ear. And again, arousal disappeared faster than it had appeared in the first place.

"We'll just be going now." Beth grabbed my arm.

"Turn around," I snapped at the man who was still watching.

He laughed.

"I will drown you."

He stood to his full height of at least seven feet.

Gulping, I pointed. "I will die trying to drown you."

He smirked but finally turned around, giving Beth a chance to jump out of the water and put on her clothes.

"Nice," she whispered, while I threw on my shirt and jeans.

"What?"

"You threatening a man three times your size."

"Let's not exaggerate." I snorted. "He's like twice my size. "

"Whatever helps you sleep at night."

"Let's go!" our guide yelled from his perch on the rock.

"Shit, shit!" I called.

"What are you doing?"

I grinned. "Calling my donkey."

Donkey, the bad ass, rounded the corner and hee-hawed.

Beth patted my shoulder. "You do realize you're riding a donkey, and you're a democrat, right? And you yell *shit shit* instead of his name?"

"Admit it." I elbowed her. "If you were undecided, you would totally vote for me if I had a donkey named Shit."

"I would. If I was undecided," she admitted.

"See?"

"But, sorry, Senator. I'm a Republican."

"What?"

"Let's go!" the guide yelled again.

"Well, shit."

Hee-haw!

CHAPTER EIGHTEEN

"You say that the senator was... peaked?" The agent cleared his throat. "In what way?"

Grandma examined her nails. "In the same way you are when you lust over that blond agent who cuffed me."

"You're good."

"I'm Grandma." She beamed.

"We should send you to North Korea."

"Lovely people." Grandma nodded. "Just lovely."

Beth

Okay, so it's possible I wasn't really a Republican. I was undecided. I was one of those people who hated making other people angry, so I just shrugged and told them I didn't pick sides. Which pissed people off even more because they said I had no backbone. But really, I hated that type of confrontation, and whenever the topic of politics was brought up, there was usually arguing, yelling, or both.

The ride back to the hotel was quiet.

Well, except for the donkey.

Hey, was it my fault I kept saying *shit*?

The poor thing hee-hawed himself hoarse, and I was pretty sure that Jace was ready to make a donkey sacrifice by the time we got back to the resort.

We only had a few minutes to change, so I took another quick shower, scrunched my hair, and threw on a white strapless sundress with tan wedge sandals. The packet Dr. Z had given us said that the only time we could express ourselves via different clothing was at dinner and on excursions. I took that and ran with it. I was already tired of my stupid linen pants and white shirt.

"Ready?" I breezed into the room, looking for Jace.

He was outside, leaning against the privacy fence, watching the ocean. His muscled back was to me, and it looked like he was smoking a cigar.

Holy Thor.

That was going to be my new curse word. Oh my Thor. Holy Thor. Good Thor! Yeah, I could get a lot of use out of that one.

His muscles rippled under the sun, and I may have swooned a bit on my feet as I watched, like the creepy boring person I was.

How the heck had boring-old-me convinced him to play the fairytale? Thank Thor, he did.

By my calculations I only had five days left.

Five days of him. And then reality.

So I watched, longer than was appropriate. And when he puffed on the cigar and blew out the smoke, I tasted his tongue on my lips.

People were rarely that good looking in person. Most actors were short, male models were skinnier than me, but Jace? He was every inch just as gorgeous, if not more so, in person.

Maybe when it came to Jace, I wouldn't be undecided, I'd probably march into the voting cubicle and freaking break the pencil while I checked the box by his name.

"Ready?" he said without turning around.

I nodded.

Idiot. He couldn't see me.

He turned.

His six pack winked.

I waved.

"Beth?" Jace's eyebrows drew together in concern.

"Yes." I steered my eyes away from Jace's abs and managed to look him in the eyes. "I'm ready. Grab a shirt, and we'll get going."

"You don't want me shirtless?"

"No." I laughed. "I don't want to cause other women to fantasy-cheat on their significant others. It would hardly be fair to the other men there to have you shirtless."

Red stained his cheeks before he quickly pulled a white t-shirt over his muscled chest.

Since when has linen looked hot on guys?

Oh right. Since Brad Pitt. Sorry, but you've just been replaced.

Jace grabbed my hand and kissed it. I tried not to sigh or look as nervous as I felt. Tonight felt more real. Maybe it was because we'd kissed a lot, or maybe it was because he seemed to actually be enjoying spending time with me.

It felt like a date.

Then again, anything would feel like a date after the whole sugarcane incident. I gave him another smile and tucked my excitement into the farthest part of my brain.

"So what restaurant is the mixer at?" Jace asked. "You never told me."

He gripped my hand as we rounded the corner toward Blu.

"Hibachi grill."

Jace put his arm protectively around me as he led me around a couple walking slower than us. And then grabbed my hand again. To him it was effortless.

But I'd never had a guy do that before. I'd seen it all around me. A guy being protective without realizing it. Or walking on the outside of the road so the girl is protected and safe. But experiencing it? Felt amazing. I felt... treasured. Crap. I needed to remember it wasn't real. He may be attracted to me, he could think I was the best thing since Netflix — but in the end, he wouldn't be waiting like Mr. Darcy.

"I love Hibachi." Jace cleared his throat.

Okay, was it me or were things awkward? Was I overthinking things?

"Beth..." Jace stopped walking and turned me to face him, placing his hands on my shoulders. "I have to tell you something."

"Okay." My throat was seriously starting to close up. He was going to bail. He was going to say he couldn't do it. He was going to abandon me; I was too boring. I knew I should have kept talking. What was wrong with me? Why couldn't I be interesting—

His hot mouth pressed against mine as his hands came around my head, pulling me into his kiss, sucking the panic right out of me.

"You look..." He shook his head and let out a string of curses. "Let me try this again." He grabbed my hands and looked down at them as our fingers intertwined. "You look absolutely... stunning."

I couldn't hide my smile.

Mars could probably see my smile.

And I couldn't care less.

"Thank you," I said finding my voice.

"No." Jace released my hands and tilted my chin so his lips were a breath away from mine. "Thank you."

"I don't understand?"

With a wink, he released my chin and grabbed my hand

again as we continued walking.

"I love white."

"Okay?"

"And I love wedge heels."

"Aw, you know what wedge heels are. Well done."

He grimaced. "Don't tell anyone."

"I'll take it to my grave."

"You wore your hair in kinks."

"Kinks?" I laughed. "You mean in waves?"

He blushed and licked his lips. "Yeah, that's what I meant."

"Thought so."

Jace shook his head and wrapped his arm around me as the door was held open for us in the restaurant. "We have reservations under Brevik."

"Right this way, Senator." The waitress had dark cropped hair and a piercing in her nose; she looked about twenty years old, and I immediately wanted to trip her for looking at Jace longer than necessary. And how did she know he was a senator? I specifically called him Mr. Brevik not Senator Brevik? Was the guy that famous?

Doubtful, it was *Oregon*, not California.

Jace held out my chair. There were eight seats around the grill. I'd hoped it would be just me and Jace, but *mixer* made it sound like we had to mix. Which totally reminded me of college orientation where you run around playing silly games, trying to get to know people in your class. I hated mixer games; I always ended up being the awkward one or, worse yet, the boring one with no boxes checked on Get-to-Know-Me-Bingo.

The restaurant looked really empty. Maybe it wasn't going to be as packed as I'd thought? Hope died the minute I heard a familiar voice.

"So you guys made it?" Brett slapped Jace on the back and took a seat, leaving Paris to pull out her own chair. Poor soul struggled sitting in it because her spandex dress was so tight her legs wouldn't lift high enough. A nicer person would have helped.

I smirked.

Not because I wasn't nice.

But because she wouldn't take her whoring eyes off Jace.

"Uh, yeah." Jace put his arm around me and tugged me close. "We thought a little food was necessary to keep going."

Would it kill him to be the smooth politician at least once today? I kicked him in the shin.

"Going?" Brett smirked.

"Like bunnies," I said without thinking. To be fair, I meant the Energizer Bunny, but that obviously wasn't how it was understood.

Jace had just lifted a glass of water to his lips and started choking.

Brett's eyes narrowed as he took us both in.

"Good evening." A server approached with a cart of tea. "I'll be your server today. Your chef will be here momentarily."

"Bunnies, huh?" Brett smirked, ignoring the waitress and his fiancée, as well as the fact that the conversation had taken a downward turn into hell. May as well get comfortable, I didn't see things improving for at least a few hours.

"Yeah." I gripped Jace's arm, digging my nails into his skin; he yelped and put his water down.

"But enough about our very satisfying sex life… what have you guys been up to all day?"

"Searching," Brett smirked, "the Internet."

"Aw, shit."

I froze, momentarily thinking I was about to hear Donkey. Instead, my blood ran cold when I realized what Brett must have been searching. He knew it was a ruse. He knew we weren't together.

Rejection sucked.

I wanted to wallow.

How was it fair that the one guy who'd rejected me when I was in high school now thought I was a lying prostitute? Forget feeling insecure — now all I felt was shame.

"How much does she charge?" Brett asked calmly as he placed a napkin on his lap.

"Excuse me?" I seethed, reaching for a knife to stab him.

"For your services." Brett grinned smugly. "Not that I'm interested, since I really am happily engaged. Besides, I'm not a fan of disease."

Paris pulled out a nail file and began filing like the world was about to end if she didn't get rid of her chip and a hangnail.

I sighed. "Your definition of happy and mine are two very different things."

"You couldn't afford her," Jace snarled.

Okay, so not the rescue I was hoping for, but it worked.

"I've got money." Brett rolled his eyes. "And I wouldn't want her anyway."

"That's it." Jace stood and grabbed Brett by the collar. "Beth, we'll be right back. Brett and I are going to go have a little heart to heart and grab a few drinks, okay?"

"Sure." My hands trembled as they reached for the water glass.

"Welcome to Blu Hibachi!" A female voice all but shouted.

I looked up in horror.

There stood Grandma, giant-ass knife in hand, a black pantsuit, and a leopard scarf tied around her head.

"Should you..." I pointed, "have knives?" Or anything that could cause physical harm to herself or anyone standing within a foot of her?

"Of course." She threw the knife into the air. I almost passed out until she caught it with her other hand and winked. "I studied for years to learn the art of the Hibachi." She said

Hibachi with way more emphasis on *chi* than I think the Japanese would say was appropriate. "Where's Jace?"

"Having a conversation." I sighed.

"With his fist," Paris interjected.

Oh wow, so airhead could speak. Nice.

"Fist?" Grandma began stacking vegetables and types of meats on the hot grill. The minute she threw oil on the heat, I was hit with a cloud of heat that should have singed eyebrows. "He's fighting someone?"

"Her fiancé." I pointed at Paris. "An old... friend."

"Please." Paris snorted. "He said you were like the nerdiest girl at his school. Doubt that makes you friends."

I wasn't sure if I wanted to grab Grandma's knife and stab it into myself or just Paris.

She giggled.

Just kidding.

Paris. I wanted to stab Paris.

"You let Grandma handle these things." She threw another knife into the air. "After all, this is your vacation, Beth, and you only have a few days left."

"Of vacation." I finished.

"NO, you only have five days to make him realize what he's worked his entire life for is standing right in front of him. A grandma knows these things."

"Grandma." I fought to keep the tears from rolling down my face. "I'm not that person. I'm not his penguin or lobster or whatever you want to call it. He's an island I'm lucky enough to be stranded on for the next few days, that's all."

"I sure hope not," Jace said from behind me. "I was hoping I was more than a damn island."

"What do you want to be?" I tried to sound like I was joking.

He gripped my face hard in his hands and kissed my mouth. "The world. I'd rather be the world."

Grandma cleared her throat.

Paris rolled her eyes and continued filing her nails at the freaking table. Seriously. Here's to hoping a piece of nail lands in her food and not mine, because heads would roll if I crunched down on something that wasn't a carrot.

Besides, Jace had just said he wanted to be my world. I just about died as his words sank into my consciousness, healing cuts I never knew existed. "Where's Brett?"

"Oh, Brett." Jace grimaced. "He got sick."

Paris grabbed her purse. "Guess that's my exit then, huh?"

"Nah, he'll be back. I told him it would be wonderful to enjoy some dinner with him this fine evening."

My eyes narrowed.

Paris shrugged. "Fine, I'm going to use the restroom. If he gets back before I do, tell him I want something with shrimp."

Her heels clicked against the floor as she sauntered away, her ass nearly falling out of her dress.

I let out a breath of relief.

"Oops!" Grandma dropped some shrimp onto the floor. She picked it up and placed it back on the grill. Then she grabbed something out of her pocket and put a few drops in the sauce for the shrimp.

I smacked Jace, "Do something! She's drugging—"

I paused.

"You were saying?" Jace laughed. "Let her eat bad shrimp. See if I care. Technically, I can't kill the guy, but that doesn't mean I want to sit here and eat with them. The sooner Grandma gets rid of them the sooner we can romance."

"Romance? You're using it as a verb?"

He grinned. "It's an action."

"So now I get action."

"Oh sweetheart, you have no idea."

My face fell. "He thinks I'm a prostitute, doesn't he?"

"No. He thinks what I tell him to think."

My head snapped up. "What did you do? Brainwash

him?"

"Baby," Jace whispered in my ear, "sometimes being a politician has its uses. Brett's a weak man. My ploy had nothing to do with punching him in the face or lying to him. But everything to do with what I could get him. He thinks we're dating, and the story is a cover-up because of another scandal in my past."

"What did you have to do? To convince him."

"I paid him fifty grand."

My mouth dropped open.

"Geez, I'm kidding..." Jace chuckled, warm against my ear. "I told him I loved you."

My world plummeted. Had he no idea? That those three words had just shattered my entire existence? Because I wanted it to be real. And he'd just reminded me yet again that it wasn't.

"Hungry?" Grandma flipped a few pieces of clean shrimp onto our plates. "Eat up!"

CHAPTER NINETEEN

"Are you really a chef and licensed therapist?" the agent asked.

"Yes." Grandma nodded enthusiastically. "I'm also a pilot."

"Licensed pilot?"

"Why do you keep saying license? Do I not look intelligent enough to have several talents and hobbies?"

"Why did you feel the need to get all of these… certifications?"

"Because I know my grandsons. At one point, I figured I'd have to learn how to fight in the MMA arena, but thank heavens that didn't happen." Grandma shifted in her seat. "Besides, a good leader always knows one thing."

"What's that?"

"If you want something done, you sure as hell better do it yourself."

Jace

"If you as much as sneeze in her direction, I will stop at nothing to destroy your pitiful existence from the ground up."

The thing I should have said instead of…

"I love her."

Brett laughed. "Right. You do realize that half the world thinks you're on vacation with a new girlfriend, and the other half's convinced you're with a prostitute."

"Well, clearly, since I love her, she isn't a prostitute. Money doesn't need to exchange hands when you're in a relationship. Not that you would know that," I sneered.

"I'll expose you," Brett threatened. "After all, what type of concerned citizen would I be if I let a state senator get away with illegal prostitution?"

"Expose away. I have no secrets." I seethed, feeling my control snapping. "But leave her out of this. Don't you think you've hurt her enough in the past?"

Brett's face pinched. "She told you about high school? That's kind of pathetic if you ask me. I mean, she's what, thirty? And she's upset about something that happened twelve years ago?"

"You're a bastard," I snapped. "And, by the way, it was me."

"You?"

"At the dance." I puffed out my chest. "Kissing her. It was me, so take your damn accusations and stuff them up your ass before I do it for you. We've been friends for an eternity, and I. love. Her. I. Choose. Her. Mind your own business before I pay a friend of a friend to cut the brakes to your car."

"Are you threatening me?"

"Of course not. We're just joking around. You, of course, are a little drunk after all those shots…" I reached for the drink on the bar and threw it in his face, "and a little unsteady on your feet after getting in a crazy bar fight." I punched him across the jaw and then grabbed at his shirt again, steadying his body so I could punch him again. "Am I right?"

His face turned a hundred different shades of red before he pushed against my chest.

I took a step back and smirked. "Now, you're going to either apologize or wish you had."

"I'll go ahead and take my chances." Brett cracked his knuckles and took a huge swing in my direction.

I ducked and then punched him in the face.

Hard.

"Bastard!" Brett almost fell over. "You don't even love her! You're just dating. Something doesn't add up here."

"It's serious, and I do..." My voice cracked on the lie. "I do love her."

The minute the words left my lips I felt like I'd betrayed something special between us. As if I'd somehow cheated her out of having that experience because I'd said it too soon. But it wasn't as if I would ever say it to her anyway, right?

I took another sip of whiskey and grimaced as the dry liquid burned down my throat. I shouldn't have told Beth that part. I should have kept it locked up inside.

Instead, she looked like I'd just told her I wanted to set fire to Donkey and eat a puppy for dinner.

"Eat, eat!" Grandma instructed loud enough to wake up the dead.

I was surprised I hadn't broken my hand — I'd never hit a guy so hard in my entire life.

"Shrimp?" Grandma asked as Brett took a seat on the opposite side of the table a good few feet away from me.

"Sure." His eyes darted from the plate to the empty seat next to him, "Where's Paris?"

"Bathroom," I said.

While Beth said, "Puking," under her breath.

"Great."

Grandma threw a knife into the air and then chopped some mushrooms in front of us and spread them out like a fan. For being eighty-six, she had quick hands.

I hadn't asked why she was our chef for the same reason I hadn't asked why she'd been our therapist. She was insane. Therefore, her cooking us dinner? Yeah, it made total sense.

I half-expected her to be our guide today for the excursion and wouldn't have even blinked if she'd walked into our room and claimed to be the maid. Hell, if she claimed to be president of her own country, I'd just pour myself a glass of scotch and ask which one.

Brett ate a few pieces of shrimp, alternating between licking his fingers and using his tongue to mate with them.

"Is he eating it or seducing it?" Beth whispered next to me.

Ten minutes later, Brett closed his eyes and moaned as he gripped the table with his hand.

"Orgasm via shrimp?" I concluded. "I may never eat again."

What I thought was Brett becoming aroused by shellfish was actually Brett moaning in pain. He teetered off his chair and with a thump fell to the floor.

"Holy shit, Grandma killed him," I mumbled under my breath, pushing my chair away from the table so I could go help him, or maybe just kick him while he was down. Jury was still out.

"I, uh..." Brett burped and reached for his water. "I don't feel so well."

"Are you allergic to shellfish?" Grandma asked, concern lacing her every word.

"No." He pounded his chest and burped again.

"Oh, heavens!" Grandma dropped the knife onto the table and rushed to his side. "I think you are! I think you're going into shock! Hurry! We need to get you to the hospital."

"Seriously?" He gripped the table again. "I do feel kind of hoarse."

Grandma nodded emphatically. "I'll get the manager. We'll have you in the hospital in no time!"

Amused, I watched Grandma lie her ass off as she escorted Brett to the waiting taxi. Paris came out of the bathroom in time to see the fiasco. She'd apparently failed to look in the mirror. White powder glowed next to her upper lip.

"Not puking, snorting. Classy woman." I took a long sip

of my whiskey and watched as the night went to hell in a hand basket.

Paris swatted Brett on the back for ruining their night. Brett, having been exposed to a foreign substance he was now convinced was killing him, started having a full-blown panic attack as they rushed out the doors and into the waiting car.

Grandma waved goodbye and walked back to her station and continued chopping. No explanation. No apology. Nothing.

"So," Beth cleared her throat, "what did you give him?"

"Nothing." Grandma kept chopping.

"Don't lie."

"Grandmas never lie." She pointed the knife in Beth's direction.

I moved out of the way, which earned me a smack on the arm.

"We merely fib, or as I like to call it, frost over the truth."

"Frost over the truth?" I laughed.

"Of course. In one hand I have the truth..." She fanned out a mushroom and pointed. "In the other hand I have the sauce. I lightly pour the sauce of the mushroom. And voilà!"

"I'm confused," Beth said.

"Can you still see the mushroom?" Grandma asked.

"Yeah."

"But you can see the sauce too."

"So?" Beth pointed at the example. "I see them both, so how is the sauce hiding anything?"

"Cloaking, my dear." Grandma scooped up the mushrooms and sauce and put them on a plate. "By the time you take a bite and discover the truth in the flavors, discover the sauce is just garlic and the mushrooms are the food of choice, you don't care anymore. Want to know why?"

"Why?"

"Because it tastes good." Grandma winked. "Frosting the truth is just like that. It may seem devious, and it may look like something else entirely, but the minute you learn the truth, you don't care anymore, because it was staring at you," she chopped a piece of meat, "the whole damn time."

Why was she staring at me like she wanted to stab me?

I popped a mushroom in my mouth and was only slightly irritated that it was amazing.

"Now," Grandma chopped up some pork, "why don't you two order a nice bottle of wine while I finish up your main course? How does that sound?"

"Are you going to be putting drugs in our wine?" Beth asked.

"The thought briefly crossed my mind," Grandma admitted. "See? I can be honest. Now, shall we order some wine?"

"What do you say?" I nudged Beth.

She blinked a few times then shrugged. I officially hated myself. How was it possible that earlier today she was blooming into this beautiful bright woman, and now she was closed off? I'd done that to her. I'd made her doubt herself all over again.

"Are you okay?" I asked dumbly, knowing that she wasn't but wanting to hear her speak so I didn't go insane.

"I think I'm just tired." Beth forced a smile.

"Do you want to go back?" I offered.

Her body slumped even more.

Damn it, how was I ruining things even further?

"Tell you what." Desperate, I said the first thing that popped into my mind. After all, she was all about having fun, right? Not being boring anymore? "Let's eat really fast then go dancing."

"Dancing? You?" Beth's smile returned.

Only this time, I figured it was at my expense.

"Just because I'm a politician doesn't mean I can't dance."

"Oh I know that." Beth patted my hand. "I was going to say it's because you're white."

"White guys can't dance?"

"I give you Justin Timberlake." Beth nodded. "He can dance."

"The man's a god." This from Grandma.

"I can dance like Justin Timberlake," I argued.

Grandma laughed.

"Do you mind?" I glared.

She pointed her knife at me and kept chopping with her left hand.

"No, you can't, Jace. You..." She shook her head. "It wouldn't be possible. It would be unfair to humanity to give you that face and body and then the ability to move your hips seductively. Seriously, I'd have words with God."

"I hope you eat your words." I kissed her cheek.

"And if I don't?"

I didn't answer. Instead, I prayed that all the women I'd dated in college hadn't been total liars.

CHAPTER TWENTY

"So let me get this straight. You sear the meat on both sides, and then you add the wine?"

"Yes." Grandma nodded. "It gives it that perfect moist center."

"Interesting."

Someone knocked on the glass.

The FBI agent straightened in his chair and cleared his throat. "So where were we?"

"Somewhere between drugging, dancing, and Justin Timberlake."

"This should be on YouTube."

"Oh, I just love the Tube! And the Facebook! And the Tweets!"

"Why do you keep putting the in front of those?"

"Out of respect." Grandma's eyebrow rose all the way to her hairline. "You never address the president as president."

The agent paused. "You have me there."

Beth

"Alright, let's see it," I yelled over the bumping music. I was thirty years old, had been drugged by a senile old woman, and I was at a club. Oh, and right, I had been accused of being a prostitute. Cool, I was officially living my own mid-life crisis. At least I had Thor. Then again, this could all be figment of my imagination. I could be tied to a giant computer, *Matrix*-style, and just making up my own dream world.

Yeah, clearly I hadn't drunk enough at dinner.

I bit down on my lip, letting the pain distract me for a brief moment while my heart stopped slamming against my chest. The last time I'd danced was at prom. No joke. I did not dance. I hadn't even danced at my sister's wedding. I'd drunk wine and hid my Kindle under the table, reading when nobody'd been looking. Which, *newsflash*: nobody had been looking until Jace had been sent my way.

He had sauntered. You know what I mean. The saunter, also known as the sensual walk of a man who knows he's been blessed with every human gift known to humanity. Good looks, good teeth, good body. Good Thor, he'd been hot.

I'd dropped my best friend that night.

My Kindle. I'd accidently dropped it onto the floor and gaped as Jace had held out his hand and asked if I wanted to dance. I'd said no; well, actually I'd just shaken my head and sighed, because I'd remembered him, and it was just like a fairytale. Having the prince of my dreams reach out to me, pick me out of a crowd. Yeah, I'd basked. Instead of dancing, we'd shared a few drinks, happily delivered via the Drugging Grandmother Express.

"Come on." Jace licked his lips and pulled me closer as we weaved through the crowd of happy couples.

Being this close to him was so not distracting enough to get my mind off the fact that five days from now I'd be saying goodbye to the one and only guy I was falling hard for.

Stupid Thor.

Stupid blond hair.

Abs! Curse you! I mentally shook my fist.

"Come on." Jace grabbed my hand and steered us

through the crowds of people having sex on the dance floor.

I wasn't a dancer. Because dancing was just another way people could make fun of me.

Elle Goulding's "Burn" came on.

My heart thumped against my chest as Jace laughed and pulled me against his chest; the lights turned down as he twirled me around and then tugged my leg up around his waist.

Oh. My.

It was the techno-version of the song, or the club version, so it was faster than what I'd heard on the radio.

Jace released me and started dancing around me.

And I was officially in a dilemma. Either I moved and tried to dance with him, or I stared as his body moved in perfect sync with the music. I'd have words with God later about that. I mean, how is it even possible that a guy that beautiful should have everything?

The song slowed.

Jace tugged me against him.

I wrapped my arms around his neck as his hands moved to my hips, helping me move with the same rhythm he was moving with. I closed my eyes and gave up.

I gave up feeling sad.

I gave up feeling embarrassed.

And danced.

Until the song changed to Jay-Z, and then I was lost all over again. I couldn't get the rhythm right.

Finally, I gave up and tried to pull away from Jace, but he pulled me back against him and whispered, "Nobody puts baby in a corner. Nobody."

I felt my grin stretch to my ears as he twirled me. Yes, twirled me to a rap song and then kept me turned around as he moved his hands against my skin. His body rocked against mine, his abs pressed against my back, his arms wrapped around me from behind. Every movement caused enough friction between us to burn the entire club down.

The song ended too soon.

Sweaty, I stepped away from Jace. "That was... nice."

"Nice?" His nostrils flared as he gripped my shoulders with his hands and licked my lower lip. He tasted like sweat and pure man. Was that my switch? A little licking, and I was ready to wrap my legs around him and yell Thor at the top of my lungs?"

"That was..." I couldn't find words. What were words again? And sentences? Nouns? Verbs? My name?

He slapped me on the backside so hard it stung then said, "I'll show you nice."

Two hours later.

And I was officially that girl. The one that walked barefoot back to her room and swayed on her feet from lack of hydration and too many shots.

Jace had been peer-pressure-personified. "Just one more shot. One more dance." But he'd kept smiling and looking so damn hot that I'd just nodded my head and smiled.

When that man got his mind set to something, he didn't give up easily. My night had consisted of him showing me just how nice he could be. From pushing me against a wall and dancing his way up my body to licking a shot off my stomach — something I'll take to my grave because it was both the most embarrassing and erotic thing that's ever happened in my existence — to making out with me next to the bathrooms. Apparently we had a thing for toilets flushing; it was the music of our love or something like that.

I swayed on my feet and felt a little nauseated. But not boring. Definitely not boring. Though I could really use a shower and more *nice* touching from Jace.

I was most likely going to regret my decisions come morning.

"I know why Grandma, or our therapist who looks scarily a lot like Grandma, made us do that exercise," Jace whispered, once we we'd both taken showers and were lying in bed.

I turned on my side to face him. "Why?"

"Because," he touched my cheek, "I memorized your body. I traced it in my mind, felt it in my hands, and when we danced… it was as if you were a part of me, an extension. Not like we were separate people, but one."

"Like a bond!" I all but shouted.

Jace burst out laughing, and wrapped his arm around my body, tugging me further into his warmth. "Yes, my little science nerd, like a bond."

"A covalent bond." I sighed happily.

"Congratulations, Beth, you're no longer chargeless."

"How do you figure?"

"Had a light bulb been touching both of us, it would have exploded."

"I think, Mr. Senator, that you just called me hot?"

"Damn right, I did." He growled, kissing my mouth. "And just so you know, getting called Mr. Senator in bed… hotter."

"Ah, so you *are* power-hungry."

"No," his eyes darkened, "just hungry. So. Damn. Hungry."

Was he talking about me or food?

He tugged at the strap on my Victoria Secret top and cursed. "Maybe in other circumstances… if I hadn't walked away from you."

"What do you mean?"

He slowly pulled away from me and rubbed his temples. "If we'd met again, after school, before my heart had been shattered and stomped into a million pieces. Maybe if we'd met before then… I'd have one intact. One I could give you. But I can't."

My lower lip trembled. His honesty was going to be the death of me. Funny, because in his line of work, you'd think it would be his lies.

"Which is why," he sighed and turned away from me, "I'm going to sleep. I'm going to keep my hands off and let you sleep too."

"What if I don't want the gentleman?" I asked in a hopeful whisper, my voice cracking from emotion.

"You do, Beth." He sighed heavily. "What good is the fairytale, if, in the end, the girl's so broken she can't even finish the damn story?"

I took a leap of faith anyway.

And moved to straddle him. His groan was all the encouragement I needed as I tugged his shirt over his head and threw it on the floor.

"Beth, we shouldn't—"

"Shh..." I brushed a kiss across his jaw, and his grip tightened on my hips. I thought he was going to pull me against him; instead he gently lifted me off his body and sat me next to him.

Voice hoarse, he whispered, "I want to, Beth. I do, but I can't. You've had a lot to drink, and it's just... that's not the fairytale you want, sweetheart."

"But I want you." I reached for him again.

He tugged me into his body and kissed my temple. "Sleep."

That was how we went to bed.

Both of us blanketed in a chilly silence. With things left unsaid. Me wanting him, him wanting me, but admitting yet again, like every other man in my existence, that although I was good, I wasn't good enough for him. Or maybe it was different with Jace. He liked me. He could give me his heart, but it seemed it had already been given very flippantly a long time ago. And I knew something about hearts, once they've claimed another as their own.

It was near impossible to forget.

My heart ached with the knowledge that it was entirely

possible that each day I spent in Jace's presence was another piece of my heart he was unknowingly taking. And I was willingly giving it. Hoping that, by the end, it wouldn't destroy me.

CHAPTER TWENTY-ONE

"*Crackerjacks!*" *Grandma slammed her fist onto the table.* "*I'm trying to tell you a story, Gus! Stop interrupting!*"

"*I'm just trying to understand how their love story ends with a kidnapping, that's all, ma'am.*"

"*No, you're frying my very last nerve, Gus, and I won't have it. I'm eighty-six, and though I look strong, it wears on me, it—*"

"*Ma'am?*" *the agent whispered.* "*Ma'am?*

He slowly rose up from his chair and tapped Grandma on the shoulder.

With a snort, she opened her eyes. "*Oh,*" *she stretched,* "*such a good sleep. You were saying?*"

Jace

"Grandma." I cleared my throat, managing to only clog further as she held out the pencil and paper. "I still don't understand what you're asking me to do."

For the last half-hour, Grandma had lectured us on how to keep a relationship strong... in the bedroom. My ears had bled, and I'm pretty sure, given the circumstances, a few of my sperm had just given up and died.

I wouldn't blame them. I'd wished for death when she'd gone into graphic detail about her late husband, Bill. Apparently in his final years he'd gone blind in his right eye, but Grandma wanted to be sure that we understood that physical ailments should not deter us from participating in what she weirdly referred to as Charades.

What followed was an actual pie chart about erogenous zones that are awakened when other parts of the body are physically... on the injured list. Our torture in hell had ended with pictures. Not normal pictures, because that would be too easy. She erected, poor choice of words, I know, a felt storyboard that I could have sworn my Sunday School teachers used to use in order to tell us Bible stories, and then told us a story about Sad Sam and Happy Hannah, and how Sad Sam turned into a Surprised Sam when Happy Hannah learned how to take Grandma's advice.

There was a poem.

And finally a song that was sung to the tune of "Mary Had a Little Lamb."

I would never eat lamb again.

I thought the torture was done, until Grandma gave us pencils and said we had a pop quiz. The questions had to be the stupidest ones I'd ever had anyone ask me, and I'd had a lot of stupid questions. It was part of the job.

"Write out your answers on this piece of paper and discuss."

"But the questions are stupid."

"So are you, and I don't go telling it to your face, now do I?"

"You have," I argued. "Twice."

"It's true," Beth chimed in.

Grandma waved me off. "Question one."

"Shit."

"How is that donkey?" Grandma sighed happily. "He's

quite old, you know."

"We know." Beth sighed. "Can we just hurry and get this done? We're burning daylight, and I really need to get a tan."

"She does," I agreed. "White as a ghost."

"Yeah, throw stones in a glass house, Viagra. Let me know how that works out for you."

"Children!" Grandma clapped. "Honestly, what's wrong with you this morning?"

Beth's face fell. "Nothing, sorry, I didn't sleep well."

Was she actually pissed I hadn't made a move on her? Seriously? Did she think it was easy for me to turn around and sleep when I knew she wanted the exact opposite? I'd heard every sigh that escaped her lips, every breath she'd taken, every moan she'd made, every damn toss and turn. I'd almost slept on the floor.

I broke the pencil in half and grimaced when Grandma threw another one at my face. I barely caught it before it impaled itself in my cheek.

"Question one." Grandma sniffed. "As a child, the cartoon character you most identified with was…?"

Grumbling I wrote down my answer.

"Question two." After a teacher pause, you know the pause teachers do to make you sweat it out for a minute before they ask the next question, Grandma spoke, "Name your most secure moment as a child."

Grimacing. My pencil hovered over the paper. I honestly didn't know how to answer. My entire childhood had been based around my parents' approval. I was secure in their love — but not secure in my success. When I was six, I'd had nightmares that my dad had told me he wasn't proud of me anymore.

I scribbled down my answer and waited.

"Final question," Grandma called. "If you were a food, you would be what? And why?"

I rolled my eyes. "Is this even real or just another one of

your ploys to get us to..." I shook my head, letting my voice die off.

"Aw, Jace, you scared you're going to get the wrong answer? It isn't a test," Beth joked. "Just answer the questions so we can hurry up and go."

Rolling my eyes, I answered the last question and gave Grandma my paper.

"I see." Grandma read my paper and then compared it to Beth's, which was a little humiliating.

What if her answers were better than mine? What if mine were stupid? Why the hell did I care?

"Lovely." Grandma beamed. "Just lovely. You're dismissed."

"What?" we said in unison.

"You may go." Grandma's smile widened.

"But..." I scratched my head and let out a nervous laugh, "you didn't even tell us how we did? I mean, wasn't there a point to that exercise?"

"No," Grandma took a sip of tea. "I was just curious. You know me, flighty as a seagull." She laughed. "Ta-ta. Use sunscreen!"

Beth jolted up from her seat, but I kept my eyes firmly on Grandma. Something wasn't right. She was tricking me, but I didn't know how. The longer I stared the more mischievous her smile became. And then she blew on her hand and winked.

"You're evil."

"Thank you." She beamed as the door closed behind us.

Beth was a good few feet ahead of me, making her way toward the pool.

"Slow down!" I called after her.

"Keep up," she called back.

"Can you just," I grabbed her arm, "stop for one damn second?"

She stopped walking and put her sunglasses on. Hell, did

that mean she was crying?

"What's wrong with you?"

"I just want to relax in the sun. Is that so much to ask?

"Yes," I snapped. "I mean, no."

"Jace," Beth put her hands on her hips, "what do you want?"

"I want you to stop yelling. I want to stop going to therapy with a senile eighty-six year old with felt pictures. I want my life back, but I want to kiss you more. So that's what I want," I grumbled.

"Your life back?"

I grabbed her shoulders and pushed her against the wall. "The second part."

"A kiss?"

"I want more than a kiss, Beth. Don't you get it? I'm trying to protect you. I'm trying to do the right thing. I want you. Don't you see that I want you? Give me a reason not to want you—"

"My cartoon character was She-Ra."

"Huh?"

"I wanted to be a warrior princess."

"That doesn't help."

"I thought it would weird you out?"

"You wearing battle gear and wielding a sword?" I chuckled. "Not even close to helping."

"My most secure childhood memory was when I got second place at the science fair. My mom and dad weren't able to make it, so my grandpa came. He told me that as long as I had a heart to go along with my brain I'd turn out okay. He said hearts and brains shouldn't work separate but together." Her eyes glistened with tears. "He said I was smart, but he kissed me on the cheek and said what was more important is that he loved my heart."

I reached for her hand.

"He, uh, died the following day. Stroke."

I pulled her into my arms and kissed her head.

"And I hate vegetables." Her voice was muffled against my chest. "If I had to be one, I'd ask to be put in vegetable soup so I'd suffer a veggie death. I hate green things. I know I'm supposed to like them. I know I'm supposed to be super-healthy, but damn it, Jace, sometimes I just want a cookie!"

"I think I can do that."

"Really?" She stepped away and wiped underneath her eyes.

"Yeah." I wrapped my arm around her shoulders and kissed her forehead again. "I'll buy you as many cookies as you want. And if your plan was to get me to fall just a little bit more for you, you succeeded."

"Oh yeah?" Beth sniffled. "Why's that?"

Grandma was a damn spy and had dug into my childhood, that's how. "I wanted to be He-Man when I was little. My most secure moment was when my dad said he was proud of me after I won Student Body President. He said all leaders should have a good head but needed to lead with their hearts first."

My hand trembled just slightly as I squeezed Beth's shoulder. "And I've been on vegetable strike since the fourth grade."

"A rebel."

"Oh yes. Every time my mom put carrots in my lunchbox, I swapped them with the girl sitting next to me. Cheetos and carrots? Same color. It helped that she was legally blind in one eye, plus she had a crush on me. I'd send her to get milk. She'd come back, and the Cheetos would be gone, leaving her with carrots. I lied for two years, Beth, I'm not proud of what I did. But sometimes a man has to do things, ugly things, to get what he wants."

"You stole Cheetos from a blind girl. How does that not make the news and me walking with you into a hotel does?"

"Easy." I grinned. "You're prettier."

Beth's face reddened. "So how about that cookie?"

"How about it?" I reached for her hand and didn't let go. We fell into easy talk of She-Ra and He-Man escapades and decided that Grandma had broken laws of national security to get the information that she had. The woman had done her homework.

"Closed?" Beth pointed at the sign to one of the snack shops lining the beach. "Why is it closed?"

Why was her voice rising? And then I remembered her reaction to cookies a few days ago. The yelling, the stomping, the throwing.

"Beth, calm down. We'll find you cookies." I patted her hand.

She turned, her angry cat-eyes flashing with irritation. Holy shit. Where was Donkey when I needed a quick escape?

"Beth! Jace! Over here!" Someone or something was waving at us.

I couldn't make out faces because of the way the sun was setting. But I didn't need to make out faces. It was too late anyway. A fist came flying into my face, and everything went very, very black.

CHAPTER TWENTY-TWO

"Did you?" The agent sounded irritated.

"Did I what?"

"Break laws of national security for personal gain?"

Grandma seemed to think about the question. "Of course not."

The agent breathed a sigh of relief.

"It was for their gain. Not personal at all."

"Ma'am, that doesn't make it legal."

"I thought we've established I'm above the law, Gus? Sheesh, you're so forgetful, and I'm the senile one."

Beth

"Char? Jake?"

I was caught between wanting to make sure Jace was okay and also wanting to hug my sister and return the punch to Jake's face.

"Hey!" Char hugged me and then shoved Jake. "You ass, why'd you punch him?"

Jake cracked his knuckles. "He kissed you. Twice. Tried to steal you away. And was inappropriately touching your sister."

"Weren't you voted Player of the Year in *Playboy*?" Char asked. "Just curious."

"I'm a reformed man and happily married." Jake rolled his eyes. "Are you okay, Beth?"

"Since when is this one defending girls' honor?"

I ignored Jake's question and put my arm around Char.

"Marriage," Char rolled her eyes, "it's cured him. Disgusting, really. He won't even answer when I call him *whore*. Tragic, really."

"Heard that!" Jake snapped then poured some bottled water over Jace's face in an attempt to either drown him or wake him up.

"Why are you guys here?"

"Grandma kept hanging up on us." Char rolled her eyes. "And Rick's been trying to track down Jake and won't stop calling him. It seems our senator has it in his head that he isn't a public figure and doesn't need to keep his phone on."

"Sort of my fault." I meekly raised my hand. "But to be fair, neither of us have even touched technology in the past three days."

"We know." Char patted her on the shoulder. "Also, that Dr. Z needs to chill out. When we were trying to reach you, she kept saying that you were not to be disturbed, which frankly just freaked this one out." Char pointed to Jake, who was leaning on his hands and knees and now lightly tapping Jace's face.

"Wake up, bastard. Fight like a man."

"Fight like a man?" Jace grumbled, not opening his eyes. "Since when is getting sucker-punched fighting like a man?"

"I breathed hard enough. You should have sensed me."

"The man has a point, Thor," I agreed.

"Thor?" Char asked then looked at Jace. "Huh. How 'bout that?"

"She calls you Thor?" Jake gave a disgusted look.

"Wanna see my hammer?" Jace opened his eyes and made a fist.

"Funny," Jake said dryly. "The dirty senator makes jokes."

"Hilarious. The drunk billionaire comes to the rescue."

"Boys!" Char shouted. "Keep your balls on, okay? Damn, it's like the honeymoon from hell."

Jake got up from his position on the ground and wrapped Char in his arms. "I'm sorry, baby."

She sighed heavily against his chest. "It's okay. I blame Grandma."

"Economy failing?" Jake swore. "Blame Grandma."

"Can't sleep?" Char added in. "Blame Grandma."

"Please," Jace tried to get to his feet. "I highly doubt you guys have been worse off than us."

"They couldn't find our reservation at the hotel so we went to another hotel. They too were conveniently all filled up," Jake growled. "And then, wonder of all wonders, Grandma finds the perfect place for us to stay, all inclusive, nice little huts…"

"Huts?" I gulped.

"There's two of these places." Jake grimaced. "I hate damn couples' therapy. Some pictures can't be unseen, some words, unheard. I need a damn drink and a—"

"She drugged me with Viagra!" Jace blurted.

"Beth Lynn!" Char yelled.

"Not me!" I held up my hands in innocence. "Grandma did."

"But Grandma's been with us!" Jake said.

"No, she's been with us, here. She's our therapist."

"No…" Char squinted, "she's been our therapist."

"Holy shit." Jake pinched the bridge of his nose. "I'm going to strangle her. I don't care what you say, Char. I'm doing it. I'm going to prison."

"Aw, baby, you know you're too pretty for prison." Char

patted his back. "They'd eat you alive."

"Drinks?" I offered lamely. "You know, before you guys decide to bury your grandmother."

"Oh good!" A voice said from the dock. "You're all here, just as planned."

I turned slowly to face Grandma. The woman had no soul.

"Well," Jake cleared his throat, "may as well get on with it. Why are we all here, Grandma?"

"Yes," another voice rang out. "Why in the hell are we all here?"

"Hi, Kacey!" Char waved.

Jake pulled her arm down and swore.

"All my kids." Grandma clapped and then did something that I'd never before seen in my life.

She burst into tears.

CHAPTER TWENTY-THREE

"Does your meddling know no end?"

Grandma squinted. "No, of course not? They need me. And by the time the story's finished, I guarantee you'll agree. Grandma's ways are best."

"I highly doubt your grandsons agree."

"I beg to differ. My grandsons love me."

"Is that why one threatened to strangle you?"

"Oh that." Grandma snorted. "He'd have to catch me first."

Jace

Funny, how a few minutes ago I was ready to kill the elderly woman, and now my heart felt like someone had pulled it beating out of my chest, stomped on it, and then placed it back inside, all twisted and dirty.

"What's wrong?" Kacey pulled Grandma into a hug and gave Travis a helpless look.

He, in turn, looked to Jake who shrugged and nudged me. Nothing. I had nothing.

"Oh, I've made a mess." Grandma wiped a few tears. "I

thought I could pull it off, but…" she sniffled, "I just… I couldn't do it. The project was too big, the minds helping me plan too damn small."

"Did she just call us stupid?" Jake asked.

"No," I answered honestly. "She'll just come out and say it if she wants to, believe me."

"And now his career's going to be over!" she wailed.

I had a sinking feeling I was the *his,* and the career was already in the toilet, but hey, ever the optimist, I kept listening.

"Jace."

Well, shit.

"Your approval ratings are low, it's true. I've been monitoring the news briefings. As of right now, everyone believes you've gone on vacation with your new family, but someone went to the reporters and said you were bluffing to cover your own ass. And when Kerry was interviewed again, she spouted more nonsense about how you weren't a family man and often paid prostitutes."

Jake's eyes narrowed.

"Yeah, cast that stone, bastard. See if it hits you or me in the ass first," I sneered.

He shook his head and crossed his arms.

"So why are we here?" Travis asked. "Seems to me that Jace needs to get back to Portland and fix this. And you need to help him."

"Well," Grandma wrung her hands together, "I may have let it slip that he was here with his fiancée and her family."

"Of course you did." I clenched my teeth, not liking where it was going.

"So that explains why you called us, and why Jake and Char panicked when Rick wouldn't stop calling them, but…"

"Oh bother." Grandma wiped another few stray tears. "I'll just come out and say it."

"Please do." Okay, my teeth were going to grind clean off.

"I told them it was a destination wedding, and that your honeymoons were cover-ups to keep the media away."

I swayed on my feet. Not a proud moment.

Grandma continued talking. "I finally reached Rick, and he said it was a good cover, but that if we could somehow leak pictures to the media of us together, it would help."

"Hmm." Travis's eyes lit up with approval. "That's actually quite brilliant."

"You think so?" Grandma beamed.

I smacked his arm. Friends don't give Grandma compliments, or access to Benadryl, or any sort of encouragement, for shit's sake.

"What?" He shrugged. "It's not like you guys actually have to get married or anything. I mean, come on, Jace, it's not like you'll ever get married again after what happened with—"

Grandma smacked him on the back of the head. He gave me a guilty shrug, while Jake looked nervously between me and Beth.

She'd been eerily quiet the entire time, driving me insane with the desire to jump into her head and find out what she was thinking. Instead, she stood there like a frozen statue while everyone else planned the next few days.

"You'll still attend therapy." This from Grandma.

"Screw therapy," Jake argued.

"Jake, you are an ass," Grandma retorted. "Which is why you still need to follow the rules. I know how hard it is for you to color in the lines, but for my benefit, you'll go to therapy. Poor Char, having to deal with all those anger issues."

"I'm NOT ANGRY!" Jake shouted.

"Stop raising your voice," Grandma said calmly. "I'm not deaf, and you will listen to me, or I'll fire you again."

He stopped talking.

"Well," Travis rubbed his hands together, "I guess that only leaves us one thing to do."

"What?" Beth asked, her voice small.

"Happy hour." He nodded. "I learned a long time ago not to argue. Things go much easier with tequila shots. Wouldn't you agree, Jake?"

His eyes narrowed, and then he did the oddest thing. He blushed as Char kissed him on the neck and laughed.

Clearly, I was missing something, but it didn't matter, because Beth was still motionless. I almost waved in front of her face.

"What say you, Thor?" Jake asked, hands on hips.

"If he's Thor, I'm Iron Man." This from Travis.

"Dibs on Green Arrow." Jake raised his hand.

"Children." Kacey shook her head. "It's like we're honeymooning with little boys and capes."

"Please, like he's cool enough to have a cape." I pointed to Jake and instantly felt judged and ten years old.

That was what being around the Titus family did to people. One minute you were a sane adult; the next you were arguing over Marvel Comics and yelling at the top of your lungs at an eighty-six-year-old woman while she blotted her red lipstick.

Somehow, I'd lost my manhood. I'd lost my maturity and everything else that went with it. Because I wanted to beat the shit out of both Titus boys for no other reason than they were arguing with me about something stupid like comics and refused to let me be right.

I felt Beth's hand on my arm.

"So, that settles it." Travis clapped. "Avengers... to the bar!"

"Best idea he's had all day." Char's amused smile was lit with humor, making me feel slightly better about the fact that my entire career was in Grandma's hands, her meddling, terrifying, little hands.

I said a little prayer and followed everyone down the dock toward the bar as Grandma paid one of the bellhops to take the luggage down to the reserved huts.

Reserved. As in, everything was planned; it had been planned a long time.

Hell, when God created heaven and earth, He created Grandma on the final day and said, "I have a plan for those men…"

And I was just unfortunate enough to be included in said plan.

CHAPTER TWENTY-FOUR

"How do you sleep at night?" the agent asked.

"How lovely of you to be concerned." Grandma touched his arm. "A tiny pink pill followed by two large glasses of merlot. Works like a charm. I sleep like the dead, except for when Charles Barkley gets agitated with my snoring."

"Charles Barkley?" the agent repeated. "In your bed?"

"Well, where else would my dog sleep?" Grandma rolled her eyes. "Some people."

Beth

My vacation was over. I couldn't bring myself to feel sorry for Jace or for anyone else. Grandma was just trying to help, though her motives were so very, very illegal. Still, she loved them, and I loved her for it.

I couldn't even find it in myself to be angry.

If anything, I was sad.

Because he'd promised me six days.

And they'd been stolen from me on day three. I was owed three more days of romance, three more days of the fairytale. Instead, I was given my sister, her new husband, his brother, and wife.

Now that Jace had people watching — people who knew a heck of a lot more about his past than I did, there was no way we'd have any more stolen kisses, caresses, fights under the stars. I shivered and closed my eyes for a brief moment as I remembered the taste of his lips on mine.

At least I had that memory.

His hands on my body.

His mouth, hot and urgent.

I'd probably retell the story to my cats once I got home and fully gave up on the male species as a whole. Maybe I should count myself lucky that I hadn't fallen in total irrevocable love with him. Because at this point, walking away would be doable. Hard, but doable. Another three days, and it may have wrecked me to see Jace turn his back on us.

"You look like you need this." Char pushed a shot of tequila toward me. "Pinch your nose and throw it back. I don't care how vile it tastes, because right now you look like someone just told you *Vampire Diaries* got canceled."

"Not funny." I glared.

"Take the shot," Char countered.

I took it and winced as the liquid burned down my throat.

"Olé!" Jake shouted, joining us at the table.

The man could try the patience of a saint. He had the most gorgeous hazel eyes and dark hair — both Titus men did.

"Beth, seriously, if you want me to assassinate Mr. Senator, just say the word. Or nod." When I didn't do anything, he continued, "Or blink. Hell, just breathe. One exhale and I'll do it."

"I doubt she wants me dead when I can make her feel things I'm doubting you've ever made any woman feel in your entire existence," Jace said in a tense voice from behind me. His hands rested on my shoulders and then ran down my arms. I shivered in response and gave Jake a cocky grin.

"So," he returned my grin, "I guess cheers are in order."

"Cheers?" Jace repeated.

"To the senator who found his heart." He held up his glass.

"Just like the squirrel who found its nuts." Jace winked.

"What?" I looked around the table.

Travis laughed. "Just go with it."

"Seems to be a common theme," I muttered, lifting my rum punch.

"Always is." Kacey clinked her glass with mine. "So what's the plan for the day?"

"Plan?" Grandma waltzed up to the table like a woman on a mission. "I've got everything settled. First a fake bachelorette party and, Jake, try to keep your pants on this time. We don't want any more elderly ladies having strokes."

His eyes narrowed. "That was one time."

Grandma ignored him. "Followed by a lovely outing tomorrow morning after group therapy. Of course we'll later have a rehearsal dinner. Would you believe I already had dresses brought in? Oh, and Javier! Javier!" Grandma yelled, breaking the sound barrier and my ear drums, for that matter. "This is Javier. He's going to be taking the wedding pictures."

"Fake wedding pictures," Jace corrected. "You're not pulling a Jake and Char on us."

"Aw, we're like a verb." Char and Jake bumped fists.

I ignored their cuteness just like I ignored the excitement bubbling around me. What would it be like to be a part of this family? What would it be like to be so in love with someone, so in sync that you were deliriously, hopelessly happy?

Jake and Char shared a kiss and laughed.

"Of course not." Grandma put her hand over her chest and sighed. "I would never. Believe me, I've learned my lesson. It's best that love happen naturally. At any rate, we'll snap some pictures and lie about the wedding, saying it's too private to share with the world."

Jace gripped my hand. "So we pretend."

"Of course." Grandma's keen eyes examined our joined hands. "After all, you have three more days of the fairytale, don't you, Jace? We wouldn't want to mess with curses and folklore, now would we?"

I bit down on my lip to keep from laughing.

"Who told you?" He slammed his fist down onto the table.

"Oh, the captain and I go way back." Grandma smirked.

I hoped to God that Jace wouldn't ask what that meant, because by the looks of the way she was blushing, it probably wasn't appropriate for the general public, or anyone for that matter.

"Now," Grandma sat down at the table, "enough of that. I've set up a few outings for us to go to as a family. Javier will take pictures, and everyone will go home with smiles on their faces. Of course, at the end of the next three days."

"Does that mean I get a new honeymoon?" Jake asked. "Since you crashed this one?"

"Ditto," Travis grumbled.

"Oh, please." Grandma waved them off. "I let you have at least three days. I thought it very generous, all things considered."

"How do YOU FIGURE?" Jake asked.

"Jake stop yelling. You should be thanking me, not scolding me." She waved him off. "So are we in agreement?" Grandma looked hopefully to everyone's faces.

Was no even an option with this woman?

"Question," Jace asked calmly. "If this is all supposed to be a ruse to save my career from tanking, and I'm supposedly at my own destination wedding, wouldn't my parents be here? And what about Beth's?"

Grandma's smile grew. "Perfect timing, wouldn't you say, Your Honor?"

Jace's face drained of all its color as he slowly turned around and swore. "Father."

"Son, we need to talk."

CHAPTER TWENTY-FIVE

"I find it hard to believe that you were able to convince the judge to make an impromptu trip to Hawaii in order to attend a fake wedding for his wayward son."

"Oh, it didn't take much convincing." Grandma laughed. *"After all, I told him it was life and death. And when that didn't work, I told the judge that his son had been kidnapped by pirates scouring the Hawaiian Islands.*

"And he believed you?"

"He had no reason not to."

"Why's that?"

"It's amazing what one can do with a microphone, voice encryption, and email these days. It truly never ceases to amaze me."

"Shall I add that to your rap sheet as well?"

"Genius?"

"No. Lying to a judge."

Grandma sighed. *"If you must. But he won't be pressing charges. I hardly think it matters, considering his son's missing."*

"The son you kidnapped."

"Details."

Jace

As a child, I'd always hated getting scolded by my father. It was rare when he had scolded me; after all, my entire goal in life had been to make him proud of me. So when I did get in trouble, it had been life-altering.

After the accident, things had gotten worse. I'd woken up with no recollection of how I'd even gotten in the hospital — my parents said a light in my eyes had died. It pissed me off that after all this time, I felt like I was still trying to get the old Jace back. The one who believed in fairytales and magic; the one who believed in optimism instead of cynicism.

I could still smell my dad's musty study. Floor-to-ceiling bookshelves lined every single wall of the room, and a green leather chair was always facing the mahogany desk. Dad wouldn't turn his own chair, not until I spoke up and alerted him of my presence. Then, ever so slowly, he'd turn in his chair, lean slowly across the table, and say, "Are you ready?"

I'd nod as tears streamed down my face, and then I'd confess what I'd done wrong. I never usually had to be told. I always knew when I was in the wrong, whether it was from disrespecting my mother or eating cookies before dinner. He was always fair in the way he scolded, always giving me a chance to plead my case before the gauntlet fell.

I was suddenly ten years old again. Waiting for the damn words I knew that he'd say in a few seconds. We walked along the beach, both of us silent as the waves crashed against the shore.

How had one week messed up my life so much? I had no one to blame but myself.

"Is mom here?"

"At one of the huts." Dad said crisply, still not looking in my direction.

I nodded, not trusting my voice.

We walked a few more feet, away from watchful eyes

and people playing in the water. Finally, I sat on one of the lounge chairs and waited.

The silence was just as heavy as the flower-scented air, thick with tension, thick with shame. He was disappointed, and even though I'd tried to do everything right since the day I'd been able to make my own decisions, it seemed it still wasn't enough. Not that he ever said that — it was always assumed in the way he barked orders and the way he held himself.

"I am..." Dad's weathered face cracked into a bright smile, "so proud of you."

"Come again?"

"Nadine, or sorry, Grandma," he rolled his eyes, "confessed to everything. How you fell in love, tried to keep her out of the media, even decided to keep her from me and your mother." He sighed. "I'm proud that you didn't flaunt it. You did it right this time, Jace. Things with Kerry..." His voice lowered. "It wasn't well done of us to encourage the match. We should have seen through her. We should have made you wait, instead of pushing you to commit in order to further your career. But. at least now, you're doing things right. I admire you for that."

Hell had officially landed on earth, and I, being an idiot, had jumped into the hand basket and was now floating around, ignorant of every single string Grandma had pulled until now.

"What exactly did Grandma tell you?"

"Everything." Father chuckled. "You're in love. You're using your friends' honeymoons as a way to cover up the wedding. I will admit, at first she said you'd been kidnapped by pirates. But to be fair, it got my attention. I was on the next flight out after we talked. That woman is something else."

"Yeah." I croaked. "She's something."

"So, now that we're here, there's really no reason for you not to get married. I figured now would be best, since the media's been placated for a while."

"Married." How the hell was I going to talk my way out of this one? "You see, Dad, the thing is…"

Tears welled in his eyes. Holy shit. Was he crying?

"I'm sorry." He sniffled. "I've just been so worried about you. I know you're so worried about your career. Hell, you wore a suit to school when you were in sixth grade."

"It was for career day," I grumbled.

"I know, son." He slapped me on the shoulder. "It's just, now it finally seems like you have everything you've ever wanted. All you have to do is grasp it. All you have to do is say yes."

"Yes?"

"To your future." Father's smile grew. "Now, what were you going to tell me?"

I should have said something. I should have told him the truth. Hell, I'd been honest all week with Beth. Why was I suddenly having issues now? Oh right, because telling him the truth would wreck him. And in turn, it would wreck me, because then he'd know it was possible I wasn't the man he thought. Because I'd stayed with a girl under false pretenses, lying to the world, and then accepted a dare in order to get her to lie to the media about her reasons for being with me.

I was an ass.

And he was looking at me like I was the perfect son. He was looking at me like I'd always wanted him to look at me.

Which was why I found myself saying, "I'm just happy you could make it for the big day."

Royally Screwed: *When the only way out is death.* **See also: Grandma Nadine.**

CHAPTER TWENTY-SIX

"He was in on it, wasn't he?" The agent smirked.

"Ah, you're getting to know me to well, Gus."

"You tricked the grandkids and somehow convinced a judge to lie to his own flesh and blood. You both must have been desperate."

"The desire for great-grandchildren is strong in grandmas and apparently grandpas. Just ask Mr. Brevik and his lovely wife."

Beth

"He's been gone for a really long time." I played with the straw in my drink and kept my eyes trained on the beach for any sign of Jace.

"Why do you care?" Char asked in an innocent voice. "Something you want to tell us?"

Kacey grinned shamelessly. Char joined in. And both men fell silent as all eyes burned holes through my person.

"Jace!" I all but yelled when he came walking up with his father.

But something was off. He looked... he looked almost guilty... and sad. Why would he be sad? Immediately, I blamed myself. If I hadn't made him go along with the challenge to stay… If I hadn't bribed him with his career and the whole prostitution rumor… Was I so wrong to want the fairytale? It had basically been handed to me on a silver platter. So what? I took it! You hear me, God! I took it!

"Welcome to the family!" Mr. Brevik pulled me into a tight bear hug.

I almost puked my drink all over him. Family? Whose family was I joining, and why the hell was he so excited about it?

"We're so happy to have you. My wife will soon be joining us to celebrate."

"Is it your birthday?" I asked lamely.

"And a sense of humor!" He elbowed Jace in the ribs. "You've really hit the jackpot on this one. And, my dear," he turned back to me, "what incredible work you've been doing for GreenCom."

"Work." I nodded. "What does that have to do with family?"

"There she is!" A loud southern voice interrupted my confusion and Jace's guilty face. A woman of about five-two came barreling toward me. She had bright blond hair and giant sunglasses. Had she not been wearing white, I would have thought she was Grandma. "My daughter!"

"I think I'm confused," Travis whispered behind me.

"I've always wanted a girl! And now I have one. Oh, this is just the best news I've had all year! It truly got me through that horrid plane ride. Oh, who am I kidding? If I have a stroke tomorrow, I'll die happy, knowing our son's settled down with such an accomplished woman!"

"Who's getting married?" Jake asked innocently as he took another sip of his drink.

"Is someone dying?" This from Travis.

"Cheers!" Mr. Brevik shouted. "To Jace and Beth!"

Grandma magically appeared out of thin air with a tray

of drinks. "I just love it when things fall together, don't you?"

Slowly, I turned to Jace.

He basically had the words *Guilty Bastard* written across his forehead as he made his way over to me and pulled me in for a tight hug, whispering in my ear, "I'm sorry."

Those two words may as well have been a knife being stabbed into my heart.

No proposal for boring Beth. No, just an apology. That's what I was. An apology, caught up in lie after lie after lie. And it was all my fault. All because I was reaching for something I never deserved in the first place.

"I'll fix it, just not now," Jace continued.

So when was he going to fix it? Before or after we walked down the damn aisle?

Everyone lifted glasses into the air, but suddenly it was too much. I wanted to run — needed an escape.

"I'm just going to go use the restroom." I forced a smile and barely made it to the ladies' room without bursting into tears.

It was all wrong.

This was not how the story was supposed to go.

Boy meets girl, boy falls for girl, boy marries girl. Never once in the story is he supposed to meet girl, tell her he can't like her, admit he'll never marry her, then marry her anyway to save his damn career.

"Honey?" Grandma's scent enveloped me, followed by her arms. "Oh honey, I was afraid you'd be upset."

"Then why did you do it?" I wiped the tears from my cheeks. "Give me one good reason."

"He's your match," Grandma said honestly. "I've known him for quite some time. He's lonely, Beth. He's afraid, but he likes you, possibly loves you. Don't deny that you've seen glimpses of what you could have together. I know about high school."

"Don't you get it?" I grabbed a paper towel and dabbed

my eyes. "This isn't high school. This is my life!"

"Is that why you compare every man you meet to him?"

"Who told you that?"

"Your sister."

"Damn her." More tears streamed down my face. "And why did she tell you?"

"You aren't the only one with struggles. She had a hard time fitting in the family, always feeling like second best. It made me wonder why you felt the same way. Funny, how we all want someone else's life and always think we're worse off than everyone else in the room."

"Your point?"

"I want you to wear red."

"Like a harlot?"

"No." Grandma pulled me into an embrace. "Like the brave, courageous, beautiful woman you are. Let Jace pull that out of you. Love always asks us to take a chance, and I won't lie to you, sugar. You may fail. But wouldn't you rather try and know you failed than wonder for the rest of your life what would have happened had you taken a little leap?"

"Grandma," I choked on the thick tears in my throat, "my love life isn't a game. I feel like you've ripped out my heart, handed it to Jace, and now everyone's just waiting to see if he's going to keep it or throw it into the ocean."

"Why wouldn't he keep it, sweetie?" Grandma kissed my forehead and smiled warmly. "What use would the sharks have for it?"

I rolled my eyes and managed a small smile. "He'll throw it, believe me. All he keeps talking about is how he can't have me, how he'll walk away."

"I know men," Grandma whispered. "After all God cursed me with loads of them. And I know how they think. I imagine Jace is trying to convince himself more than convince you."

"So where does that leave me?"

"I imagine," Grandma looked thoughtfully into the mirror and fluffed her hair around her face, "it leaves you exactly where you've always wanted to be."

"Stuck on an island with a lying politician?" I joked. "Sorry, Grandma, that was never my fantasy as a little girl."

"Of course not, sweetie. That was mine." She winked. "Your fantasy has always been the white horse, the fairytale, and the happily ever after. No story is ever the same. How boring would that be? To always have a happily ever after? How unoriginal." Grandma tucked my arm in hers. "I want magic."

The tears threatened again.

"I want mischief." she continued. "I want madness. I want red dresses and red lipstick followed by starry nights and fireworks. And Beth, I think you do too."

"You think I want madness?"

"I don't think it." Grandma patted my hand and started walking away. "I know it. So what are you going to do? Are you going to risk it all for him? Or are you going to walk away from an opportunity to do the one thing that fairytale books don't teach."

"What?"

"Fight for your man."

"I thought he was supposed to fight for me?"

"How can he when you won't even show up for the battle?"

My eyes narrowed as Grandma sauntered off toward the crowd. I wiped my tears, pinched my cheeks, and followed. Jace lifted his head and gave me a breathtaking smile.

With the ocean crashing behind him, he looked like some sort of Greek god on vacation. Smile still in place, he stalked toward me, his muscles glistening in the sun.

"Holy Thor," I whispered. "I'm going out guns blazing." I smiled to myself. Good Thor, I'm going out with a fight.

The number of steps I took? Three.

The number of seconds I waited before my lips touched his? Two.

The amount of time it took for Thor, God of Thunder to respond? One.

I wrapped my arms around his neck and held on for dear life as he lifted me in the air and twirled me around.

"What was that for?" He set me down, his blue eyes sparkling.

"My fairytale isn't over yet." I kissed his mouth again.

"Who said it was?"

I shrugged.

His forehead touched mine. "I gave my word. I don't go back on my word."

"I know that now."

"I'm sorry about… everything. I'll find a way to fix it. I swear."

"Even if you don't." I shrugged. "The fun's in the adventure, right?"

"Right." He cupped my face and kissed me lightly across the lips. "But you deserve more."

"I have more," I answered honestly. "And it's time you realized you can have more too."

With a deep breath, I took a step around him and joined everyone else for drinks, wondering how in the heck I was going to survive another three days without getting my heart broken. Because after making the decision I've made, I was going to fight until I couldn't fight anymore. And if he still walked away in the end, I would let him.

CHAPTER TWENTY-SEVEN

"Interesting logic. Trickery and then seeds of wisdom." The agent nodded thoughtfully.

"Well, I'm not so bad." Grandma shook her head. *"Had I set them to their own devices, they would have taken years to get together. Now look at them."*

"Right. Look at them. Both missing."

"I didn't say I had all the kinks worked out. I am eighty-six."

"So you keep saying."

Jace

"I'm going to hell."

"Say hi to Jake when you get there." Travis slapped me on the back and ordered a beer.

We'd decided on going to a luau instead of doing a typical bachelor or bachelorette party. After all, the only things we needed were pictures, and it was easy enough to convince the parents that I wasn't interested in that sort of thing.

Beth seemed relieved.

Beth... Just thinking her name got me aroused in all the

wrong places. It made me want her, not just physically but emotionally, which was ridiculous. I was three days into our relationship, and it was a fake one at that. And here I was, drinking my sorrows away and lying to not only my parents but the world.

"For what it's worth," Travis slid a beer toward me, "Grandma's two for two."

"Yeah, not helping." I took a long swig. "I'm still going to hell for lying to everyone, and I doubt Jake will be there, considering he's fully turned over a new nauseating leaf."

"Right?" Travis laughed. "It's like he's a new man."

"What about you?"

"Me?" Travis's eyebrows shot up in surprise. "I've always been the good one, no changing necessary, other than being so humbled by Grandma that I was an embarrassment to not only myself, but society."

"Ah," I winced, "that's encouraging."

"Sorry, your best bet is to marry her, fall in love, and produce as many great-grandchildren as possible."

"Never." I pushed the beer away, suddenly feeling sick to my stomach. "You know I can't, Travis. You know I don't want to be vulnerable like that again. You know I don't do commitment."

"Did you and Jake trade brains?" Travis leaned in, "or are you high?

I pushed his chest and rolled my eyes. "Please."

"It was two years ago, Jace. Move on. Let yourself be happy."

"I know how to let myself be happy. I just choose to do it without a woman by my side."

"Because you secretly prefer men?"

"Are we done here?" I rose, but Travis pulled me back down onto my chair.

"Look, I know it's only been three days. We can easily fix the marriage so it's not legal. Your parents won't know the difference, but to the world you'll still be married. You can go your separate ways once you land in Portland. Beth can go back to her really fun life playing with diseases and start herding cats. And you can go back to your insanely large penthouse and big-screen TV."

"Well, when you put it that way…"

"Marriage isn't so bad, and I know you like Beth. Hell, everyone knows you like Beth. And I, for one, know you could love her."

"Oh, this I gotta hear. After three days? Did Grandma slip something in your drink?"

"Easy, Viagra." Travis patted me on the back. "Before the wedding, you and I went golfing. It was freakishly hot, so we called it a day and went to get drinks."

This story wasn't going to end well.

He smirked. "I asked you about the one that got away."

"I think Grandma's calling me." I stood.

Travis pulled me back down.

With a grunt, I jerked away and waited.

"You said—"

"I know what I said."

Travis ignored me. "You said there was only one girl whose kiss you couldn't forget. One girl you compared all the rest of the girls to, even Kerry. In fact, didn't you call Kerry *Beth* one time?"

"No." I lied. Yes, I'd done that. She'd slapped me., Then again, she'd been sleeping with my best friend, so she really wasn't one to judge.

"You cried."

"I did not cry." I winced. I think I had cried. Or at least shed one drunken tear. So what? Sue me! "I was dehydrated, Travis!"

"Good excuse, man. See if that holds up in court." He took another long swig of beer and then set the empty bottle back onto the bar. "You said, and I quote, 'If second chances were possible, she would be mine.'"

Blood roared in my ears. My body felt absolutely numb. Was this what a panic attack felt like? "So you sold me out? To that one?"

I pointed to Grandma as she did the hula around the table where the girls were sitting. She pulled a fire dancer down into a chair and started chanting, "Light it up!"

Travis chuckled and then winced when the fire dancer started crying. Apparently his outfit wasn't fireproof. "I can neither confirm nor deny your suspicions."

"You did this to me." I pushed against his chest.

"Misery loves company."

"If this is miserable, sign me up," I grumbled, and then immediately wanted to take it back.

Travis grinned. "My point exactly."

"You don't get it. I have to choose." I sighed. "Beth or my career. And I'm sorry, Trav, I really am. I know she's your sister-in-law, but I've known adult Beth for only three days. Why would I throw away my entire life based on sixty-four hours?"

Travis frowned. "Who the hell told you that you had to choose?"

"But—"

"Nobody said choose your career or Beth. In fact, the best thing for your career is to choose Beth. You, my friend, have your priorities way screwed up, and if my point hasn't just been proven at least four times, check it out." He pointed to the stage, where Beth and Grandma were being handed fertility necklaces, just like the one that I'd been given on arrival. Though hopefully, these weren't plagued with curses.

"Jace," Grandma screeched into the microphone, "come up here. Grandma has a blessing for you."

"Or curse." Travis coughed. "It's all in how you look at it."

"Funny." I pushed past the crowds and made my way up

to the stage, hoping I wasn't about to have to do any sort of hula dancing.

Once I was on the stage, Grandma put the damn necklace over my neck and then gave one to Beth.

"A blessing to the happy couple. Love is the combination of life's treasured moments tied together in the infinite circle of life. It never ends. It's a constant reminder when you're weak and tired, and it never fails. When you want to quit, love continues. When you want to cry, love uplifts, and when you want to run away, love remains. Each of you are wearing a symbol of fertility, but it's more than that. They are love beads. They bring good luck and favor in your relationship. May you wear them wisely, and may your lives always be filled with love."

I turned to give Beth a kiss but was hit with the sensation of the wind shifting. Ever so slowly it picked up Beth's hair, wrapping it around her shoulders. Her eyes glowed in the moonlight, and I couldn't have looked away had someone paid me.

I had to touch her face. My fingertips grazed the soft part of her neck as I leaned in and whispered, "You look beautiful."

She smiled and ducked her head.

"Look at me."

Swallowing, she lifted her head, meeting my gaze with a piercing one of her own. Grandma had spoken of moments. If I could just hold onto this one, I'd be happy for an eternity. I wanted to keep it for myself. I wanted to remember the way Beth smelled. I wanted to remember the way she felt in my arms.

"Cheers!" People lifted glasses in the air, and a camera flashed. It may as well have been an electrical shock to my nervous system. I snapped out of the spell and remembered my predicament.

I could fix things for Beth.

And I would.

She deserved the fairytale. She deserved the chance to have a happy ending.

I walked her back to the table we were sharing with the rest of the family, more determined than ever to make things right.

"Beautiful speech, Nadine." My father clinked Grandma's glass and kissed my mom's forehead.

Maybe my curse was to be surrounded by happy people until I got my head out of my ass and made a choice.

"Great party." I licked my lips nervously.

"It's a luau," Grandma corrected. "We Hawaiians do not party. We feast."

"You're not Hawaiian," Jake pointed out.

"Am too."

Jake sighed, "How do you figure?"

"I visit every year."

"Which would make you a tourist," Travis took a sip of his drink, "not a local."

"I joined a local tribe."

"Do they call them tribes here?" I asked. "I don't think that's politically correct."

"Thank you, Mr. Senator," Jake said crisply.

"What the hell is your problem?" I pushed back my chair. "Do you really want to fight again? Do you want to get your ass kicked in front of your entire family? I'll do it, Jake. Don't tempt me. I'm sick and tired of your pompous attitude!"

The table fell silent.

My chest heaved.

I looked around for support. Jake was grinning like a fool, as if he'd done it on purpose. What the hell?

And then he clapped. "Finally."

"Finally?" My voice was hoarse. "Get there faster, man, before I strangle you."

"It's not normal to be calm all the time," Jake said in that same calm, irritating voice. "If I wasn't convinced earlier, I sure am now."

"Convinced?"

"You need a wife."

"You need to stop talking. Now."

"Why would I stop talking when I know it pisses you off so much to fill the air with my voice?" He stood. "Let's go talk."

"Do you really trust me not to kill you and build a sandcastle over your dead body?"

"Of course." He shrugged. "Politicians hate prison."

With a sigh, I stuffed my hands in my pockets and followed Jake, the ass, out onto the beach. Great, another heart-to-heart from a Titus brother. I was cursed all right, or maybe just haunted.

Once we reached the beach, he took a seat on the sand. I followed, waiting for the gauntlet to fall.

"We all have our shit we need to deal with. Nobody's perfect, Jace."

"I know."

"No, you don't." Jake grimaced. "Because if you knew that, you wouldn't be acting like such an asshole to Beth. You wouldn't be thinking about what this situation is doing to your polls. You wouldn't be planning out your entire workweek, while she's sitting there staring at you like you hung the moon and freaking stars. You sure as hell wouldn't be sitting around the table with your parents watching, while you played pretty with our family."

"Wow, you know me so well," I said dryly. "You done?"

"Nope." Jake laughed out loud. "I know I'm not usually the voice of reason, but hear me out."

"Five minutes."

"You like Beth."

"Yes."

"You want Beth."

"Yes."

"You want to spend time with Beth alone?"

"Yes."

"Yet you're letting people control your decisions because you want to make everyone happy. Because you can't stand the fact that you may let your parents down, or even Grandma, who you've only known for a year."

"Are you telling me to come clean?"

"Not at all." Jake shrugged. "I'm saying only someone truly stupid would worry about what everyone else thought when the woman of his dreams was sitting right next to him. So you want to kiss her? Kiss her. You want to touch her? Touch her. You want to run away with her? Sneak out? Get crazy? The only person stopping you right now is you and your damn ideas about perfection."

"It's like you're giving me permission to do drugs or have sex."

Jake let out a bark of laughter. "Well, drugs aren't the way to go. Just look at Grandma."

I smirked.

"And while I wouldn't suggest another one-night stand… it wouldn't hurt to kiss her instead of making her cry."

"She was crying?" My heart slammed against my chest.

"Grandma told Char who ended up telling me. What you do with this information is all you. But word to the wise? Grandma's never been wrong."

"Why do people keep telling me that?"

"Because it's true."

We sat in silence.

Groaning, Jake smacked me on the shoulder. "Go on, Thor, steal her away."

"Not you too."

"It's a catchy nickname." He snickered.

"Everything okay out here?" Grandma nearly fell on her face as she maneuvered through the sand like a drunken sailor.

"I'm sick," I blurted.

"Was it the fish?" she said in a low voice. "'Cause I'll tell you one thing, that ladies' restroom won't be the same after I went in there and—"

"He should go to his room. I'll send Beth," Jake said, coming to my rescue.

"But what about the party?" Grandma moved her hips from side to side.

I coughed wildly.

"Quick, Grandma, he's going to puke!" Jake put his arm around me and walked me briskly toward the opposite end of the beach. "Better make a run for it. I'll send you Florence Nightingale. Oh, and P.S., you owe me for distracting Grandma tonight."

"Thanks." I jogged off toward the hut, smiling. Who would have ever thought Jake had a thought in that brain of his?

CHAPTER TWENTY-EIGHT

"So your grandson pulled the wool over your eyes?"

"No," Grandma said. "I allowed him to think he had. I purposefully told him about Beth, hoping to get him to do something about it. I knew Travis would intervene, bless his heart. He's always been the softie. But Jake? Jake has a way about wording things. He's honest, and he's brutal about it. I think the senator needed to hear it from Jake."

"Hear what?"

"To get his head out of his ass."

Beth

I ran to the hut. Jake came back without Jace, claiming that he was sick and was puking up fish.

Not a mental picture any one of us needed, considering we were all eating the same fish.

"Should I go see him?"

"Someone needs to!" Grandma started toward the direction of the huts, when Travis began choking on his food.

A few things happened in that moment. All of which, I

am one-hundred-percent convinced were planned strategically by the Titus family.

"Oh no!" Kacey hit his back. "Travis! Grandma, help him!"

Travis's eyes widened as Grandma yelled and pushed people out of the way to reach her grandson. Much like a cheetah flies through the brush, in a flash of spots, Grandma was there, arms around Travis as she started the Heimlich.

Of course, that was at the exact time that Jake spilled rum punch all over Jace's dad, pushed out of his chair, and ended up smacking Jace's mom in the face with his cup.

Chairs fell.

People were shouting.

I could have sworn I saw a few tears.

And in the midst of it all, Char leaned over and whispered, "I don't think they'll notice if you leave."

Which was why I ran to the hut. It wasn't for fear that something was wrong with Jace. It was a fear of Grandma Nadine. A healthy fear. The type of fear that keeps people from getting eaten by bears. I was running so I wouldn't get caught.

I scurried to a halt in front of our door, slid the key in and entered, then slammed the door behind me, breathing heavily as I leaned against it.

"Being chased by wild donkeys?"

"No," I heaved. "I didn't want Grandma to follow me."

"Ah, that explains the panic."

"She's faster than she looks." I leaned over and took a few deep breaths through my nose. "I think I need to start doing more cardio."

"Or eating less cookies." Jace felt the need to say.

"And to think I came here to nurse you back to health." I lifted my head long enough to give him a glare then stretched my arms above my head.

"Take off the necklace, and you can nurse all you want."

"The necklace? Why?" I fingered the brown necklace and tugged it over my head.

"I have a theory."

"Oh, this should be good."

"Do you want to hear it or not?"

"Yes." I took off the necklace, placed it on the nightstand, and sat on the bed.

"If you wear the fertility necklace at the same time I do, and we sit on the same bed, we'll—" He waved his hand in the air.

"Sleep?"

Jace rolled his eyes. "You know… we'll… you know."

"Do your speeches always go this well, Mr. Senator?"

"Have sex." He coughed, "and we should probably not, not with the sex."

"Not with the sex?" I repeated. "Eloquent."

"I'm sick. Bad fish." He coughed again.

"You're a liar, and you're going to hell."

"Funny, I told Travis that exact same thing today."

"No sex?"

"Cute." He threw a pillow at my face. "No, that I was going to hell."

"Well, at least Grandma won't be there," I offered cheerfully.

"Point, Jace." He closed his eyes and moaned.

"Are you really sick?"

"Do I look sick?"

He was still in all his clothes but lying across the bed; his eyes had dark circles underneath them, and he looked pale.

"Kind of."

"So I look like shit?"

"Of course not."

He gave a relieved sigh.

"Shit looks like Donkey."

He closed his eyes and mumbled a curse. "It's like the

Island of Misfit Toys."

"And you're the king. Yay, you!" I offered a playful punch to the arm.

"Jace!" A hard knock sounded at the door. "Jace, it's Grandma! I brought you tea!"

"Shit!"

"Hee-haw." I chuckled.

"Not the time for games, Beth. I'll pay you. I will do anything you want. I'll go find Frank. I'll let Frank bite me — just don't let her think I'm healthy. Please, I can't take one more thing."

He looked too pitiful. Too beautiful. And honestly? I wanted to be stuck in the room with him. I wanted him all to myself.

"Lie back."

"Wait, what are you doing?"

He struggled against me while I pulled his shirt over his head and pulled the covers over his body.

"Just a minute, Grandma!" I ran into the bathroom and got some hot water and a washrag. I threw it at Jace's face and whispered, "Fever of a hundred, your muscles ache, you've lost vision in your left eye, are sensitive to loud noises and light, and have a sore throat."

"So I'm dying?" he snapped.

"No. You have the flu. Stop being such a guy and cough."

"Oh, if I had a dollar for every time a doctor told me that."

I smirked and gave him a pointed stare before marching to the door and throwing it open.

"Oh, Grandma, I'm so glad you cared enough to come, but I have everything totally under control."

"Do you?" Her eyebrow shot up as she peered around me. "Have you used the honey?"

"Er, no."

"Or the onions and mustard?"

"He's sick, not planning a picnic."

Grandma pushed past me. "And the tea? Did you make the tea?"

"Not yet, but—"

"Move."

Grandma shoved me aside and breezed into the room, carrying something on a tray. Something that smelled like shit, actual shit, not Donkey.

"So you say you're sick?" Grandma paced in front of Jace's bed. He had that deer-in-headlights look that people get when they don't know how to lie to save their lives.

I made wild gestures behind Grandma, grabbing my throat and then touching my forehead and finally covering my left eye. Unfortunately, she chose that exact moment to turn around.

"What are you doing?"

"P-pirate."

"Role play," Jace interjected. "When I was a kid, my dad used to do a pirate voice to make me feel better."

"Oh, how lovely." Grandma took a seat on the bed. "You may proceed, Beth."

"Yes, Beth," Jace's stone face cracked into a smile, "proceed. You know how much better it makes my tummy."

I was going to kill him. No, better yet, I was going to leave him to Grandma, see how he liked her as a nurse when she was stabbing a needle in his godlike ass.

"Well?" Grandma urged.

I pasted a smile on my face and swung my arm in front of my body. "Ahoy, matey. Thar be booty t'seek."

Jace covered his mouth with his hands and started coughing.

Grandma's face drew together in concern. "Dear, maybe a career in theatre isn't in your future. But who am I to judge? If that makes poor Jace feel better then..." She shrugged. "Besides if that doesn't work, I brought my magic tea."

"Magic tea?" I asked, peering over her petite shoulder. She lifted the top of the container and pointed inside. "See the chicken feathers?"

Jace's eyes widened in horror.

"Why yes," I grinned, "I do."

"It's an ancient recipe, passed down through my family. What you do is, you boil the feathers in hot water then drink the hot water once the feathers have been boiled for at least eight minutes."

"Tasty." I almost threw up in my mouth.

"We should count our lucky stars that the restaurant had some live chickens out back. I plucked a few of these beauts and steamed them right up."

"I bet Jace is counting his stars right now."

He flipped me off and glared.

"Here, Jace," Grandma poured some cloudy liquid into a white cup and handed it to him, "this will make you all better. You do want to get better, don't you?"

"Yes." His jaw flexed.

Holy crap. He was going to do it. He was going to drink the tea. I almost didn't want to look, but I couldn't help it. He brought the cup to his lips, took a small sip, and grimaced before pulling it back. A small feather attached itself to his lips.

"Oh dear, it was a male chicken. I can always tell these things." Grandma pulled the feather from Jace's lips and chuckled. "Back when I sexed chickens, well, it was my job to figure out which was which."

"Sexed. Chickens?" Jace repeated, his voice hoarse. "That's not a job, Grandma. And I doubt this works."

You'd think Jace would have already learned his lesson: Never doubt Grandma. And when she says something that just shouts crazy, don't engage. Just back away and leave it alone. Because it was a guarantee that something insane, illogical, and, nine times out of ten, illegal would be shared in her presence.

"It works, and it is too a job. Want to know how to tell the difference between a female chicken and a male chicken?"

"No. No, I don't." Jace shook his head. "I'm sick. I want a good night's sleep without visions of you sexing chickens."

"Not until your tea's finished," Grandma instructed, urging the tea closer to his mouth. He seemed to pale as the cup was brought closer to his lips.

Jace's eyes darted to mine. I knew that look. It was fear, pure fear. I took pity on the guy; after all, he was drinking feather tea.

"Tell me, Grandma," I grabbed her hands and had turned her toward me, while behind me, Jace slowly poured the tea into the potted plant next to the bed. We'd just committed murder via feather tea. Poor plant would be lucky to survive the next five minutes, let alone an entire day.

Best bet, the plant dies or turns into a hybrid chicken plant that Grandma takes credit for discovering.

My imagination was running away from me. I really needed to get normal friends.

"Well, the males' are jagged, whereas the females' are smooth," Grandma said, serious as a heart attack. "You see, there's feather sexing and feather venting."

I had no words.

Jace cleared his throat, "Venting?"

"Oh yes." Grandma chuckled. "But there's a school for that."

I felt my eyes widen in horror as Grandma chuckled and pulled a feather from the giant tea pot.

"After all, doctors don't graduate high school and start performing surgeries! They need expertise. So do sexers."

"Is that what they're called?" I shouldn't have asked, but my curiosity was destroying me.

"Yes." Grandma nodded. "Sexers. But like I said, I wasn't a chicken sexer, per se. I sexed the feathers."

Jace pursed his lips together. "You… sexed the feathers?"

"How does one—"

"Beth." Jace started coughing wildly.

"Oh dear!" Grandma reached for the kettle. "Do you need more tea?"

"No!" Jace and I said in unison.

"Sleep." Jace yawned. "Beth will take care of me. Promise."

She turned just as Jace brought the cup back from his lips and held it out. "Well, good job!"

He beamed.

I rolled my eyes behind Grandma.

"Now, I'll leave you to sleep. Beth, if his throat keeps getting sore, be sure to make him a mustard sandwich with onions. It's hell when you wanna kiss your honey goodnight, but it works like a charm. Ta-ta!" She took her tray and left.

"I think she just killed my stomach." Jace burped and then groaned. "Holy shit, it tastes like chicken feathers. I'm dying! She poisoned me!"

"Stop being dramatic. She was just trying to help."

"No, that woman is a lunatic!" he yelled. "Chicken feathers? Sexing chickens? She was trying to call our bluff! Need I remind you that she put Viagra in my tea?"

"Well you showed her," I said dryly. "So brave."

"Tell me, Captain Jack, where's the rum?"

"Arrgh."

"Nice." Jace laughed. "You sound like a pirate with a cold, and, by the way, your accent sounded like a cross between an Australian and very confused Canadian. Good job, eh?"

"I hate you."

"You nicknamed me Thor — you love me." He grinned. "Thanks for taking care of me, by the way, and for helping me kill the plant."

I should have slit his throat when I had the chance;

instead, I picked up a feather.

"Thirsty?"

"Are you threatening me?" He seemed amused at the prospect.

"Yes, better be on your best behavior, or I'm calling Grandma in to nurse you back to health."

"She'd kill me."

"I know."

"My death would be on your hands."

"I'm aware of that."

"Asphyxiation via feathers."

I smirked. "Oregon State Senator Jace Brevik Found Dead in Hawaiian Hut, Surrounded by Chicken Feathers and Viagra."

His amusement faded before my very eyes. "You don't think she put more... stuff in my tea, do you?"

"Why?" I scooted across the bed and lay down next to him. "You feeling inspired again?"

"*Inspired* makes it sound like I'm rarely inspired, which is ridiculous because I'm inspired a hell-of-a-lot more than usual."

"Maybe it's me," I offered. "Then again, it could be the chickens."

"Not the chickens, not the pool toys, not any of those things." He reached for my hand and sighed. "I'm sorry, you know."

"For what?"

"Everything."

The room was completely silent except for my stupid heart as it rammed against my chest. He kept holding my hand, and I wondered if it was because he wanted to give me the fairytale, or if it was because he actually wanted to hold it.

"I shouldn't have run," Jace whispered.

"What are you talking about?"

"Prom." He squeezed my hand harder and then pulled

me into his lap. "I should have stayed."

"And done what?" I laughed nervously. "Fought for my honor?"

"Something like that."

He dipped his hand into my hair and ran that same warm hand down my neck, sending chills to my toes.

"It was never that I didn't want to fight — I just hate letting people down. In theory, it sounds good. I don't like people being disappointed in me, but that's only partially the truth. I hate disappointment, but it's only by those I deem worthy of approval in the first place. And because I didn't know you, other than the taste of your lips and heat of your mouth, it wasn't worth it to me. You weren't worth it."

"Are you trying to make me cry?" My chest felt like an elephant had just decided to camp on it and invited all his friends and family.

Jace's eyes softened. "I'm trying to apologize."

"Try harder," I urged.

"Second chances are rare."

"Unless you're Grandma and have God's ear. Then you have as many chances as she allows, until she kills you herself."

"True."

What was happening, exactly? Was he apologizing for high school, or was he apologizing for now? And why was he looking at me like I'd just declared my undying love for him? Yes. I liked him, possibly loved him now that I'd gotten to know him, but it was more of an irritating love. The kind that pokes you until you finally give up and accept your fate. And I wasn't ready to admit anything yet, especially to the one guy I knew would be walking away from me in a few days.

"You're my second chance." Bomb officially dropped.

I wasn't sure whether I was supposed to cry tears of joy or slap him in the face. His grin was cocky, as if I should be thankful that he was finally bleeding his feelings all over the place. I wasn't thankful. I was irritated. Irritated that his epic speech wasn't that he couldn't live without me, but that I'd finally worn him down, like some sort of cold that takes control of your immune system.

"Say something." He kissed my mouth.

It was a tie between wanting to kiss Thor back or throw him in the bathtub with his hammer on.

"Was that it?" I asked calmly.

"What?"

"Was that *the speech*?" I pulled away from him and stood.

"No?"

"Is that a question or an answer?"

"Um," he scratched his head and looked helplessly around the room, "I thought you liked me."

"Oh, dear Lord." I closed my eyes and pinched the bridge of my nose. "Of course, I like you. Of course, I believe in second chances, and I accept your apology for partially getting us caught in this fiasco. But Jace," I fought to keep my voice even, "girls don't work that way."

"What do you mean?"

"You can't just give us the words and expect a pat on the ass and a cookie."

"How about just a pat on the ass." He smirked.

"Be serious!" I almost stomped my foot. Good one. "You expect me to fall all over myself because you said sorry? You expect sex because you want a second chance, yet you haven't even told me why you want one. You said you were walking away in a few days. Is that still true?"

Jace stood and reached for me, his hands digging into my shoulders as he pulled me into his embrace. "That depends on you."

"What? So we play at being madly in love, and if it ends up being true, you don't walk away? But if things don't work out, then what? Then I'm left with a broken heart. Don't you see? The problem isn't the second chance. The problem is you want to have your cake and eat it too. You want to test the waters because you want *safe*. And I'm sick and tired of *safe*."

Jace shoved his hands in his pockets, swaying on his feet as if the world had just dropped onto his shoulders. "What do you want?"

"Danger," I snapped. "Spice. Crazy." My lips trembled. "I want crazy. I-can't-get-you-out-of–my-head lust. I want Romeo-and-Juliet-type of love. I want Mr. Darcy to ride his damn horse into my life. Words aren't enough. I need actions too. And I think I deserve it."

Jace was oddly silent during my rant. And then his face broke out into a giant grin.

"Stop smiling." I was about two seconds away from choking the life from his body. Was he making fun of me?

"Done."

"Done?" My eyebrows shot up. "What do you mean *done*? You're going to suddenly Thor yourself all over the place and get romantic?"

He shrugged.

"Find a white horse and sword?"

He shrugged again.

"Stop shrugging!" This time I did stomp my foot. Yes. I was a thirty-year-old foot-stomper, so sue me. We all have our moments.

"Let's go." He grabbed my hand.

I stood my ground.

So he threw me over his shoulder and marched out the little hut door. And I hated to admit I was grinning like a fool the entire way.

CHAPTER TWENTY-NINE

"Do you think that Mr. Brevik felt outside pressure to romance the young girl?"

"Well, of course he did! Leaving that man to his own devices is like giving children a quad-shot mocha. They run into walls and scream at the top of their lungs."

"So in your mind, Mr. Brevik is a child?"

"He's a man," Grandma said slowly for the agent's benefit.

"Your point?"

"Men, children — there is no difference, only that you change one's diapers while the other just lets loose in public."

"I don't know how to respond to that."

"Like I said, men."

Jace

I was going to need a hell of a lot of Gatorade if I was going to pull everything off. She wanted crazy? I'd give her crazy. There I was, pouring my feelings out all over the place like some Lifetime Christmas movie, and she still wasn't impressed?

Fine. I'd keep romancing the pants off of her until she realized that I was in it; I wanted a second chance. Then again, I didn't blame her. Why give me a second chance when I'd told her to her face that I was walking away from her?

I wouldn't trust me either.

And there was that small problem of my profession.

"Jace," Beth snapped. I was still carrying her. I liked carrying her. I wasn't putting her down anytime soon.

"Shh…" I slapped her ass. "I'm thinking. Don't interrupt a man when he's thinking."

"I want to lick you."

I tripped and almost went sailing into the wall. All thoughts left my mind. All thoughts except her tongue on me, my tongue in her mouth, licking. Lots of licking.

"Why'd we stop walking?" Beth said innocently.

I slapped her ass again. "You'll pay for that."

"Yes, please."

More licking.

"Damn it, Beth!" I huffed. "Stop doing that."

"What?"

"That," I grumbled, setting her on her feet. "Now climb."

"Climb?"

I turned her around and pointed to the cliff. "Climb."

"You're kidding, right?"

The cliff was a rocky climb. It led to a ledge that was about thirty feet high. I'd seen locals jumping from the cliff for the past few days and figured if they could do it without dying, we could too. She wanted crazy? This was insane.

"Nope." I crossed my arms. "Not kidding. Where's your sense of adventure?"

"Must have left it back at the hut with your feather tea," she said through clenched teeth.

"I'm making a big gesture." I tilted her chin toward me and brushed a soft kiss across her lips. "The least you could do is go along with it."

"Fine, but if I die, I'm going to haunt you for the rest of your days."

I helped her on to the rocky trail and held her hand as we made our way slowly up the cliff. Luckily, the path was lit by a few torches, so it wasn't like it was this creepy abandoned area that was booby-trapped or something.

A warm breeze picked up once we reached the ledge. Waves crashed against the rocks below us. I had to close my eyes.

"What are you doing?" Beth squeezed my hand.

"I forgot to tell you something."

"What?"

Shit, I was sweating. "I'm terrified of heights."

"Then why are we here?"

"You said you wanted crazy. You said my apology wasn't good enough, and let's be honest, you have absolutely no reason to trust me."

"All true." She looked nervously over the edge then back at me. "So what's your point?"

"My point is you need vulnerable."

She bit down on her bottom lip and released my hand.

"You don't need crazy." I sighed. "You want crazy for you."

Beth still refused to look at me.

"Heights terrify me," I continued. "If you had asked me last week what my biggest fear was? I would have said heights. Two days ago, I would have said Frank."

Beth's warm laugh made my stomach flip.

"Ask me what I'm scared of right now."

Beth's gaze flew to my eyes. "What are you scared of now?"

"You," I whispered. "I'm scared I'm not who you think I am. I'm scared that you really have convinced yourself that I'm some sort of hero, when we both know that's the last thing people would call me. I'm terrified that if you give me a second chance, I'm just going to screw it up. I'm afraid that you'll wake up and not want me. That you'll decide I'm not worth it. Because the truth, Beth? Guys want to be fought for too. We want to be worthy of the women we love. I want to be the Romeo, Mr. Darcy, and Avenger. But those shoes? They're pretty big ones to fill, and although I love difficult situations, I don't like the idea that one day you're going to wake up and realize how damn beautiful you really are. You are worthy of those guys and more. I know where I land on that totem pole, and it's on the very bottom, underneath the dirt and worms and crap. You'll see me waving.

Beth laughed.

"I'm serious." I pulled her into my arms. "I'm serious about you. What would you say if I told you that you were the one that got away?"

"I'd say you're crazy."

"Mission accomplished," I whispered. "And what would you say if I told you I wanted more than a few days?"

"I'd say you're out of your mind."

"What would you say if I told you I burned for you? What would you say if I told you that even before this week, you consumed my dreams?"

Beth shook her head and opened her mouth to say something.

I kissed her roughly across the mouth. "And what would you say if I told you I was going to jump?"

"Jace—"

"I'm jumping. If only to prove to you that I'm going to start conquering fears, starting with jumping and ending with you."

"Jace don't—"

I couldn't hear her words as I jumped; my blood was roaring too loud, and the wind whipping by my face wasn't helping anything. The water slapped against my body as I landed, far away from the rocks and into the warm ocean.

I didn't have time to enjoy my accomplishment, what with Beth throwing herself off the cliff in such a fashion that I was a bit concerned she was going to belly flop.

Three seconds of cursing like a sailor, followed by mind-numbing screaming, and Beth splashed right next to me. She gasped for air, and then her hands were around my neck.

Holy shit. She was going to drown me!

"Beth!" I croaked, unable to actually breathe.

"Don't you dare," she shook me in her tiny hands, "do that to me again! I thought you were going to die!"

"Alive," I wheezed, "until you murder me."

"I want to murder you."

She released me. Thank God.

"But I'm too impressed by your speech and stupid death wish."

"Really?" My chest puffed out.

"Really." Beth swallowed. "So what now?"

"We get married."

"Be serious."

"We pretend to get married."

"Better." She grinned.

"And we get even."

"Oh?"

"I'll give it to Grandma. She knew what she was doing, but I hardly think the couples' therapy and Viagra were necessary to get our attention."

Beth gave me a doubtful look.

"Okay fine. It was probably necessary because I'm a man. Happy?"

"Thrilled."

"Inspired?" I pulled her into my arms.

"Not as much as you are." Beth wrapped her legs around me and jerked my body against hers.

"Three more days."

"Of the fairytale," I whispered. "Guess what happens at

the end?"

"What?"

"The prince wins."

"And the princess?"

"She lives happily ever after."

"In a castle?"

"Apartment."

"NO deal."

"Beth…" I growled.

She released her grip on my body and started swimming for shore. "Come on, Thor. We have to sneak back into the hut without Grandma seeing us. You're supposed to be sick, remember?"

"Why would I go back to the hut when everything I want is right here? In my arms?" He reached out and gently caressed my hand, I shivered in response.

"That was a good speech." Beth exhaled.

I could feel her heart race as we swam back toward the beach. Once we could touch the ground, I pulled her into my arms and kissed her, wrapping her legs around me in the process.

"I could love you," I whispered.

"I could love you too."

I finally gave in. I forgot about my career, forgot about prom, forgot about Kerri — I forgot about everything, purposefully, and focused, purposefully on the curve of her hips as I held her against me, on the softness of her skin as my lips brushed across it. I focused on the sound of her soft pants when my tongue licked the salt water from her neck.

Beth arched her back as I kissed down the front of her chest, causing our bodies to fit together perfectly. She was on fire, and I wanted nothing more than to remember this moment — since we'd somehow screwed it up so badly the first time.

She dug her nails into my head, touching part of the scar

from the accident. And for some reason, I froze.

Something felt familiar.

Something wasn't right.

Beth. The accident.

Beth and the accident.

"Bye, Dad!" I called out and ran to the car. "Beth," I smiled, "I'm going to marry her someday."

I jerked back from her as if she'd just burned me.

"Jace?" Beth held my face. "What's wrong? Are you okay?"

I shook my head, unable to find my voice. It had been a memory. I'd been dressed in the same tux I'd worn to prom. What the hell?

"Jace?"

"I, uh..." I couldn't catch my breath. "I think I really may be sick."

"It's okay." Beth pulled me in for a hug. "Let's just go back to the hut, alright?"

"But—"

"Jace. It's fine, plus you look really pale."

"Right." I gripped her hand like a lifeline and waded through the water to shore. The memory was still there. I'd said her name. I'd gotten back into my car that night with her name on my lips. Why?

CHAPTER THIRTY

The agent yawned. "So, the senator admitted his feelings. Good for him."

"No," Grandma sighed, "not good. You see, there was one thing I wasn't counting on happening, one person I wasn't able to..." she shrugged, "manage."

"You mean one person you couldn't control?"

"I prefer manage." She glared.

"Manage, it is."

Beth

I didn't sleep all night. It had nothing to do with the fact that sex-personified was snoring next to me. I was even partial to the snores. It had turned into my white noise, my soothing sound.

Something wasn't right.

I wasn't sure if it was me, if it was Jace, or if it was just the situation. But the more I thought about it, the more I realized it was the situation.

Everything had been going fine until things got heated

during our moonlight swim. It was almost as if he'd seen a ghost. I tucked my knees under my chest and sighed. Was it me? Or was it something more?

I stole a glance at him, knowing that I was being the creepy girl that watched a hot guy sleep. I was totally pulling a Bridget Jones. The scar near his eye was more evident in the moonlight; it made me wonder where he got it? Football, maybe? Or getting punched in the face by Travis? I smiled to myself.

Two more days, and this vacation would be over. Whatever Jace and I felt for each other would be tested.

The experience had almost felt like something off *The Bachelor*. In fact, the more I thought about it, the more it seemed exactly like a reality show. From the dates to the excursions. I frowned.

I don't know why I hadn't thought of it before, but the minute the little light bulb turned on — I almost started crying.

She was *Bacheloring* us. And yes I was totally comparing my life to a reality show.

We'd had the romantic getaway, the action adventure, the silly couples' therapy followed by the whole vulnerable Jace moment, even down to the fact that Brett had shown up. Both Jace had I been so ridiculously played that it wasn't even funny — nor was it real.

None of it was real.

I'd gotten exactly what I'd asked for.

Something fake.

My money was even on Grandma putting Jace's parents up to the task of making him feel guilty. After all, he'd very openly written down on a piece of paper that he never wanted to let them down. Not marrying me would let them down.

I was a smart girl. I'd always been smart. Sadly, during the last week all I'd done was ignored my feelings and my gut when it had told me something wasn't right.

Jace and I, back in the real world? With cameras flashing and people all around us? The fairytale would fade into the blackness, and I'd be left — exactly how I'd started off. Alone. Only this time I'd have a broken heart on top of everything else.

I was letting my insecurities take control. But I couldn't help it, because it still didn't make sense. Why would he want me? Why would he look at me as if I was his long-lost love?

Jace stirred next to me. The blanket fell off his golden skin. It wasn't real. He wasn't real. Because in what world would a guy like him actually be interested in me?

I was about to break a promise.

Being as quiet as humanly possible, I went over to my suitcase, pulled out my phone, and grabbed my charger. I tiptoed into the bathroom and locked the door.

My phone wasn't completely dead, so I plugged it in and only felt a twinge of guilt when I typed in Jace's name.

Senator Jace Brevik.

Most of the pages that popped up described his perfect childhood, loads of money, and ability to charm the pants off just about anything that walked.

A few brief paragraphs about his ex-fiancée who'd accused him of cheating on her with paid escorts.

And then a news article from yesterday…

Sources close to Senator Brevik say he had this trip planned for months and is vacationing with family while he enjoys a brief respite from his busy schedule. His parents are expected to join him. Sources say last week the senator was seen going into a hotel with an alleged prostitute. Friends of the senator identified the girl as Beth Lynn, a friend in town for her sister's wedding. The senator also attended the wedding, serving as a groomsman for Travis Titus of Titus Enterprises.

That was it.

The rumor had died down.

Clearly, it had been fixed.

So why were we still in Hawaii faking a marriage? And why was Grandma still urging the cover-up?

I clicked the link to the next article, this one from an entertainment blog.

This week's polls show that Senator Brevik's approval ratings are likely to take a jump if he settled down and got married. Sources say he's just sly enough to pull off a wedding in the near future. After all, the man isn't nicknamed slick for no reason.

Lies. They had to be printing lies. Right? Was Grandma in on it too?

Suddenly unable to breathe, I turned the phone off and started pacing the bathroom. What if he and Grandma were in on it? Was I just a pity case? Available? Easy? The crazy cat lady!

I stomped back into the bedroom and flicked on the light. "Get up."

"Wha—"

I threw at pillow at his head. "Get up."

"You better be dying..." Jace grumbled in a low voice as he sat up in bed and glared. "What's wrong?"

"Everything." Panic welled in my chest as I clicked open the article and threw the phone at his face. He caught it before it nicked his perfect chiseled jaw. Damn him. "Read."

"Okay." Jace held up the phone. "And didn't we say no technology?"

"We did," I agreed. "And now I know why you were so eager to put everything away."

Jace's eyes about bugged out of his head as he read through the article. Finally, he set the phone down and rubbed his face with his hands. "You believe this?"

"Of course I believe it!" I knew I was shouting but couldn't help myself. "Why else would you have stayed? You saw an opportunity and took it! You even have our parents in on it!"

"What?" Jace roared. "What the hell are you talking

about? You think I planned this? You think I lured you here under my fairytale-voodoo magic and decided that, hey, you'll do? My polls really aren't that important. Geez, do I look that desperate?"

I reared back as if I'd just been slapped. "So you'd have to be desperate to marry me?"

"No!" Jace yelled. "Of course not! I told you today how I feel. I mean it. I like you. I want a second chance with you. What do I have to do to prove it to you?"

"Let me walk away."

"What?"

"Let me. Walk. Away." I shrugged. "Out the door. Let me catch the next flight."

"Why the hell would I do that? Why would I let you get away again?" He looked panicked as he held his head in his hands. "I just found you again and… you want to leave?"

"Because, it's the only way I'll believe you. If you make me stay, it means you had it all planned out. If you let me go—"

"I can't do that." Jace shook his head. "If I let you go, you may never come back." He looked absolutely petrified.

But I was too! I needed to know I could trust him!

"Am I worth the risk?"

"I don't know if I could survive it, Beth." He rubbed the back of his head. "Something's off. Something's wrong."

"Am I worth the risk?"

Jace was silent, his eyes wide and thoughtful.

"Guess we're lucky you didn't fall in love, huh? I guess you were right all along. In the end, one of us is walking away. Only this time, you're going to be the one watching, while I do what I should have done the first day I got here."

"What's that?" His voice was hoarse.

"Leave."

"Don't," Jace whispered, taking a step toward me. "We'll figure it out. Just don't walk away." His eyes flickered with uncertainty.

"Give me a reason to stay. Give me something. Give me truth."

Jace opened his mouth, but nothing came out. That was the part that hurt the most. He was able to give me the words when it was for his benefit. He was ready to do the big gestures, but when I needed him the most, he didn't pull through. He froze, because in the end he still wasn't sure about us, and if he wasn't sure now, he never would be.

"Let's talk about this," he tried again.

His smile made me sick.

"Come on, Beth, don't do anything rash. Just give me a few minutes to gather my thoughts. You did wake me up out of a dead sleep, you know."

He looked so disoriented I almost felt guilty. *Almost* being the key word.

Ignoring him, I walked into the bathroom and started putting all of my belongings into my suitcase.

"Beth—"

I stepped around him. "Jace?"

Again, he had no words.

"Enjoy the rest of your vacation." I threw my clothes into my suitcase and zipped it up. The clock near the bed said 5:15 a.m. If I was lucky, I could catch the first flight out. Then again, I hadn't been lucky in a very, very long time.

"If you go—" Jace's voice cracked.

"If I go, what?"

"If you walk away, it's your choice. You're choosing to be afraid. You're choosing to walk away from us."

"Meaning?" I whispered, my back to him.

"I'm not going to chase someone who doesn't want to be chased. I'm not going to pursue a girl who doesn't even realize why she's worthy of a pursuit. I care for you, Beth, but in my line of work, trust is the number one factor that builds a relationship, and if you already don't trust me, we're doomed before we even start."

Warm tears spilled onto my cheeks. "I know."

The door clicked shut behind me.

CHAPTER THIRTY-ONE

"Are you crying?" Grandma leaned forward over the table an offered the agent a Kleenex.

"Gnat, it, uh, flew into my eye."

"Both of them?"

"So she left?" The agent sniffled. "And it's your fault."

"Yes. To all of the above."

Jace

I about banged the door down before it finally opened.

"Three seconds before I murder you," Jake whispered, his voice hoarse.

"She left."

"Who did?"

"Beth."

"So what the hell are you doing standing here in front of my hut ruining my sleep?"

"I panicked." And I'd had a nightmare about prom, one where there was blood, and I was in that same damn car. Where the hell had I been going anyway? And why was I saying her name? It made me sick to my stomach that I couldn't remember. I wanted to punch a wall. And then to be woken up in the dead of the night and see tears in her eyes? It had about destroyed me.

"Oh, dear Lord." Jake opened the door wider and let me in.

Char was still sleeping. I grinned when she made a little mew in her sleep.

"*My* wife," Jake growled.

"Easy, tiger. You won, remember?"

"Damn straight." Jake yawned again. "So, explain, what did you do to Beth to make her leave?"

I gave him a run down. "And she woke me up out of a dead sleep."

"I know the feeling."

"And expects me to be able to form coherent thoughts?"

"How dare she," Jake said dryly.

"I'm serious."

"So am I."

I swore. "I don't know what to do." I wanted to chase her down and punish her for leaving then kiss her senseless for doubting me.

"Well, at least now you know what you shouldn't ever do. Don't ever stare at a woman like she's crazy when she asks you to give her a reason to stay, and don't tell her to her face—"

"It was her back," I pointed out.

Jake rolled his eyes. "Don't tell her in any way that you aren't going to chase her. What the hell is wrong with you? Do you wake up this stupid, or does it develop throughout the day?"

My stomach dropped down to where my balls had conveniently disappeared. "This morning, I'd have to say I woke up that way." Either that or the thirty-foot jump jarred something in my head.

A loud bang was heard on the door.

Swearing, Jake ran to open it and came face-to-face with Grandma. She was wearing leopard silk pajamas and had a creepy green mask covering her entire face, except her eyes.

"What did you do?"

"Me?" Jake sputtered. "Try him."

He pointed at me. He may as well have put a giant-ass target on my back and handed Grandma a shotgun.

"You." She joined in the pointing.

I started sweating.

"I basically handed you happiness on a platter!"

With a groan, I hung my head in my hands.

"And how do you thank me? You let her just walk away."

"She's already gone?" I jumped up from my seat. "But how did she get on a boat so fast? How—"

The slap sounded like a crack of thunder. Did she? Had I just been slapped by Grandma?

Jake winced as if he knew firsthand how hard that eighty-six-year-old woman could hit and took a protective stance, covering his man parts. Yeah, I'd probably never father children. That slap killed sperm; it made my balls recoil so far into my body I was pretty sure I would walk funny for at least a week.

"You. Are. A. Jack. Ass. Jack. Ass!" Grandma shouted.

More laughing from Jake.

"You're worse than Shit!"

Jakes laughter turned to confusion.

"She means the donkey," I explained.

"Was your plan just to let her walk away when things got too hard? When things got difficult? Now look what you've done! All my hard work, for nothing! I flew your parents here. I staged your wedding! I dropped crumbs every few minutes so that you'd follow the trail, and what do you do?"

"I crapped on the trail?" I offered lamely.

"You did worse than that."

"I really don't know what could be worse than crapping on the crumbs you're supposed to be eating," Jake said.

"Not now, Jake!" Grandma shouted.

"Someone crapped in trail mix?" came a gargled voice from the bed.

"Char!" Grandma wailed.

Char closed her eyes and ducked under the covers.

"Char!" Grandma tried again.

"What?" Char sighed.

"You can't let Beth leave."

"She's leaving?" Char jumped out of bed. "Why? What happened? The plan was working perfectly!"

"YOU KNEW?" I yelled.

"Whoa!" Jake held up his hands. "Don't get your panties all twisted. We all knew. Well, I mean, we knew once Grandma told us, and to be fair, Travis has known since the airport, but since he's a selfish bastard, he figured if Grandma concentrated on you guys, she wouldn't be texting him every five minutes asking if Kacey's pregnant yet."

"Nothing wrong with a little enthusiasm and encouragement." Grandma sniffled.

"No offense, Grandma," Jake rolled his eyes, "but having your eighty-six-year-old grandmother texting you about sexual positions kinda kills whatever enthusiasm said grandson may be experiencing. It's like sword fighting with noodles. Nobody's going to get poked, and you'll sure as hell get bored real fast."

"Noodles?" Char smacked Jake on the arm. "You're comparing sex to noodles?"

"Keep up!" Grandma stomped. "We have to fix what Jace ruined."

"I can fix it," I raised my hand, "if one of you or all of you tell me what the hell is going on."

"These plans," Grandma began to pace, "they take months to come up with. I can't simply snap my fingers and fix it."

She stopped pacing and smiled, the same one I had come to recognize as the all-knowing smile. People should run when that smile appears; countries should just give up — it's not worth the bloodshed.

"Do you love her?" she asked simply.

It should have been a simple question; instead, the question made me get itchy and squirmy as if I wasn't comfortable in my own skin. It made me afraid and made me feel stupid. Saying yes seemed too hard. Saying no? Too easy.

"He does." Jake sighed irritatingly.

"How do you know?" I snapped.

"Because you're itchy."

"Huh?" Char and Grandma said in unison.

"Players, we know the game well. Believe me, he's all uncomfortable with his feelings. It's why he's so twitchy. His mind is manifesting a physical response to his inability to commit emotionally."

Something happened that night.

Something I'm not sure any of us were willing to purposefully talk about.

Jake Titus, manwhore of the century, not only found his heart, but somewhere deep inside that brain, he found psychology.

It scared the shit out of me.

"Are you drunk?" Char whispered under her breath.

"Admit it." Jake ignored his wife and crossed his arms. "What I said made sense."

"I—" Sweating. Definitely sweating.

"Jace, if you like her so much, why are you hesitating?" Grandma asked sweetly.

"Because I want to get it right." I sighed. "I want to be what she deserves, and I don't think I am. I know I'm not, because if it was her or my future, I think I'd still pick me. Okay? Are you guys happy that you've just discovered what a selfish bastard I can be? I choose me! I don't choose the really pretty girl with bright green eyes. I choose what I've worked years for. I want a second chance. I guess I just wanted it on my terms."

The room fell silent.

"Oh, honey," Grandma pulled me into a tight hug, "it's good for you to admit that."

"It is?" I pulled back.

"Yes." Grandma patted my back. "It's only when we admit what scares us the most — we can conquer our demons. You're afraid of failure, but most importantly, you're afraid of success."

"Success?" I snorted. "I already have that."

"I meant emotional success. Nothing scares you more than knowing, in the end, you are the reason for your own unhappiness. Not some woman, not your career, not anything but your own stubborn self. I believe, Mr. Senator, that you've made your choice. I just hope, in the end, it's worth it."

"A reflection doesn't keep you warm at night," Jake said, all teasing gone from his voice.

"You're right." I hung my head defeated. "But the risk is nothing."

"I'm sorry." Grandma wiped away a tear.

"Grandma, it's fine it's—"

"Not you." She turned. "Her. I'm sorry, Beth."

It was then that I looked at the door. It had been cracked open the whole time. Beth stood there, bags packed. And she'd heard the whole damn conversation. So she'd run, but it hadn't been to the airport. She'd run to the woman who'd brought us here in the first place. She'd run to Grandma, hoping she could fix it, fix me. And she'd failed.

"Beth I—"

"Save it." She nodded her head and gave a sad smile. "I'll just..." She backed away slowly, rolling her suitcase behind her.

I waited for Jake to punch me. But it seemed even he was too disappointed in me to waste any energy.

Grandma kissed me softly on the cheek and whispered, "Be happy."

The problem? I'd never felt so alone or disappointed in myself in my entire life, and I still had to go tell both my parents that not only had they been duped, but that I'd failed them.

CHAPTER THIRTY-TWO

"Disappointing, that the senator shows such little character."

"He's just a boy." Grandma held a tissue up to her eye and dabbed. *"He wants to piss on the world and claim it as his, all the while forgetting that at the end of the day, when your home is empty, what do you really have to show for the success you've had? The life you've lived? Success fades. Family? It's forever."*

Beth

I always pitied those girls you saw at the airports. The ones that had tear-stained cheeks, were saying goodbye to friends or family or even significant others as they put on the old red, white, and blue and flew overseas.

My eyes were swollen, my bags packed like I was fleeing the country, and, of course, in my current state of distress I hadn't even realized that I had sweats on and no makeup.

The conversation I'd overheard? Not my favorite. In all my rashness I'd decided to talk to Grandma. I know, I know. She didn't sound like the voice of reason, but I wanted to thank her for the trip. She'd easily got it out of me, why I was upset, and said she'd fix it. She'd grabbed my hand and led me to the hut. It hadn't been hard to find Jace; the yelling had helped. She'd told me to wait outside.

I wish I would have gotten in the damn taxi. Because after hearing Jace's voice, the words from his mouth? I knew the truth. In the end, he would always choose himself; he'd let me walk away, and although he'd be sad about letting me go... to him? His job was his mistress, his wife, his everything. Even if he was guilt-free in the entire scenario, he still couldn't admit how he felt.

To me, that was weakness. Not being able to share your innermost feelings with someone? It's inexcusable, especially when that person does you the great honor of doing the exact same thing in hopes you'll return it.

I wiped away another tear and walked toward security.

"Beth?"

Kill me now.

"Beth?"

Seriously, God, send the lightning, I wanna go down in flames.

"Where's Jace?" A hand gripped my arm. I had a momentary vision of me turning around, grabbing Brett by the balls, and twisting until I heard either a pop or a tear.

"Not here," I said dryly.

Brett grinned seductively. "Paris is sleeping."

"Your point?" What? Did he want a cookie for getting his wife to go to bed on time? Fresh out, buddy. Sorry. And, let's be honest, even if I had a cookie, I wouldn't share. I was so not in the sharing mood. Unless the cookie had arsenic; I'd stuff it in his throat and smile the whole damn time.

"Well..." Brett reached up to cup my face.

I tried to jerk back, but he held my chin firm within his fingers.

"You're here. I'm here. Your little senator is missing, and it seems I have some free time. You wanted me all those years ago in high school, and I'm like a fine wine. I taste better with time… We could go kill a few hours. What do you say?"

"You can't afford me." I glared.

"Try me."

"It was a joke." I finally jerked free. "I'm not a prostitute, you bastard! And I'm sorry, but cheating husbands don't really appeal to me."

"And cheating senators do?"

"Pardon?"

"Please." He laughed. "You really think you're enough to keep a man like Jace Brevik occupied? He'd cheat on you within the first year of marriage."

Grandma was going to have to bail me out of prison.

I reared back to slap him, when someone grabbed my hand and jerked me against his chest then twisted me around. A hot mouth met mine with force and urgency; he tasted like rum. Jace.

What? Here?

Jace released me and turned. "You rotting bastard. I should kill you."

And then I heard a yelp.

Jace released me just as Jake landed a blow to Brett's face, sending him sailing to the floor.

"Thanks." Jace held out his hand to Jake. "Nice hit."

"Yeah, well," Jake shrugged, "not the first airport fight I've gotten into."

"Titus men," another voice chimed in.

"Char?"

My sister waved and gave me a sad smile that just screamed guilt.

"Where are you going?" Jace asked calmly. "I want to give you a reason to stay. I need you to stay." He cupped my face in his hands. "Stay for me."

"That's a good reason." I nodded, tears pooling in my eyes.

"Listen," he licked his lips, "I have something to tell you, something to explain. I'm not really sure I understand it myself, but I think it will help. Full honesty, full disclosure on my part. Don't leave."

"Jace, I can't—"

"Who's not worth the risk now?"

Maybe he was right. Maybe in the end I was running because I was scared.

It happened too fast. The photographers, the lights, the cameras going off. I blinked, and then we were surrounded. I looked like hell, and Jace looked so stunned his mouth opened and closed three times before he could form words.

"Mr. Senator? Is this the woman you've been hiding from us?"

"Mr. Senator, is she a prostitute? Or truly a family friend?"

"Mr. Senator, was this a planned destination wedding, or are you just joining in a publicity stunt to help with your approval ratings?"

Question after question was fired at him.

I waited for him to defend me, for him to explain to them exactly what had happened with Grandma, not that they'd believe it.

Instead he looked directly at me and said in a sad voice, "She's an old family friend. No wedding, no prostitutes, just the happy coincidence of being on the same vacation. Isn't that right, Beth?"

His eyes pleaded with mine, while tears clouded my vision so much that I couldn't see straight. I gave a pathetic nod and turned away, knowing this time he wouldn't come after me, and I wouldn't turn back.

He'd been given a third opportunity in a day to make his choice.

And for the third time, he'd failed to choose me.

CHAPTER THIRTY-THREE

"Did you send the reporters?" The agent rubbed his face and sighed.

"It's possible."

"So that's a yes."

Grandma picked at her sweater. "I'm elderly, memory's not what it used to be."

"And just how was ratting out the senator supposed to help the relationship? If anything, it made it worse."

"It didn't." Grandma smirked. "Because clearly the senator is still missing, and so is she."

Jace

The look on Beth's face devastated me like a punch to the gut. I tried to catch my breath, but every inhale was filled with utter disgust and panic. I'd just told her to her face, for the third time that day, that she wasn't enough. But I'd done it to protect her — to give her time to decide what she felt about me. Instead, she'd walked away. Not me. Her.

Every insecurity she must have felt about herself was

probably scratching to the surface, and it was all my fault. All because I was selfish careless bastard. Every instinct told me to run after her, but what would that do? She'd probably slap me and end up on the six o'clock news. So I stayed rooted to the ground and did my damn job — I smiled pretty for the cameras, and I smoothed things over. Never in my life had I had to work so hard to pretend like my world wasn't crashing down around me.

"Senator." Another reporter shoved a microphone in my face. "Channel Five, can you tell us why you're visiting the islands?"

A flash went right off in my line of vision...

I heard screeching tires all over again, and then glass went everywhere. A flashlight shined in my eyes. "Son, are you alright?"

I forced a tight smile. "Much needed vacation."

"But our sources say that—"

"Excuse me." I pushed away from the crowd to Jake and Char. They'd come as reinforcements to help convince Beth to stay.

The reporters followed me.

Char opened her mouth, but Jake covered it with his hand. "Not here."

We walked outside and got into a cab.

I was tense as hell.

"Why?" Char whispered.

"What did you want him to do, Char?" Jake jumped to my defense. "Call her out on national television? Say that they were together? Steal the last shred of privacy she may have had? The way I see it is he made it easier for her to run."

"She's not running!" Char fired back. "She's hurt!"

"So am I!" I yelled, realizing too late that I had given myself away.

Char grabbed my hand, but I couldn't feel it. I couldn't feel anything.

I'd told myself I wouldn't get attached, and look where

that had gotten me. In the exact predicament I hadn't wanted to be in. I wasn't heartbroken. I was too angry with myself and angry with the situation to feel anything worthwhile.

The anger didn't dissipate. If anything, it intensified when we pulled up to the resort, and my parents were waiting in the lobby with Grandma in tow.

I expected lots of yelling and confusion. What I didn't expect was for my dad to pull me in to a giant hug and pat my back, like he was still somehow proud of the ass his son had become.

My mom smiled sadly and squeezed my hand.

"Let's go have a nice morning chat." Dad led me toward one of the restaurants.

I ordered black coffee and stared mindlessly into it while he ordered breakfast for both of us.

"A month ago," Dad stirred some milk into his coffee, "I had a nice chat with Travis."

Not what I expected. Warning bells went off in my head.

"He was worried about you, said you'd been drinking more and acting careless. I immediately assumed it was all that Kerri-business coming back to haunt you. Then Travis said something interesting."

"I'm sure he did." Numb. I was so damn numb.

"He said, you'd drunkenly told him about the best night of your life."

Well, hell.

"And imagine my surprise when it wasn't the night of your election, but the night you took your cousin to prom."

I shifted uncomfortably in my seat.

"A girl with green eyes and dark hair had captured your attention, and for some reason, maybe it was the kiss, or maybe it was the way she fit perfectly into your arms, you fell."

I rose to get up.

"Sit down."

I sat.

"Funny," my father nodded, "because I remember the story a little differently."

I looked out at the crashing waves and waited.

"Your mother and I forced you to take your cousin to her senior prom. You fought us on it until I finally put my foot down. She didn't have a date, after all. A few hours later, you came back to the house in such a frenzy I thought something had happened."

Squinting, I looked up into his eyes. "I never came back to the house, Dad."

He sighed. "You did. The therapists said that telling you about what you didn't remember could cause emotional damage, so we kept it quiet. Never in my life did I think it would be so important."

"I don't understand." I scratched the back of my head, feeling the scar from the surgery.

"Of all the things to forget, you forgot the accident and things leading up to it, but you remembered that damn kiss you shared with that girl, and it wrecked you."

"You're telling me this now because?"

"Because it will help. I hope to God it helps, because I'm about at my wit's end with you." He smirked lovingly. "You ran into the house and said, 'Dad, I've met the girl I'm going to marry.'"

Suddenly, I was in my parents' living room again.

The memory hit me full force. I tried to stuff it back into my mind. I tried to ignore the pain in my chest as it sliced me completely in half...

"Dad!" I ran into the house. "I need the cell phone, and I'm going to take the car."

"You're back already?" He straightened his tie. "You sure are in a hurry, son."

"I met her," I said, grinning like an idiot. "You and mom were right. It happened just like you said it would. It was like... it was

magic!"

"What was?"

"The kiss!"

"You kissed your cousin? Son, sit down..."

"No!" I yelled. "I kissed Beth. She goes to Macy's school and was there with some other guy and... I want to catch her in time!"

"And what's your plan once you catch her?"

"I haven't thought it out," I admitted. "But it's going to involve kissing."

"Keep your pants on, son." Dad laughed. "And be careful."

"I will!" I promised and ran out the door yelling, "Dad, I met the girl I'm going to marry!"

I was driving too fast, not caring that I was breaking so many laws that my license could get revoked. I accelerated through a yellow light. And that's when I heard the screeching metal of steel on steel.

My world went completely black.

I woke up three months later from a coma. And the first word that trickled out of my mouth was, "Beth."

But she had already gone, already left for school. She hadn't cared enough to look into how I was. Hell, she probably hadn't even known who I was or that I was the same guy she'd kissed. The same guy who had almost died trying to see her again.

I felt like I couldn't breathe. All this time I thought I'd walked away from her, but I'd gone back. I'd gone back to make the big gesture because those few minutes were enough to make me believe in something I'd always told myself wasn't real.

Dad placed his hand on mine. "Love at first sight."

"Doesn't exist." I snapped, jerking my hand back.

"That experience changed you." He shook his head sadly. "You poured everything into the next two years of high school and then graduated early from college. You lived and breathed your job."

"Because my job won't ever let me down. It's consistent.

The one time I took a chance in my life, and I almost died."

"You afraid of a little coma, son?"

"My brain was swollen for three months, Dad. I could have been a vegetable the rest of my life, all because I was careless."

"With a car. Not with your heart."

"Are we done?"

"Don't disappoint me." I froze.

"How the hell is me walking away from Beth disappointing you?"

"Because, I know you, son. You wear your heart on your sleeve. You want to take that leap for her, but you're too chicken shit to do it. Tell her the truth. Tell her what happened."

"And if she rejects me? Like I deserve?"

"Think of it this way." My dad took a long sip of coffee. "What if the car would have made it to prom? What if you would have walked into that gym and seen Beth with those pretty green eyes staring at you."

"I would have kissed her," I croaked. "And probably made an ass out of myself."

"You would have told her you were going to marry her someday."

I didn't respond. I couldn't. My chest felt so heavy with emotion that I wasn't able to take deep breaths. I wheezed, coughed, and took a few steps away from my dad before stopping and turning.

"Were you in on it?"

"On this?" Dad spread the napkin across his lap. "Why, son, it was my idea."

He said it so calm that I thought he had to be joking.

He took another sip of coffee and smiled.

Holy shit.

"Grandma?"

"Offered her expertise. How else do you think I was able

to plant the media outside the hotel? Grandma can't be in two places at once. She slipped something in your drinks, made sure you made it safely to the hotel, and I took care of all the rest of the details. Right down to sending media to the airport."

"But—"

"Grandma was with you the whole time," Dad laughed, "texting me details."

"But the resort we're staying at? She's a therapist here."

Dad looked at me like I was stupid. I hated being looked at like that. "Titus Enterprises owns several hotel chains. You're staying in one. How else do you think Grandma could infiltrate the staff so effectively?"

"I think I'm going to be sick."

"Good." Dad's eyebrows quirked. "At least you're finally feeling something."

"But…"

"Son… it's when you're at the end of your life that you start thinking about the beginning. Choices made, things you should have said, people you should have forgiven. I don't want that for you. I saw you going down a path that I knew would end in heartache. Travis and I went golfing soon after you confessed about second chances. That's when I put two and two together. It was easily done, and when I saw you at the wedding. I knew…"

"You mean when you drugged us at the wedding."

"My idea was to get you caught in a compromising situation on camera, not drug you, fly to you to Hawaii make you bleed your feelings all over a therapist, and get your first experience with Viagra."

I winced.

"But Grandma had a point. You two needed time to get to know one another, and she provided a safe media-free environment for exactly that to happen. My only question is… did it work?"

"Did what work?"

"Our plan?"

I was silent for a few seconds.

"Son, do you love her?"

"I do." I licked my lips, feeling like a thousand-pound weight had been lifted off my shoulders. "I really do."

"Then chase her."

"What if she doesn't want me back? How do I even know that she would have dated me had my car made it back to the gym?"

Dad smirked. "Son, that's why they call love a leap. It's a bit like faith. You know it exists, though you can't feel it."

"I have no faith in myself."

"That's okay," Dad nodded, his eye welling with tears, "because I have enough faith in you for the both of us."

CHAPTER THIRTY-FOUR

"Well," the agent scratched his chin, "you can keep a secret. I'll give you that."

"Thank you."

"But the senator is still missing, and by the looks of it," he checked his watch, "it's been over forty-eight hours."

"One more hour." Grandma smiled.

"One more?"

"And then I'll bring you the senator and his lovely wife."

"Wife?"

Grandma smiled. "Then again, I can't be in two places at once, or can I?"

"I may need more coffee."

"Trust me. The rest of the story is my favorite part."

Beth

Two weeks had gone by, and I hadn't heard anything from Jace. Though, lucky me, I kept getting really pathetic and sad looks from Jake and Char every single time I went over to their house.

We had dinner every Sunday.

They thought they were helping me get over my sadness by feeding me enormous amounts of wine and food. Jake, bless his heart, also felt the need every once in a while to pat my hand. You know, like I was a three year old. Other times, he'd just stare at me really hard as if by him staring and giving me one of those *Aww*-looks, I'd soldier on.

This Sunday I just wanted to forget everything that had happened. I expected to have a nice quiet meal, where Jake sent me concerned looks while filling my wine glass to the brim, and Char cursed men everywhere, except for her husband, who, since getting married, had earned saintdom in her eyes.

So when Grandma threw open the door to Jake's giant house on Lake Washington, I almost fell ass-backwards.

She pulled me in for a hug and squeezed so tight I think I felt a rib pop. "Oh, honey bug! How are you?"

"Great," I lied, forcing a smile. Emotionally I was feeling a bit wrecked. Add that to the whole flu bug I'd somehow caught the day before last, and I was just one giant ball of fun.

I wasn't sure if it was the rib-popping squeeze or maybe just the emotional stress of seeing Grandma again, but I suddenly felt like I was going to puke. I pushed past her just in time to throw open the bathroom door and empty the contents of my stomach into the porcelain toilet that probably cost more than my rent.

"Beth?" Grandma knocked softly on the door. "Sweetie, are you alright?"

I flushed the toilet, rinsed out my mouth with water, and opened the door. I hated puking. Nothing was worse. I hated the way it tasted, and I hated how it made my stomach clench so tight that I wanted to curl into a ball and die. Plus, puking always made me want to cry.

Why was Grandma smiling? My eyes narrowed.

"A touch of the flu?" Now her eyes were twinkling as she

rubbed her hands together.

I nodded slowly. "Yeah, I've been queasy these past few days."

"Interesting." Grandma nodded, her smile growing by the second. "Positively... perfect."

"Perfect that I'm sick?" I asked, confused as my stomach clenched again.

"Oh, honey, you just let me take care of you." She patted my hand then shouted so loud my eardrums nearly burst. "Jake! Grandma's staying a few weeks!"

"The hell you are!" Jake shouted back from somewhere in the house.

"He's teasing." Grandma winked "I'm ALWAYS WELCOME IN MY GRANDSON'S HOME!"

"YOU BELONG IN A HOME!"

"WHAT? YOU BOUGHT ME A HOME?"

Cursing followed, and then dishes banged together before Jake rounded the corner, his eyes narrowing in on Grandma and then me.

"You're pale."

"Jake thinks himself a doctor now." Grandma rolled her eyes.

"Why are you pale?" He reached out and grabbed my wrist and then felt my forehead. "You don't feel hot."

I shrugged. "I don't think I have a fever."

"She puked." Grandma felt the need to add.

"I'm fine." I was going to lose my mind if they both kept staring at me like I was in a museum. Just let me be sick and feel sorry for myself, damn it!

"What's wrong with Beth?" Char ran down the stairs.

"She puked," Jake said at the exact same time that Grandma declared, "She's pregnant!"

"What!" we all said in unison while Grandma clapped her hands in glee.

"I'm not! No, I'm not." I started getting hysterical. "It's

impossible."

"You've been having the sex." Grandma nodded.

"Grandma stop putting *the* in front of everything."

Char grabbed her husband's hand. "The Jake is right. It's getting weird. And Beth, do we need to have a little talk on how babies are made?"

"Oh, I have a chart for that!" Grandma held up her hand.

"I burned that chart last week," Jake shot her down.

"But they were color-coded," Grandma said dejectedly. "I spent hours on them."

"Listen," I held up my hands in innocence, "I don't need charts, and I don't need help. I'm not pregnant. I didn't have *the sex* with Jace, or at least I didn't while in..." My head suddenly started pounding. Would I be that stupid? Would Jace be that stupid? The night of the wedding? Holy crap, holy crap. I reached for something to hold onto and latched onto Jake like a leach. He looked panicked as I gripped the front of his shirt.

"Hello?" Grandma said.

I turned slowly to see her leopard cell phone attached to her ear.

"Yes, Jace."

"No!" I shouted, launching myself at Grandma.

She hung up and chuckled to herself. "Well, that was easy."

The doorbell rang.

Seriously. Was I hallucinating?

Grandma all but skipped to the door and threw it open.

Jace.

I opened my mouth to speak just as Grandma shouted, "Beth's with child!"

"What?" Jace roared, his face turning red. "Who the hell did you let touch you, Beth? I swear I'll kill him. I'll rip him apart with my bare hands! You hear that, bastard? I'm coming for you!"

"I'm not—"

"Aren't you a little late to be playing hero?" Jake said smugly. "What the hell are you doing here anyway?"

"I came for my wife."

"You're married!" Char shouted, launching herself at Jace.

He held up his hands in panic. "Not yet!"

"You have a freaking fiancée!" I shouted, my voice carrying across the giant house like a firecracker.

"Oh, I feel faint. I do feel faint." Grandma patted her head.

Char swayed on her feet next to Grandma, turning an interesting shade of white before passing out in Jake's arms.

"Hospital!" he yelled.

"For the last time, I'm not pregnant!" I countered.

"BUT CHAR IS!" he screamed in my face.

"Yay!" Grandma did a little dance. "I knew those beads would work."

"A little help?" Jake motioned to Jace, who was already opening the door and grabbing flip flops for Char.

She was starting to come to. I was too worried to do anything but pray. Why hadn't Char told me? She could only be a few weeks along!

"I took a taxi," Jace said in clipped tones.

"Garage." With his free hand, Jake dialed the garage pad, and it opened.

If I hadn't been in such a panic, I probably would have passed out. He had more cars than a dealership, and they all looked expensive.

Which one were we supposed to take?

Jace ran to where the keys were hanging, grabbed a pair, and unlocked a new Mercedes SUV.

"Get in," he barked.

I got in the front while everyone else piled in the back.

Tears burned at the back of my throat. "Is she awake?

Coherent?"

Jake's voice cracked, "Yeah, her eyes just opened. Baby, are you okay? Talk to me. Do you know where you are?"

Grandma reached up to the front seat and patted my shoulder. "She'll be alright, honeybug. This sometimes happens."

Jace pulled into the closest hospital in record time. I didn't even realize I was holding his hand until I tried to sit down and realized I'd have to sit on his lap with how close I was leaning against him. Abruptly, I let go and shook the familiarity of his touch away.

Wife? His wife?

The man was quick. Two weeks, and he was moving on?

Jake went back with Char, while Grandma left to call Travis.

"She'll be okay," Jace said confidently. "She's strong."

"Yeah."

"I don't have a wife," he added a few minutes later.

"I don't care."

"You do," he said confidently. "I meant you, by the way."

"What? We're secretly married?"

"Not yet," he said smoothly, "but we will be."

"What gives you that idea?"

"Well, first of all, I love you."

My breath caught in my throat.

"And second? I didn't walk away."

"I know, I know. I did. But you didn't give me a reason, and then you denied everything in front of the news! What was I supposed to do?"

"Stay." He turned in his chair and grabbed my hands. "You were supposed to stay."

"But—"

"I didn't walk away."

"So you keep saying." I tried to jerk free.

"Ten minutes. That's all I need. And then I will walk

away. If I can't convince you in ten minutes, then…" his face fell, "then I'll go if you want me to."

"Is that why you're here? To plead your case?"

"I'm here because I wanted to make the big gesture. I wanted you to see that I wasn't going to run with my tail between my legs. But the minute I got back, I had some things to fix, some choices to make. I wanted to make sure I had those firmly in place before I talked with you. I wanted to be sure you knew that I was fully committed."

Okay, so as far as speeches went? His was pretty dang good.

"It was your white dress." He framed my face with his hands as we touched foreheads. "It fit you so perfectly. The way the lights danced across your body — hell, I thought I was seeing an angel. And then those eyes." He muttered a curse. "They were like a drug. I couldn't look away. I'd always believed in this silly little fantasy that when you found the one you wanted to spend the rest of your life with, you'd experience this incredible pull toward that person. You'd just know — things would just click. It was that way for my parents. And my mom, from the day I could understand her nonsense, convinced me it would be that way for me too. So when I saw you that night, I knew."

"Knew what?" I whispered.

"I knew I wanted you. I knew I wanted to marry you. I knew I wanted to spend my life watching that smile, gazing into those eyes. Then again, I was only sixteen and stupid, so I can't totally blame it on love at first sight. We'll just call it lust. I wanted to touch you so damn bad that my hands were shaking."

I shuddered as he moved his hand to my neck and rubbed softly. "I promised myself that I'd dance with you. I'd ask for your name, and that would be that."

"But you kissed me."

"I couldn't help it," Jace whispered, brushing his lips

across mine. "You tasted so good. I was hooked the minute my mouth met yours, and then I panicked. Again, I was sixteen, so let's give me a little credit. I didn't want to get the shit beat out of me by the other football team, so I left."

"You walked away." I sighed dejectedly.

"I came back," Jace argued. "But I never made it."

"What do you mean?"

Jace closed his eyes. "Remember when we jumped off the cliff?"

"Yes, I thought you were dying."

"And you almost did a belly flop."

"Jace…" I warned.

"Fine."

His warm chuckle made my stomach flip.

"When you kissed me, for some reason it jolted a memory, one I'd forgotten until now. My dad, who, by the way, can give Grandma a run for her money any day, told me what really happened that night. I ran home, told him I'd found the girl I was going to marry, and quickly got into my car and drove headfirst into another vehicle after running a yellow light."

I gasped, putting my hands over my mouth as the tears welled in my eyes.

"You see…" he smiled sadly, "there was this pretty girl with bright green eyes that I really wanted to see again. I wanted to kiss her and tell her how gorgeous her dress was. I wanted to apologize for being an ass, and I wanted to tell her just how good we would be together, if she'd only give me a chance." He swallowed, his Adam's apple bobbing. "Instead, I woke up three months later from a coma."

Warm tears slid down my cheek.

"So here's the thing, Beth. Your whole life has been based off thinking you didn't have a charge, assuming guys weren't into you, wrongly assuming I had walked away — when the very opposite was true. I almost died trying to get to you, and the truth?" His voice shook. "I would go through it all again, as long as I knew you'd still be waiting for me on the other side."

With a sob, I threw my arms around his neck, letting the tears spill over my cheeks. "You could have died!"

"But look," Jace squeezed me tight, "I'm right here. And I'm waiting."

"Waiting?"

Jace pulled away and with a grin, took off his long black trench coat, revealing a tux. "For the last dance we should have shared. For the moment that was taken. I want a do over. Because, maybe, in this cold senator's chest, there's a heart that believes in second chances, and quite possibly the fairytale."

"You're re-creating prom?"

"Kind of." Jace winked. "Minus all the lusty teens with acne. I hadn't really planned on dancing with you in a hospital."

Tears streamed down my cheeks as I took his hand and started swaying with him.

"I'm sorry," I said, wrapping my arms around his neck, holding on for dear life. "I'm so sorry."

"You did nothing wrong. Hell, all you did was look pretty, and I was lost."

"And then I opened my mouth, and you wanted to smack me?" I teased.

"Nah," Jace's gaze turned serious. "You opened your mouth, and I fell in love."

CHAPTER THIRTY-FIVE

"Sorry." Grandma dabbed her eyes. "I just love that part." She blew her nose loudly and shook her head. "It seems true love finally does win in the end, doesn't it, Gus?" She stood and yawned. "Lovely talk. We'll have to do it again sometime."

"Sit."

"But I told you everything I know."

"Sit. Now."

Grandma rolled her eyes but sat.

"The ending. I need to know where this story ends, because where this story ends tells me where you end. In prison? Or in the free world."

Jace

I would be content holding her for the rest of my life. It had taken me awhile to work out the kinks. After all, taking more vacation? After being gone for a week? It wasn't sitting well with people, but I'd worked my ass off the last fourteen days so I could do this with her, so I could go to Seattle and sweep Beth off her feet the way she deserved.

I was planning on staying until she relented. I went as far as to buy a Thor costume in hopes it would sway her plan. If that didn't work, I was going to have to resort to wine, and lastly Benadryl.

"What's going on?" a female voice demanded.

I pulled away from Beth and smiled as Grandma slowly walked into the waiting room.

"Dancing." Beth sighed happily.

I kissed her head.

Grandma's eyes narrowed. "And you two are... reunited?"

"Yes," I answered for both of us.

"And the child?"

"For the last time, I'm not pregnant!" Beth shrieked.

"But, honey bear, do you even remember your night with this one? For all you know, he could have put on a raincoat and chanted around the bed before he rutted you—"

"Oh, good Lord, did you say rut?" Jace half-whispered.

"It's what animals do, and we are animals."

"NO." Beth shook her head. "No, we aren't."

"At any rate, I'd get checked." Grandma sniffed. "Besides, I need more great-grandchildren."

I wasn't about to explain that technically they wouldn't be her great-grandchildren. I had a feeling that there wasn't a way I was going to permanently exorcise her from our lives, so I may as well go with it.

"Oh," Grandma clapped, "and I'm happy to announce that Char is just fine! Low blood sugar! Pregnancy messes with you."

"So, she is pregnant?" Jake was probably scared shitless.

"Yup." Grandma beamed. "Grandchild number one, though I gave good ol' Travis an earful about how he clearly isn't doing things right in the bedroom, if Jake and Char are breeding first."

"Breeding?" Beth repeated under her breath.

"At any rate. I'm sure he's just fine now. I explained a few of the mechanics that I'm sure he was confused with. After all, a Grandma knows these things. To think he wasn't even aware of the best positions for conception! I sent him pictures."

"Of?"

"Kama Sutra." Grandma nodded "From the Google."

"Aw hell," I muttered.

"What?" Grandma shrugged innocently.

"Since everything's okay, I guess Beth and I will just go—"

First thought? Drink wine, followed by sex, more wine, more sex, no unplanned pregnancies, and hopefully I'd finally get to pull her hair. Thank God.

"Well, the media is having a frenzy. They watch poor Jake's house like it's the Netflix. The story's already been leaked, wouldn't want you guys getting caught up in it."

"Oh." Beth's face fell.

"But never fear." Grandma straightened her jacket and smirked "I've got a plan." She turned the full force of her frightening gaze to me. "How good are you with driving vans?"

CHAPTER THIRTY-SIX

"So you're saying he kidnapped himself?"

"That's what I'm saying."

"No drugs involved?"

Grandma shrugged. "That van has many uses. I may have hid the ruffies under the seat to keep them from the feds, but really, Gus? I panicked!"

"So where is the senator? A reporter saw the van drive off. They saw you get in the van."

Grandma rolled her eyes. "Of course I got in the van. I promised them I'd take them to the airport!"

"The airport?"

"Yes." Grandma yawned. "Really, it has been such a pleasure, and I do mean that, Gus, but I have better things to be doing rather than sitting here telling you love stories. If you don't believe me, call this number. I think by now," she checked her watch, "yes, by now the rest of the three days are up."

"Three days?"

"Of course." Grandma stood. "Jace promised Beth six full days of the fairytale, and she only got three. They're in Hawaii, you ass."

Jace

"You sure you're ready for this?" I asked, gripping Beth's hands in mine.

"Yes." She beamed. "I am."

"It's a big risk."

"It's worth it," she whispered.

"Well, then I guess there isn't anything more to say." I grinned. "Shit, shit!"

The donkey moved forward with Beth atop it. Perfectly content that if he were in a race with a turtle, he'd lose by a long shot. He made his way down the small aisle.

I decided to walk alongside Beth and the annoying little ass. It seemed right that it wouldn't be her walking toward me or me waiting for her, but us traveling on the journey together. Because sometimes, that's how love is. It isn't a man chasing a woman, it isn't a man storming the castle, and it isn't the girl waiting for love to happen.

It's two people making a commitment. It's two people realizing that they hold the keys to their own happiness in their own damn hands. The problem? Most people forget that they have the power to live the fairytale. I'd forgotten I had the power, and in the end, I'd been willing to walk away from my future.

Beth had forgotten too.

So we walked hand-in-hand. She on Donkey and I next to them, you know, just in case the little shit got spooked and took off running with my future bride on tow.

"I see you've found it." The ship captain's face lit up with a smile, helping Beth off the donkey and into the boat.

"Found it?"

"Your *keiki*."

"*Keiki?*" Beth repeated.

"Long story," I muttered, jumping into the boat.

The captain took us out into the middle of the water and

turned off the engine.

"Alright, let's make this quick, shall we?"

"Not very romantic is he?" Beth winked.

"I told him to make it quick," I admitted.

"Why?"

"Because I couldn't care less about saying the words — I just want to show you what you mean to me. I'm sick and tired of words, Beth. I've been using words my whole career. I think it's time for a little action, don't you?"

"Yes," she said breathless.

"Do you take this woman to be your bride?" the captain asked.

"Yes." My voice rang out loud and clear in the warm afternoon air. "I do."

"And do you take this man to be your husband?" The captain cleared his throat. "You don't have to take him, you know."

"I do," Beth grinned and then said, "Thor," under her breath.

"With the power vested in me by the state of Hawaii, I now pronounce you man and wife!" The captain grabbed two beautiful leis and placed one over each of our heads.

"May your womb be fertile," he said happily.

"Um... let's not get carried away." I laughed nervously.

"Grandma specifically said that in order to break the curse, I had to give you a blessing." The captain grinned mischievously. "I bless you with children — lots and lots of children."

"Take it off! Take the lei off!"

"Let it go," Beth whispered. "After all, it's best to just go with it when it comes to Grandma."

"Fine," I grumbled, fingering the damn fertility lei.

"Look on the bright side." Beth wrapped her arms around my waist. "If getting married was going to help your polls, imagine what children would do. Plus, that means we get to have all *the sex*."

"Side note." I cleared my throat. "If you keep quoting Grandma, I'm going to need one of her magic blue pills in order to perform."

"Aw, no inspiration?"

"None," I grumbled.

"I'm pretty sure I can take care of that." Beth's hot mouth pressed against mine, her tongue coaxing my lips apart.

"Where to?" the captain asked.

I swept Beth into my arms and pointed back to the shore, not wanting to pull my mouth from hers for one damn second. I was going to love her, cherish her, and honor her, and I was going to damn well remember it this time!

"Alrighty, then." The captain chuckled. "Back to the hut it is."

CHAPTER THIRTY-SEVEN

"Hawaii? This whole time? Are you saying you've successfully evaded the FBI and put us on a wild goose chase, all because you wanted to give the senator time to..."

"Play." Grandma stretched "But, of course. Every couple deserves time to discover one another. And I gave them that time."

"But we're the FBI."

"And I'm Grandma." She winked. "It's best to know your place in the world. Oh, and be a dear." She sighed. "Tell the president to call me back when he has a free moment, such a lovely dear man."

The agent blinked and then stood.

The door to the room opened. "Let her go. Her information checked out."

"But—"

"Nadine, we are so very sorry for this inconvenience."

Grandma patted him on the back. "It really is nothing. I'm glad Gus and I could spend some time together. I do love a good love story."

He grinned as Grandma waltzed out of the federal building.

"She's insane," the agent remarked to his superior.

"That woman helped us win the Cold War. Insane does not

even begin to describe her."

Beth

Jace slammed the door to the hut behind him and stalked toward me. His hands moved over my white dress and down my bare arms.

"Are you attached to any thing you're wearing?"

"What? Why?" I shivered.

"Yes or no?"

"No."

"Good."

With a rip he pulled the dress from my body. *You've got to be kidding me.* That crap happened outside of movies. I was witness to it.

Let that be a lesson to women everywhere: When your man looks like Thor, he has superpowers in the bedroom.

The dress fell to my feet, leaving me in nothing but my white wedge heels and my lacey underwear.

My entire body felt heavy with need.

He reached out and fingered the lace material, his fingers grazing my breasts, making my entire body ache with need. Jace's eyes darkened and then turned questioning. "And this? Are you attached to this?"

"N-no."

"Good." With a tug, he had my bra off and my panties in a bunch on the floor.

"Holy Thor."

"What?"

Crap on a stick! Did I just say that out loud?

"Did you just say Holy Thor?"

Instead of looking horrified, Jace seemed... I looked down... quite inspired at the thought. Apparently, visions of Grandma were long gone.

"Yes, yes I did."

"Hmm." He bit down on his lip and grinned. "I think I like it."

"Yeah?" I felt myself blushing. Not only was I standing in front of him naked as a jaybird, but I'd just totally turned our first sexual experience, that we would remember, into something mildly embarrassing.

I licked my lips nervously and waited for him to touch me.

He stared instead.

I was getting more and more fidgety. Why the hell did he get to keep his clothes on? I moved to cross my arms, but he jerked my hands away, his eyes drinking in every inch of my naked skin until I was ready to squirm. He made me want him by just looking; one gaze and I was ready to jump him.

"I would have remembered this — I should have remembered this." Jace traced the outline of my breasts and moved down to my hips, worshipping me with his hands as he pulled my body against his. "Drugs or no drugs, a man should never forget perfection."

"I don't remember either," I said shyly as I wrapped my arms around his neck. "I remember the cookies." Lame, someone shoot me now.

"You remember cookies, but not me?" He grinned.

"They were good?"

"I'll show you good."

"Show me great," I dared.

"I can do that."

He gently pushed me away and started doing a naughty striptease. Okay, so it wasn't naughty, but in my head it was, because every movement was slow, teasing me with glimpses of golden tan skin and rock-hard abs. I wanted to pinch myself.

By the time the last shred of clothing was thrown to the floor, I was almost panting.

And then he touched me.

Our mouths collided.

Yeah, we would have remembered this? Wouldn't we?

His hands dipped into my hair as his tongue drew lazy circles down my neck. My knees buckled just as he swept me into his arms and carried me to the bed.

I closed my eyes when his godlike body hovered over me. "I'm only going to go slow once." His face was strained. "And then I'm taking you in the pool."

"For a swim?" I said innocently.

"Right." His eyes darkened. "For a swim, followed by taking you in the shower, something I've been dreaming about since the day you pressed your naked body against mine."

I gasped when he pushed inside me.

"I'm not a patient man when it comes to you, and the way I see it, I have three whole days to drive you wild."

He pressed further.

I winced in pain.

And froze.

Jace's eyes widened. "Well, hot damn." He gave me a smug grin. "It seems all we did that night was eat cookies. How about that?"

"But—"

"So maybe I'll have to go a little bit slower."

"I'd rather you go fast." I winced even more.

Jace laughed. "How about I just make you forget?"

His mouth was on mine, and I was flying as his body fully joined with mine. Yes, yes. I would have remembered this. I would have remembered the way our bodies fit perfectly together. I would have remembered the way I wanted to cry with each movement, not out of pain but sheer pleasure.

"I love you." The friction of our bodies was seriously going to be the death of me; it felt too good. I thought I was going to explode.

Instead, I gave in, gave in to my husband, to my future,

and joined with him in what was sure to be one of many times
we worked on those great-grandchildren for Grandma.

CHAPTER THIRTY-EIGHT

"The coast is clear." Grandma checked her watch. *"Tell me, dear, just between the two of us, did he perform well? If not, I managed to save a few of those nice little charts. I'd be happy to book you for a morning session where we can pow-wow on ways to better communicate with your body?"*

"Bye, Grandma."

"But, dear! Do you even know what you're doing?"

"We'll figure it out."

"Beth, really, be reasonable! This old bird has been around for ages! Trust me, I know the sex."

"I'm hanging up now."

"Oh well, I'll send some photos just in case you get confused about which parts go where. Hell, the first time I was in a bedroom I—"

Beth

Chuckling, I hung up the phone and shook my head. "So, that was Grandma." I laughed. "She said the coast was clear." I wasn't about to tell him about the advice she'd given me or pictures that were going to traumatize my cell phone for life. Talk of Grandma had a way of making my husband less godlike.

Jace yawned and stretched out next to me, completely naked. Thank Thor.

"And?"

"She said that if you ever get elected president, she wants to make some guy named Gus your... vice-president?"

"Tell her I'll think about it." He smirked. "And what the hell does she mean *if* I get elected?"

"Aww..." I patted his firm stomach, "I'm sure she was teasing."

"Damn straight. I have to be president, if only for the purpose of making Brett's life a living hell."

"Let it go, babe."

"Nobody messes with my wife."

"I like the sound of that."

"Babe?"

"No."

"Wife?"

"That one." I sighed happily and patted his chest. "I think I'm ready now."

"Are you sure?" Jace's eyebrows drew together in concern. "I mean, it's normal to take a break, Beth. Really, I'll understand."

"Nope. It's time."

"Fine." He held up his hands in surrender.

"Cookie me."

Jace pulled a chocolate chip cookie from the box and placed it in my mouth. "Your wish is my demand. Damn, you have a nice mouth."

"You should know." I blushed.

"Yes, I should."

A piece of hair fell across my face. He brushed it away and chuckled.

"What? Do I have cookie on my face?"

"No. It's not that."

"What is it?"

"Can I pull your hair?"

"Will you wear that Thor costume you brought while pulling it?"

"Only as long as you wear the She-Ra one and pretend to drown while I save you and your cookies."

"Deal."

EPILOGUE

Five years later

"Damn it, Grandma! We said no ponies!" Jake looked about five seconds away from losing his mind.

Travis chuckled and took a swig of eggnog, not caring that his house was getting blown to shreds by four small children or that Grandma had, in fact, bought each child a pony. Two for Jake's twins, one for Travis's little girl, and one for Jace's little boy.

Grandma had said every child needed a pet.

Travis had been thinking more along the lines of a turtle or something. Not a horse. But arguing with Grandma was ridiculous — she'd always win. And he was done fighting; he was too exhausted after staying up with their two year old last night when she'd had a nightmare. To be fair, the nightmare had been Grandma's fault anyway. She'd let Arabella eat her weight in cookies, and sugar had a way of making her have bad dreams.

"How about I tell everyone a story!" Grandma shouted.

Travis winced.

Kacey gathered all the kids around in a circle, though it looked more like a corralling of adrenaline junkies. Sasha was pulling Taryn's hair, Arabella was yelling *fornicate* — a word Grandma had mistakenly used a few minutes previous, and little George was eating popcorn off the tree.

"Come on, kids." Jace took pity on Kacey and helped her round them up while Grandma grabbed a storybook.

"Now." Grandma smiled. She was nearing ninety-two but still looked beautiful. "I'm going to tell you each a story. A special story about your mommies and daddies. You see, they weren't always married, a long time ago, in a land far, far away—"

"Portland." Travis coughed, earning a glare.

"In a magical land," Grandma's eyes narrowed, "there was this beautiful grandma who decided that her grandsons needed a bit of help. So she did what any grandmother would do. She created special stories for each one of them, even taking pity on Uncle Jace when he was sad."

"Why was he sad?" the eldest twin asked.

"Yes, why was he sad?" Beth said in an amused voice.

"That's easy." Jace smirked. "Aunt Beth ate all my cookies."

"Not the only thing she—"

"Grandma!" everyone shouted.

"Anyway, where was I?" She beamed. "Sometimes children, magic does exist. Love is just like magic. It takes special care to discover, but once you have it in the palm of your hand, it spreads throughout your heart and soul. When you find love, you have to hold on to it. You have to promise to never let it go."

The eldest raised her hand again.

"Yes, Sasha?"

"Grandma, what if we miss our magic? What if we don't get it on time? What if it passes us by and we don't notice! Grandma, what do we do when we can't find it?"

"Well, dear," Grandma patted her head, "that's easy. Grandma already knows where your magic is." She poked Sasha in the chest. "It's right here, and if all else fails, I'll always be around right there, watching, waiting, and helping you every step of the way."

"Promise you'll never leave?" She sniffled.

"Promise." Grandma winked. "And grandmas never lie. Besides," her sharp gaze snapped up to Travis, Jake, Kacey, Char, Beth, and Jace, "it seems my work here isn't quite done yet."

ABOUT THE AUTHOR

Rachel Van Dyken is the New York Times, Wall Street Journal, and USA Today Bestselling author of regency and contemporary romances. When she's not writing you can find her drinking coffee at Starbucks and plotting her next book while watching *The Bachelor*.

She keeps her home in Idaho with her husband and their snoring boxer, Sir Winston Churchill. She loves to hear from readers! You can follow her writing journey at www.rachelvandykenauthor.com.

OTHER BOOKS BY RACHEL VAN DYKEN

The Bet Series
The Bet (Forever Romance)
The Wager (Forever Romance)
The Dare (coming July 8)

Eagle Elite
Elite (Forever Romance)
Elect (Forever Romance)
Entice
Elicit (August 11, 2014)

Seaside Series
Tear
Pull
Shatter
Forever
Fall

Wallflower Trilogy
Waltzing with the Wallflower
Beguiling Bridget
Taming Wilde

London Fairy Tales
Upon a Midnight Dream
Whispered Music
The Wolf's Pursuit

Renwick House
The Ugly Duckling Debutante
The Seduction of Sebastian St. James
The Redemption of Lord Rawlings
An Unlikely Alliance

The Devil Duke Takes a Bride

Ruin Series
Ruin
Toxic
Fearless
Shame (October 6, 2014)

Other Titles
The Parting Gift
Compromising Kessen
Savage Winter
Divine Uprising
Every Girl Does It

21173491R00173

Made in the USA
San Bernardino, CA
08 May 2015